THE RELUCTANT HEIR

WILLIAM SAVAGE

Ridge and Bourne

This is a work of fiction. All characters and events, other than those clearly in the public domain, are products of the author's imagination. Any resemblance to actual persons, living or dead, is unintended and entirely co-incidental. Where actual place names are used, I have changed the geography on several occasions to suit my story.

England in 1795 was an unhappy country. The revolution just across the channel had changed everything. When it began, many of those with the time and money to read the newspaper reports had welcomed events in France. They saw it as the necessary cleansing of a land that had suffered under the dual domination of a corrupt aristocracy and an equally corrupt church. When the revolution turned bloody, they were shocked and appalled. Hopes were now fixed on the other major continental powers — Prussia, Austria and Russia — stepping in to restore order and some semblance of good government. That had not happened. Instead, the French somehow quelled the excesses and emerged eager to export their constitutional innovations throughout the rest of Europe. After a shaky start, their armies grew in confidence and power until France was dominant enough to start to defeat the forces arrayed against it.

Then the French government declared war on Britain and began preparations for an invasion.

Britain's only effective defence was its navy but keeping such a large fleet at sea and ready for action cost a great deal of money and consumed scarce resources. Prices rose and the poor suffered everywhere.

You might think that Norfolk would be relatively remote from the frantic activity to protect London, the South Coast and the great dockyards at Portsmouth and Chatham. If so, you would be wrong. Norfolk's gentle beaches and unpopulated areas behind them were considered to be ideal for a major landing. If not for the full-scale invasion, then to land a force large enough to mount a worrying diversion and draw defences away from the channel coast.

It was against this background that Sir Adam Bascom returned to his home in Aylsham with his new bride. Though he was well aware of the parlous situation facing the country, that was not what worried him most in the days after his return. It was idleness and boredom.

Adam had been a busy country doctor, working hard to earn his living, like almost all his countrymen. Then he had married an extremely wealthy young widow and been unexpectedly elevated to a baronetcy for services to his king and country. As a result, his status had changed out of all recognition. Now, like the tiny minority of landowners who controlled and dominated politics, the armed forces and the government, and whose mansions and estates spread thickly across the county, he no longer had any need to work at all.

Younger sons like Adam had to make their own way in the world. His elder brother, Giles, had been raised expecting to take over the modest Bascom lands when their father died. Thus indeed it happened. Giles became a local squire and magistrate and loved the life. Adam became a physician and loved his work as well. Giles was now heavily involved in the organisation of the local militia — England's force of largely untrained rural conscripts and amateur officers, which was supposed to hold back the battle-hardened regiments of the French army should they land. Adam, mostly by chance, had been instrumental in solving a number of crimes and helping the authorities frustrate a number of attempts by seditious groups and French spies to establish secure routes into and out of the country. Now his newly acquired estate was larger than his brother's, while he also owned lands and houses elsewhere, all by reason of his marriage to Lady Alice, the young and beautiful widow of Sir Daniel Fouchard of Mossterton Hall. Those lands, extensive as they were, represented barely half of his wealth, the rest being made up of investments and loans. Sir Adam and Lady Bascom were exceedingly rich.

Lacking the experience and knowledge to manage all of this, Adam had hired agents and advisors, selecting them carefully enough to allow him to place his faith in their skill and honesty. Meanwhile, his new wife had thrown herself, heart and soul, into the rearrangement, refurbishment and extension of their new home, Wrigsby Hall. While she consulted Adam from time to time, he was mostly content to leave the arrangements to her. She had lived in grand houses from birth. The modest dwelling in the little market town of Aylsham, to which the couple had returned after their wedding and a trip to Bath, was the only property Adam had ever owned before.

He was idle, listless and bored, with nothing to occupy his mind or stir his curiosity. His days ahead were empty, offering only a prospect of endless, luxurious leisure.

It appalled him.

ADAM'S MEMORIES OF HIS TIME IN BATH WERE A BLEND OF NEAR-ecstatic happiness and acute discomfort. To be able to take Lady Alice in his arms and treat her as a husband is expected to treat his wife brought him moments of bliss and fierce ardour. To discover that her passion matched his — sometimes even surpassing it in joyous frenzy — was both unexpected and deeply, overwhelmingly satisfying. Many of their nights together began with passionate lovemaking, then progressed to the kind of sleep only an exhausted, satiated body and spent emotions could produce. Lady Alice shone in society, dressed in the finest silks and arrayed with glittering jewellery which drew envious looks from the other ladies. Adam, unused to such high-society entertainments, tried his best as her escort but ended up feeling dull and provincial. By the end of the first week, he was also sick of the braying emptiness of much of the conversation. By the end of the second, he found himself counting the hours until they could make their escape.

The journey to and from Bath had been notable for the discomfort of bad roads and lumpy beds in wayside inns of generally mediocre quality. Unfortunately, no one amongst Lady Alice's wide circle of relatives and friends owned a house close enough to the turnpike to be able to offer them accommodation along the way. The actual stay in Bath, from Adam's point of view, proceeded from a day or two of appreciative viewing of the fine new buildings, passed through typical evenings at the various events with which the towns many wealthy visitors amused themselves and ended in rising levels of boredom at the realisation that what had been novel on the first day was now to be repeated ad nauseam.

After purchasing Wrigsby Hall and estate, Adam had hoped to be able to move into the new house quickly. His new wife had other ideas. The Hall was a handsome building of which she heartily approved, but she had been brought up in grander mansions and looked on Wrigsby Hall as rather too small for their future life together. As wealthy landed gentry, they would be expected to entertain on a lavish scale. There was also the question of a future family. Lady Alice's elderly first husband had been unable to father the longed-for heir and had more or less chosen Adam in his stead. Since she had yet to reach the age of three-and-twenty and her new husband was but thirty-two, Lady Alice had high hopes of becoming a mother very soon.

Adam missed the news of the killing near Kessingfield Hall altogether. It had taken place only a day or so after his wedding to Lady Alice, when they were away enjoying themselves in Bath and were not due to return home for nearly two weeks. Even then, there had been no particular reason for him to take special notice. Frederick Dalston had been killed not far away, it was true, but his life had recently been spent entirely in Norwich; nor was his death entirely surprising. He was not a popular young man in most quarters. He was known to be erratic and impetuous. He gambled heavily, indulged in wild escapades and was the kind of young man no father would willingly allow to have contact with his womenfolk. He was constantly in debt and increasingly unlikely to pay his creditors. Add to that his arrogance and reputation for shady dealings and you had something more worrying than a typical young 'blade' of the type produced in abundance by aristocratic and gentry landowners in the 1790s.

Worst of all, he seemed to have a magnetic attraction for women of all ages; a trait he exploited to the full.

What finally brought the killing to Adam's attention was an unexpected visit to his house by the dead man's father, Mr William Dalston, the squire of Kessingfield Hall, a modest estate lying somewhat to the east of Aylsham and, therefore, nearer to the coast. Adam only agreed to see him because he could think of no polite reason to send the man away.

'I'm extremely grateful that you are willing to receive me in this way, Sir Adam,' Dalston began, after the usual pleasantries. 'Especially without any prior arrangement. I realise you must be an extremely busy man. I assure you; I would not have come at all if you had not been my last hope.'

Adam interrupted at once.

'I should tell you at once, sir, that I am no longer practising as a physician. I have handed over all my patients — well, almost all — to my colleague Dr Henshaw. If you have come about a medical matter you should see him, not me.'

'It is not a medical matter, I assure you. Would that it were. Then, at least, I would know where to begin.'

'The beginning is usually a good place,' Adam said dryly. He had not much wanted to see this fellow and was already wondering how best to send him on his way without giving offence.

The late middle-aged man sitting in the chair opposite him in his library, formerly his consulting room, had arrived without warning barely five minutes after Lady Alice had left for yet another meeting with the architect to inspect his plans to transform and modernise Wrigsby Manor. When handing over his card to the butler, all the visitor had said was that he needed to speak to Sir Adam on a matter of the gravest consequence. Adam turned his head slightly to the right and looked again at the visiting card. It was singularly uninformative. It merely announced his visitor was Mr William Dalston of Kessingfield Hall, Eastwick, Nr Aylsham. The name meant nothing to him.

'My son has been murdered. The magistrate is content to treat it as a failed robbery. I am not. There are too many strange circumstances surrounding Frederick's death to support such a convenient notion.'

'Strange circumstances?'

'Let me explain. Where to begin ... Yes, nothing was taken. His purse, his rings, all untouched. The horse he was riding — quite a valuable beast — was found by one of my grooms several hours later and brought to our stables at the Hall. A strange robbery, you'll agree, when nothing is stolen.'

'Perhaps the robbers were disturbed and fled before they could do what they had come for?'

'That's what the magistrate charged with bringing any prosecution said. I'm a Justice of the Peace myself, you'll understand, but can hardly be responsible for prosecuting whoever murdered my own son. A colleague called Mr Stephen Palfrey is in charge.'

'You disagree with Mr Palfrey's conclusion?'

'I do indeed. It's an extremely quiet stretch of road, even during the daytime. At night it would have been virtually deserted. Who would have disturbed a robber there?'

'So, your son was attacked in the dark?'

'Yes. It must have been sometime between midnight and dawn. Most days, I can't imagine there would be more than one or two people, if that, passing along that road at such a time.'

'Was he armed?'

'He always carried a brace of pistols in holsters on either side of his saddle. They were still in place when he was found.'

He hadn't tried to defend himself then. Either he was taken too much by surprise or he'd been knocked from his horse before he could draw his pistols.

'Unarmed and on the ground,' Adam mused. 'Effectively helpless, save for his fists. Why would any robber have run away?'

'The robber, or robbers, might simply have thought they heard someone coming. I imagine they would have been extremely nervous, having just killed a man. There might have been no one there at all.'

'Just a noise from an animal or bird.'

'Palfrey suggested it might have been a poacher,' Mr. Dalston said in disgust.

'It might have been, if it was not a regular footpad,' Adam replied. 'Poaching must be common enough in these parts and the gamekeepers on many estates are prone to shooting on sight rather than risking injury during a fight. Is that an area where poachers are especially likely?'

'I suppose so. However, the next circumstance is much less easy to explain away. At the inquest, the medical examiner said that my son had probably been face down on the ground when he was stabbed. It was something about the angle at which the blade had entered and the force with which it was driven home. I can't really remember all the details. The point is, if he was pulled off his horse, then turned over onto his face, why didn't he fight back? He was a sturdy young man and quite capable of defending himself. You would have expected there would be signs on the ground of some sort of struggle. Personally, I think it would have taken two or three burly men to force him onto his face. Wouldn't the ground have been scuffed or churned up by his attempts to hold them off? At the very least, you would have expected his knees to be muddy and the toes of his shoes marked and scratched, wouldn't you? Yet there were no marks on him at all. Neither on his hands, his knees or his toes.'

'Anything else?'

'Indeed so. First of all, poor Frederick's body had been dragged a short distance into the tangle of coarse grass and weeds which lay at the road's edge. Then his saddle and saddlebags had been carried to the same place and thrown a little way further from the road, where they landed in a patch of furze and blackberry.'

'To hide what had been done?'

'You might think so, save for the fact that the body had been left where it was, clearly visible to anyone passing by. It is quite dense woodland at that spot with plenty of gorse bushes and holly trees where a body might have been hidden, to say nothing of all the bracken.'

'But if the attackers had been disturbed, might they not have left before hiding the body adequately?' Adam replied. 'But let us return to the way your son was killed. His attackers may have stunned him in some way. Hit him with a club, perhaps, then grabbed him as he began to fall so that he turned onto his face.'

'Would that not have required a hard blow to the head? According to the evidence given at the inquest, there was no sign of such a blow, nor of any other injuries to the body. Why drag him off the road? None of that sounds to me like the actions of a group of footpads.'

'Very well,' Adam said. 'Anything more?'

'The doctor who gave evidence at the inquest said he was surprised at the force with which the blow had been delivered. According to his testimony, the attacker must have raised the blade high above his head and driven it down with all his strength.'

'I suppose that must have been possible,' Adam said. 'Can you recall who it was who carried out the autopsy?'

'It was a Dr Henshaw. He was your partner, I believe.' Adam nodded assent. 'Quite a young man, yet one who spoke with a good deal of authority. You will best know the extent of his skill and expertise.'

'He is a most capable fellow who would have said nothing without ample evidence to back it up. Tell me, did he say anything else about the manner of the attack?'

'No,' Mr Dalston replied wearily. 'The coroner was quite short with him. Said he was only required to certify the cause of death not speculate on the circumstances that might have brought it about.'

Adam frowned. He had encountered that kind of coroner himself. 'One thought occurs to me,' he said. 'Why was your son on the road at such a late hour? Do you know where he was going?'

'He must have been coming home,' Mr Dalston sounded even more dejected. 'The road does not really lead to anywhere else. As for the time, Frederick was not a man to keep regular hours. He could well have been up late drinking or gambling. Dr Henshaw said there was a smell of alcohol about the body. He could easily have been with a woman.'

Adam asked. 'Didn't he live with you at the Hall?'

'Not for some months. He told me he hated the countryside; preferred the city, with all the noise and bustle. His presence at the Hall had also become extremely disruptive. He demanded things at all hours of the day and night, shouting and quarrelling if they were not produced on the instant. He was also a menace to any female servant under the age of fifty. He was bored, belligerent and disruptive. In the end, I told my attorney to find suitable rooms for him in Norwich. I even paid the rent at first.'

'Were you expecting him?'

Mr Dalston hesitated. 'Frederick came and went as he wished,' he said after a moment. 'It was impossible to predict his movements.'

'Do you know how he spent his time in Norwich?'

Mr Dalston smiled grimly at the question.

'He preferred to spend his time, wherever he was, drinking, gambling, wenching and getting into fights and brawls. I gave him a perfectly adequate allowance and he would spend it within the first week. Rather, he would lose it gambling. I imagine he was coming home that night to ask for more money yet again. In the seven or eight weeks he had been in Norwich, I had already paid off his debts twice. The last time I told him there would be no more; he must live within his allowance or find money from elsewhere. Our family tree stretches back for many hundreds of years, Sir Adam. In all that time, it is probably fair to say that the Dalstons have never been more than dull, respectable, local merchants. Every couple of generations, one has got into trouble. Then the next in line has married well enough to repair the family fortune, though never to increase it significantly. It was my grandfather who decided to invest the money he had made as a brewer in buying a gentleman's estate. My own father then mismanaged the land and overspent on renovations to the Hall. This he did to the extent that, when I inherited, most of my inheritance had been mortgaged. Fortunately, I married an heiress and was able to settle those debts. The estate was just about on a sound footing until I had to start paying off my son's debts. Now it is mortgaged again and more heavily than I would wish. There is little surplus. A run of two or three poor harvests would bring us to the brink of ruin. My son's wild behaviour has imperilled the financial stability I had been able to achieve. It has also meant that finding him a suitable heiress to be his wife has become impossible. No man is going to allow his daughter to marry such a wastrel, especially if she is likely to bring a substantial dowry for him to fritter away.'

'Is there anything else you can tell me to substantiate your belief that this was not simply a robbery which went wrong?' Adam said.

'Only that I know it in my heart,' Mr Dalston replied. 'Frederick would not have allowed himself to be pulled off his horse and done to death in such a craven manner. He would have fought and struggled. His clothing would have been torn and disarranged, not left as if he had laid down in the mud willingly to wait for the final blow.'

He shook his head violently and stared at Adam with tears in his eyes.

Adam was at a loss for words. The man's pain was palpable, yet everything he had recounted was capable of a simple explanation. Suddenly, Dalston sprang to life.

'I forgot the most peculiar circumstance,' he cried out. 'I told you that the doctor said my son must have been lying face down when he was dealt a mortal blow. Yet that was not how the body was first found, or how it lay when I arrived. My servants were adamant they had not moved the body in any way.'

'Can you describe how he was lying then?' Adam asked.

'Frederick was lying on his back, his eyes closed, his legs stretched out neatly and his hands crossed over his chest. He looked exactly as if he was ready to be laid in his coffin. Would any cutthroat have done that before removing his victim's valuables? Would he or they have spent time laying out the body neatly, then run away, empty-handed, if they heard a noise to startle them?'

'That's certainly most peculiar,' Adam admitted. 'I suppose some people, especially simple people, become frightened in the presence of death. They fear the ghost of the man they have killed will come to haunt them. Most highway robbers do not set out to murder their victims. They may bluster and threaten, but few of them are willing to carry out their threats in cold blood. It sounds as if your son's attacker may have believed that treating the body with respect would ward off the evil consequences of his deed.'

'I cannot believe that, sir. Neither are you convinced of it, I imagine. Even if each individual circumstance can be explained away, when you add them all together, I believe there is a powerful case to prove that this was a planned and premeditated murder, not the act of some roving blackguard intent merely on robbery. Nevertheless, I failed to convince the magistrate by my argument, so he has done little to find my son's killer, beyond putting up the usual notices offering a reward for information. So far as I know, no one has come forward to claim that reward. In his mind, therefore, the case is closed, and the verdict returned by the coroner's jury of "murder by person or persons unknown" will be the final word. Have I also failed to convince you, sir?'

Adam chose his words carefully.

'I agree that each individual circumstance you have related to me can be explained away, Mr Dalston. I also agree that, taken altogether, they suggest that a simple robbery gone wrong may not be the appropriate way of viewing your son's death. However, it is now more than two months since that death occurred. All the evidence you have given to me is circumstantial. No one has come forward who might be willing to stand up in court and testify to facts that would disprove the simple explanation. I do not say that no such facts exist but, if they do, they have not yet come to light.'

'So, you will not help me?' Mr Dalston asked.

'I have not said that. What I'm trying to point out is that this would be a complex and difficult case to investigate, probably requiring a great deal of time and the questioning of many people. I am a busy man, Mr Dalston, with many commitments. Let me think about what you have said and discuss it with my wife. This is not something I can agree to on the instant. I'm sure you understand that. As I said, let me think about all that you have told me. Only then can I give you my answer.'

'Very well, Sir Adam,' Mr Dalston said with resignation. 'Let me at least express my gratitude that you have not dismissed me on the instant as the magistrate did. I will await your decision, sir.'

When, after dinner that evening, Adam related everything that Mr Dalston had told him to Lady Alice, he didn't quite get the answer he expected.

'Why are you hesitating?' she said once he had finished. 'The man needs your help. However difficult and reckless that young man was, he remained his son. Losing a child is a terrible thing which must turn your life upside down.'

'But he may be imagining the whole thing!' Adam protested. 'All the supposed evidence he could present was circumstantial. There were simple explanations for everything.'

'What would you do if some patient came to you complaining of severe pain and told you another doctor had dismissed what they said as imaginary?' Lady Alice asked. 'Would you simply send him on his way?'

'Not without satisfying myself that was the explanation!' her husband replied.

'How is this situation different?'

Adam was silent. He had no answer to that.

'You could at least speak to Dr Henshaw!' she continued. 'You say he did the autopsy. If he found nothing suspicious, you can tell Mr Dalston you can see no basis for taking the matter further.'

AFTER BREAKFAST THE NEXT MORNING, ADAM SENT A NOTE TO DR Henshaw's house asking him to call when he had finished his medical business for the day. The young doctor arrived just before four in the afternoon looking somewhat harassed. James Grove, the cheerful butler who had followed his mistress from Mossterton Hall, took his hat and coat and brought him through to where Adam was seated in his study. A moment later, Grove reappeared with a large jug of strong ale and two mugs.

'You have just saved my life,' Henshaw said to him. 'How you knew what to bring I have no idea, but you have my profound thanks.'

'A bad day?' Adam asked.

'Not particularly so. More a day of constant frustrations.' Henshaw paused and drained half of the mug of ale before setting it back on the table and filling it up again. 'It began badly with a patient who asked for my opinion, then told me at length why I was wrong. That, I could cope with. I simply made a note to add five guineas to his bill! Then I missed any food at midday in order to visit an old farmer who had fallen down in the stockyard and twisted his ankle. He began yelling in pain before I even laid a hand on him and kept it up until he saw me safely on the other side of the room. What made it worse was that the reason for his fall came down to drinking four large glasses of strong cider with his breakfast, before stumbling out of doors barely able to stand upright. It's all very well for you to laugh. You don't have to deal with any of this nowadays.'

'But I used to,' Adam said. 'It's what we must all face when we choose to set up practice in a rural area. Hopefully, however, that marked the end of your problems for the day.'

'Not at all!' Henshaw replied. 'I had barely returned home when a servant lad arrived to bid me go in haste to the house of Mr Heal, the attorney, whose wife was supposedly suffering from severe complications during her labour. It turned out that the only complication was loss of nerve on the part of the prospective new father. When his wife went into labour, he sent for the midwife. She had failed to arrive promptly enough and, in his view, his wife's labour had gone on far too long.'

'How long had it been?'

'As far as I could ascertain, about two hours. I told him I could find nothing amiss and that nature must be allowed to take its course, but I could see he didn't believe me. Fortunately, the midwife finally arrived about fifteen minutes later. She had come directly from another confinement and, during the journey, a wheel had come off her dog cart. Showing a great deal more fortitude than the father, she then climbed out of the ditch and stopped a passing farmer and his son to help her put the wheel back on the dog cart so she could continue with her journey. She agreed with me that there were no problems with the birth, terrified the father into retiring to another room until he was summoned and then prepared to usher another life into the world. I stayed until the baby was born, more to improve my knowledge of midwifery than for any other reason. When I got home, I found your note ...'

'Let me ring for the butler to bring you some victuals,' Adam said at once. 'If you drink any more of my ale on an empty stomach, you'll be twisting your ankle on the way home. We'll talk while waiting for the food to arrive, then take a rest so that you can eat it without ruining your digestion.'

'What was it you wanted to know?' Henshaw asked. 'Surely you have not called me here to give you medical advice?'

'Nothing like that,' Adam said with a grin, 'though you're gaining experience all the time, while I'm gradually forgetting many of the practical aspects of being a physician. I want to ask you about the murder of Frederick Dalston. I gather you carried out the autopsy.'

'That's right. The man was stabbed coming home late at night. How has it come about that you are involved?'

'His father came here yesterday in considerable distress. It seems he cannot convince anyone that his son's death was not a bungled robbery but premeditated murder. He wants me to carry out some kind of investigation. I had to tell him that his evidence is circumstantial and easily explained away. However, you examined the body. If you found anything that might support his contention, I'd like to hear it. I gather the coroner wouldn't let you say any more during the inquest than what was needed to establish the cause of death.'

'Indeed so,' Henshaw replied. 'He and the magistrate seemed to have decided precisely what happened before the inquest even began.'

'But you're not so sure?'

'I am not. There's no doubt the man met his death from a single deep stab wound, which entered just below his shoulder blade, passed through his heart and came close to breaking the skin on his chest. It must have been delivered with either a very long dagger or some kind of sword. Something with a narrow, thin blade like a rapier. It must also have been administered with amazing force. Had I been allowed to, I would have pointed out that the angle at which the blade passed through the body precluded the blow being struck by anybody standing on the ground. It could only have been made by someone on a horse, striking with a level blow. Given that such a blow would have relied entirely on the strength in the attacker's arm, we must be talking about a person with the strength of Goliath. The only alternative explanation — and one that I find rather more convincing — is that the man was lying face down on the ground while his attacker stood over him, probably raising the weapon with both hands above his head and driving it downwards with all the force he could muster.'

'What convinced you of that?' Adam asked.

'The blade struck a rib as it pierced the skin. It was not then deflected either over or under that rib. The rib was neatly snapped in two. The blade passed onwards, pierced completely through the heart, chipped a large piece from the top of another rib, ripped through the muscles of the chest and finally managed to come close to piercing the skin and driving a hole in the murdered man's waistcoat. Dalston would have died instantly from such a fearsome blow. What I don't understand is how his attacker managed to keep him face down before delivering the coup de grâce.'

'You examined the man's head for any signs of a blow sufficient to render him unconscious?'

'Of course. He was wearing a hat which might have prevented any surface damage to the skull, but there was no indentation or clear evidence of bruising. It may have been that being pulled from his horse caused him sufficient bewilderment to render him incapable of action for just long enough to suit the murderer's purpose. It was also evident from the smell about the body that he had been drinking — probably heavily. Whether he was too drunk to gather his wits about him in time, I cannot say.'

'Was there anything else that aroused your suspicions?' Adam asked.

'Were you told that the body was found lying on its back and laid out neatly as if for a funeral? Have you ever known a highway robber to do such a thing before?'

'Most certainly, I have not. From what you have just told me, I am beginning to feel that Mr William Dalston is fully justified in believing that this was no simple highway robbery. Besides, he assured me that none of the valuables his son was carrying had been taken. It sounds much more like a case of murder, carried out with uncommon violence and passion and followed up by an almost tender care for the corpse. I can make no sense of it.'

'Neither could I, then or now,' Henshaw said. 'If you do decide to investigate the matter, please tell me the outcome. I have been puzzling over this death for some time and would be grateful to be allowed to put it out of my mind.'

THAT NIGHT, ADAM WOKE, FLUSTERED AND TENSE, AS DAWN arrived. He must have been dreaming of all he had been told during the day for, in his dream, he saw a man standing against the trunk of the tree a little way off a lonely road. It was hard to see him in the uncertain light but the occasional noise from shifting feet confirmed he was there. The man waited, as still as the trees all around him. Only the occasional rustling of woodland creatures going about their business and, once, the wavering call of an owl some distance off prevented the silence from being absolute. Before him, the road ran left and right, a narrow ribbon of dull, rutted sand and flints in the moonlight, then disappearing into dense shadows from the great trees, whose massive shapes and lives measured in centuries mocked the petty world of men.

Then, far off in the distance, came the sound of a horse coming along at somewhere between a walk and a slow trot, picking its way carefully between the ruts and potholes, which spread everywhere across the road's surface. The man by the trees stirred a little and moved forward a few steps from his hiding place. For a brief moment, he stepped into the road and turned to look in the direction of the approaching horse. Then he went back again and moved out of sight behind a holly bush.

As the rider came up, Adam had seen it was a young man, too fashionably dressed for this remote, rural location. He sat slouched in the saddle, allowing the horse to pick its own way forward, so wrapped up in his own thoughts that he looked neither right nor left and let the reins lie slack over the horse's neck. The hidden watcher by the side of the road let him pass, then moved clear of the holly bush. Now he was on horseback too. A giant of a man, broad in the chest and arms. He urged his horse forwards and came up swiftly behind the young man. As he did, something moved in his hands; a long, thin blade glittered in the moonlight for an instant and was at once plunged with tremendous force into the rider's back. He gave a sudden, deep grunt, his whole body stiffened and arched from the strength of the blow, then he went limp and pitched forward over the horse's neck onto the ground.

Next, Adam saw the killer go up to the rider, now lying face down on one side of the road, and kneel by the body, presumably feeling the neck for a pulse and finding none. Eventually he stood up, seized the corpse by its feet and dragged it off the road.

That was when Adam awoke. He lay quiet in his bed, replaying the vision in his mind once or twice more. Was that how it had happened? It matched most of the facts he had been given. Sadly, the dream had come to an end before it dealt with how the killer had arranged the corpse. That was the point which worried Adam most. If the killer had been a footpad, why waste time arranging the body neatly, then have to run off when he heard someone approaching? Would he not have robbed first and dealt with the body after, whether from superstition or some other cause?

Adam swore quietly to himself. Like Henshaw, he knew only one thing would serve to set his mind at rest. He had to investigate this death, however bothersome that might prove to be. He had little else to do anyway. His statement to Mr Dalston that he might not have the time to do as he asked was a white lie aimed at making it easier for him to refuse.

Very well, he would write a letter to Dalston and perhaps set his mind at rest as well — at least for a time.

❦ 2 ❧

Adam had rediscovered his friend Peter Lassimer, the apothecary, when he first arrived to set up his medical practice in Aylsham. Years before, both had attended the same Scottish university to obtain medical degrees. Sadly, Peter's source of funds had been cut off before he could complete his studies. Unknown to Adam, he found a new profession by undertaking an apprenticeship in an apothecary in the little Norfolk market town of Aylsham. On the old man's retirement, Peter took over the business. Nowadays, it was not just a thriving concern as an apothecary's, it was also the hub for gossip for the whole of the town and its surrounding villages. Adam had found that useful on several previous occasions when he was investigating some mystery. He also valued the opportunity to talk over his progress — or the lack of it — with his friend. Peter's sharp mind and pragmatic outlook was the ideal foil to his own, more complex thought processes. He was determined that neither his marriage nor his elevation to the baronetcy was going to interfere with this.

That was why, on that morning of the day after he had spoken with Dr Henshaw, Adam was to be found in one of his favourite places — the compounding room of Peter's apothecary store. That was where he mixed his medicines, made his pills and suppositories, and decanted various dried herbs and spices into bags and boxes for sale in the shop next door. Aside from the long counter at which Peter was currently working, there was a sink and a draining board, a water pump on the wall above and racks pulled up to the ceiling on which branches of herbs were drying. Most of the other walls were lined with shelves and drawers containing a cornucopia of dried roots, powders and exotic liquid ingredients, all neatly labelled with their names in abbreviated Latin. A single window, protected by bars, let light come in over the counter, while a small grate in one corner held a coal fire. The gentle light, the constant warmth from the fire and the mingled scents from the herbs turned the room into a wondrous place. Adam's imagination had made it into a secret cave; a refuge from the world as well as a source of knowledge and enlightenment. Naturally, he had never shared this fancy with Peter, who would have responded with hilarity. For the apothecary, it was his daily work room, equipped to meet all his specific needs.

Adam was sitting in his normal position, perched on a tall stool close to the counter. Peter was also in his habitual state of working at the counter while they talked. As Adam explained all that he had learned from Mr Dalston and Dr Henshaw, Peter's attention seemed to be on the fiddly business of rolling paste into pills. However, Adam knew his friend would be listening carefully and taking it all in.

'Are you going to do what this Mr Dalston asks?' Peter said, when Adam finally reached the end of his explanations.

'Yes,' Adam replied. 'My wife thinks I should and so does Henshaw. I sent William to Kessingfield this morning with a letter for Dalston to that effect. There's certainly something odd about this killing. To my mind, the magistrate, backed up by the coroner, has simply taken the easy way out.'

'That would be typical of Palfrey. He is well-known to be a lazy bugger when it comes to anything other than shooting game or hunting foxes. The only time you'll see him eager to bring a prosecution is when some villager is accused of poaching. Then his approach is more like a relentless avenger than a dispassionate dispenser of justice.'

'I suppose I'll have to deal with poaching myself, now I own an estate,' Adam said in wonder.

'Just see you act fairly,' Peter told him. 'Some poor soul desperate to feed his family is quite a different matter to these organised gangs who can strip an estate of game in a single night. They don't act out of necessity. Their purpose is to sell all they catch to butchers in Norwich and London. I'd happily see them transported or hanged. Thieves and brigands, all of them!'

'Quite,' Adam replied, 'but I haven't come here to talk about poaching. What do you know of the murder? It took place while I was away in Bath.'

'Doubtless in a haze of happiness in Lady Alice's arms.' Peter caught the warning glance and returned to Adam's question. 'As for the murder itself, no more than you, I expect.'

'And of Frederick Dalston?'

A wastrel, a bounder, a cad and a fool, all rolled into one. He showed his true nature when, aged fourteen, he got a twenty-year-old parlour maid at his home pregnant, quickly followed by a young milk-maid on the Home Farm and a fisherman's widow on the coast near Eastwick. All hushed up, of course, though both the parlour maid and the widow died in childbirth. Frederick was quickly sent away to live with an uncle who was a clergyman and, by all accounts, a ranting puritan as well.'

'Puritan he might have been,' Adam said, 'but he clearly had no effect on the boy.'

'None whatsoever. Frederick was found a place at the University of Oxford but lasted little time there — only two terms I think — before his father was requested to remove him. He was said to be a bad influence on the other undergraduates.'

'In what way?'

'I have no idea. If I had to guess, I'd start with whoring and move on to gambling.'

'I wonder what made him so wild? His father seemed to me to be a rather placid fellow.'

'The younger brother, George, takes after his father, or so I'm told. Sadly, Frederick was born restless. An insignificant estate in a remote part of Norfolk is no place for a lad desperate for excitement and the good things in life.'

'Any other brothers or sisters?' Adam asked.

'I believe there is a much younger sister who must be about fourteen or fifteen. Dalston's wife died soon after the girl was born and he has not married again. I would describe the family as prosperous rather than rich, though that may have something to do with what Frederick has cost his father over the years.'

'What of Frederick's life in recent years?' All this background information might prove useful, but Adam felt that the reason for Frederick Dalston's murder was more likely to lie in recent events.

'I know much less about him since he left his home and went to live in Norwich,' Peter replied, 'though what I do know is not good. It seems he transferred his attentions from servant girls to the wives and daughters of the gentry and rich merchants. I daresay many fathers and husbands breathed a sigh of relief when they heard Frederick Dalston was dead. He was devilishly attractive to women, though Lord only knows why, given his history was well known.'

'He didn't marry?'

'Not for want of trying by his father,' Peter said. 'I have heard the estate is becoming impoverished. The only way out is for Frederick to secure a good marriage with a woman who has a substantial dowry. Yet all attempts to find him a suitable bride have so far foundered on the same rock. Once the girl's family learn of young Frederick's behaviour, they will have none of him. The fellow is not only ruining his family, he's preventing the one means of rescuing it. Now, my friend, that's all I know, and I'm needed in the shop, I expect. Unlike certain wealthy gentlemen I know, I have to earn my crust by actual work and it's high time I did some more. I suppose you want me to fish for any gossip I can pick up about young Dalston?'

All Adam could do was agree he did indeed want Peter to keep his ears open for any fresh gossip and then return home to ponder more direct ways of discovering about Frederick's life in Norwich.

FOR THE FOLLOWING TWO DAYS, ADAM FRETTED AND FUMED WITH frustration, imagining himself to be stuck already. He had no contacts amongst the young blades who were probably Frederick Dalston's drinking and gambling friends in Norwich. How was he to collect information beyond common gossip? Only on the third morning did he realise the answer. He could have kicked himself for not thinking of it at once.

Peter had told him that Frederick had shifted his targets for seduction to the wives and daughters of prosperous merchants and minor gentry. Adam's own mother was a member of a group of Norwich ladies who met regularly to take tea and discuss anything and everything of note in the city, especially gossip about those outside their circle. Some of them had helped him once before by sharing what they knew. If he contacted his mother and explained the circumstances, he felt sure she would be able to use her contacts to collect as much information as she could. That is if she could stop boring them with all her constant references to "my son, the baronet"!'

Ruth Scudamore, Lady Alice's niece, was also now living in Norwich. In fact, she was sharing Mrs Bascom's house. She had also assisted Adam in a previous investigation and would be certain to have her own friends amongst the younger set in the city. Between the two of these ladies, there should be little difficulty in discovering nearly all there was to know about Frederick's recent amours.

Thinking of Ruth reminded Adam of Charles, her twin brother, now practising as a lawyer as his father had done for many years. Unfortunately, he did so from his new home in Holt. Would that be too far away for him to hear anything useful? Should he put Charles from his mind? Of course, there was his own lawyer. He resided in Norwich and might well be worth speaking to, though all lawyers tended to be close-mouthed about their other clients. He could also approach his banker, though bankers were, if anything, even more secretive. Still, the fellow must be aware of the most important events amongst the city's financial houses and the businesses that he supported. It was a faint hope, yet a visit might produce something relevant.

What Adam decided he really needed was access to someone in the city who could make confidential enquiries far more widely than he could do himself. Ideally, it should be someone who could talk with shopkeepers and tradesmen, even with servants. Servants always knew far more about their masters and mistresses lives than their betters believed. Such people, like artisans, were most unlikely to be willing to talk with Adam openly. All his wider acquaintances were either gentry or wealthy members of the merchant class. In the society of the time, most people at Adam's level would never deign to speak to people amongst the lower classes; sometimes, not even to their own servants, save to issue orders. While Adam himself did not believe in such foolishness, and would have been happy to speak with anyone, the same was not necessarily true in reverse. Most ordinary people would be so overawed by being confronted with a baronet that they would say no more than they were forced to.

That night, as Adam lay in bed and recalled with delight the earlier hours of darkness when he had visited his wife's bedroom, the answer sprang into his mind. Wicken! Of course! The man controlled the most amazing network of informers and agents. Surely he could be persuaded to loan out the services of a suitable person for a few weeks?

Next morning, the moment breakfast had been completed, Adam hurried to his study and began to compose the necessary letters. He was thus somewhat chagrined to discover at dinner that his new wife had reached the same conclusion well before him and dispatched a whole series of letters herself while he was talking with Peter the day before. Not only had she already alerted Ruth and Charles, she had written to a number of her other friends and acquaintances amongst the county elite, many of whom would have family members at risk of falling prey to a man like Frederick Dalston. Only when Adam told her about writing to Sir Perceval Wicken did she admit, with a shy grin, that she was not able to forestall him in all respects.

'I can see I surprised you nevertheless, my dear,' she said. 'Indeed, I hope I shall always be able to do so at times. I would not like you to think of me as entirely predictable.'

'Never!' Adam said. 'You have managed to surprise me in one way or another almost every day since we've been married.'

'And what about the nights?' she enquired with a look of innocence. 'I hope you have not been disappointed then, husband.'

'Definitely not,' Adam said, blushing furiously. 'I ... well ... let us simply say that anyone who meets you in the normal course of events would never suspect ... I mean ... you seem so proper and ...'

Lady Alice took pity on him. 'So I should hope, husband,' she said, interrupting his stumbling efforts. 'Surely you would not have me behave thus with anyone else?'

'Indeed not, my dearest,' Adam mumbled. 'I just had not anticipated ...'

'Speak no more of it, my dear. You will embarrass the servants,' Lady Alice said with a giggle. 'I have no idea why you think it proper to raise such delicate matters over the dining table.'

'But you ...'

'Enough. I ought to enlighten you in another area, I think. You said a day or so ago that you could not understand why so many respectable ladies were willing – even eager — to respond to Frederick Dalston's advances. I did not then have the opportunity to explain, but I can suggest at least two reasons. There are always those who believe they will be able to reform such a reprobate with the power of their own personality and — yes, though I blush to say it — their love. It is a delusion, of course, but a flattering one. I imagine he would encourage such notions as much as he could. By the time they discover their mistake, it is too late for those ladies. Then there are others whose lives have been cumbered round by tyrannical fathers or husbands. They will have been warned again and again not to allow themselves to be led astray by the sins of the flesh. Never having had the chance to learn what exactly those sins might be — or why they should be such as to overwhelm all restraint — they secretly harbour a longing to find out for themselves. Forbidden fruit always seems the more tempting the more it is described as deadly. Along comes the tempter and, like Eve, they are more than ready to believe. Surely what men indulge in quite freely cannot be as harmful as they have been told. Frederick sounds like the perfect reincarnation of the serpent from the Garden of Eden.'

'You've done it again!' Adam cried. 'I swear you are full of wonders, my dearest wife. A perfectly simple set of explanations for what has been puzzling me for days. I think I shall retire from my investigations and leave all to you from now on.'

Despite feeling greatly pleased by her husband's words, Lady Alice was careful to avoid any appearance of seeking to come into competition with him or make him feel that she was criticising his abilities. She had known for some time that he was far more sensitive to criticism than he appeared on the outside. His self-confidence could be easily shaken by an ill-considered remark.

'It is merely that you speak of the feelings of women, husband. As a woman myself, I am bound to understand them a little better than you do. In all other ways, I could never hope to be your equal as a solver of mysteries. Now, if you have eaten sufficiently well, let us leave the table and go into the drawing room, where I shall drink a dish or two of tea and you may enjoy your usual glass of brandy.'

⚜

THE MAJORITY OF THE RESPONSES FROM LADY ALICE'S FAMILY AND acquaintances proved to be swift in coming, but uniformly disappointing. They reported what was already well-known, then hurried on to add that no one in their family had ever had any dealings with Frederick Dalston, nor would any of them do so in the future. After the fifth such a response, Lady Alice was heard to complain that, unfortunately, everyone she knew was altogether too dull and respectable.

'The whole crowd of them are as dull as ditch water,' she complained to Adam. 'Not the slightest sense of adventure or even of curiosity. See how keen they all are to assure me that none of them have had more than the slightest contact with Frederick Dalston.'

This disappointment was followed by the first response arriving from the letters Adam had sent out the day after his wife sent hers. It came from his attorney and was equally unhelpful. He wrote that he suspected he knew nothing beyond what was common knowledge in the city. He would, of course, enquire amongst his own friends and contacts, but had little hope of discovering any more. Just like the responses that Lady Alice had received, this letter then hurried on to assure Adam that he had never had any dealings with Frederick Dalston and thought the same would prove true of any others he might contact. He would write again if he had anything more useful to report.

'There we have yet another boringly respectable Norwich professional,' Adam remarked to his wife. 'Like all attorneys, he never says yes or no to anything if he can avoid it. I recall an old friend of my father's used to say that you should always look to do your business with an attorney who had lost an arm.'

'Why on earth should he say that?' Lady Alice asked in astonishment. 'It makes no sense.'

'I once asked him that myself,' her husband replied. 'What he said was that attorneys usually answered questions with the phrase, "on the one hand ..." followed by suggesting the opposite beginning with "but on the other hand ..." Now, if your attorney only has one hand ...'

At that point, Lady Alice interrupted him, called him a fool and, in defiance of all propriety, kissed him on the lips in full view of any servants who happened to be looking.

'We have learned one useful fact though,' Adam said, disentangling himself before worse could happen. 'Everybody assures us they have never had any dealings with young Dalston. That surely argues for a fellow whom respectable people are eager to avoid. They act as if any contact with him, however humdrum or remote, would leave a stain on their reputation. Does that not argue for a fellow of the very worst character?'

'Yes, but you knew that already.'

'I knew he was said to be immoral. I just didn't know how debauched his behaviour was.'

The first indication of a source of truly useful information did not come until the fourth day. It arrived in the form of a letter from Sir Henry Barnes, one of those to whom Lady Alice had written.

'Who is this Henry Barnes?' Adam asked her when she told him about the letter.

'A pleasant man, now of advanced middle-age I would reckon. He was really a friend of my first husband. Sir Daniel thought very highly of him. Unlike some of the others who claimed to be friends of ours, he made sure to stay in contact with me after Sir Daniel died. He never forced his acquaintance on me; simply made it clear that he would always be ready with help or advice should I need them. I'm surprised that you don't recall him since he came to our wedding.'

'There were so many new faces on that day I quickly abandoned any attempt to remember them,' Adam replied. He was not the most sociable of people. Being introduced to perhaps twenty or thirty new faces in quick succession had been his idea of torture. He looked at his wife as he spoke, afraid that she was going to call him to task. Fortunately, she simply smiled and patted his arm before continuing her explanation.

'Sir Henry is a widower with two sons, one called James and the other Edward. I don't think he has any other surviving children, though there may be a daughter I haven't met. I think I heard him mention one. The sons must both be in their early twenties by now. The family home is close to the southern fringes of the city, so I suspect both those young men spend the bulk of their time within the city itself.'

'What does he tell you in his letter?' Adam was growing bored with all this biography. All he really wanted to know was whether or not Sir Henry and his sons could offer him any useful information.

'He writes that he has spoken to his elder son — that's James — and James will speak with Edward. He thinks they might have something useful to contribute, since both are members of what he calls a "fast set" of young men from good families living in or around the city. He admits his sons are rather wilder than is quite proper, though he also writes that they don't appear to get involved in anything excessively dangerous or likely to lead to embarrassment for the family.'

Here she paused and started to smile broadly. 'This next part is typical of Sir Henry. I told you he was a kind and thoughtful man. He writes that he himself got into some wild escapades when he was the same age, though he would never admit that to his sons. Then he goes on to say that there is no real harm in any of the members of this group, although he does wish his own sons would not lose quite so much money at the card tables.'

'But did they know Frederick Dalston?' Adam did wish she would get to the point.

'Don't be so impatient, husband! I'm telling you what Sir Henry says while trying to read his letter at the same time. I can't help it if the man tends to wander a little in his narrative.'

'My apologies, my dear,' Adam said in mock contrition. 'Please continue.'

That earned him a hard stare with a slight but definite indication of a tongue being poked out between closed lips.

'Now we get to the crux of the matter,' Lady Alice continued, relaxing her frown. 'It seems they did know Frederick Dalston quite well and thought him — here I am quoting Sir Henry's actual words — "a mad fellow, unhappy with his situation and always seeking to earn money with no effort". Sir Henry writes that both his sons would be willing to speak with you at greater length, if you thought it would be useful. Unfortunately, Edward is away for a few days. If you would prefer to see them together, he can arrange this for Wednesday of next week. They would even come to Aylsham if you wished it.'

'It might be most convenient, though I would happily go to Norwich,' Adam said. 'It's a good many weeks since I've been there and there are various small tasks which I might accomplish at the same time. It's only a shame that we can't meet them both sooner.'

'Do not say "we", my dear. I'm sure my presence would be sadly inhibiting, particularly if you want these young men to talk with you openly about their set's activities in the city — let alone those, possibly far wilder, that involved Frederick Dalston. I will confine myself to questioning any ladies who might be able to offer us useful information. They would similarly be reluctant to speak openly if a man were present.'

She paused, folded the letter from Sir Henry and placed it on the table in front of her. Adam noticed there was another letter lying there but, before he could ask about it, Lady Alice had picked it up, broken the seal and began reading the contents.

'This is a note from my niece, Ruth,' she said after a moment. 'She says that she and your mother would like to speak with you as soon as convenient. The two of them have collected what they hope may prove to be a good haul of gossip about Frederick Dalston's amorous adventures in recent times. She says that they will both be at home on Friday afternoon — that's the day after tomorrow — and throughout Saturday. Why don't we go and spend a few days at our house in the city? You can do whatever it is you need to do and then arrange to meet with James and Edward Barnes on our return. Next day, we can both talk with Ruth and your mother. I haven't seen either of them since the day of our marriage. It will be delightful to spend some time in conversation with them. Visiting Norwich will also give me an opportunity to call on certain purveyors of fine cloth material for upholstery. I have completed this set of discussions with our architect — at least for the time being — and he has returned to his place of business to draw up the revised plans for the renovations and list the changes in cost involved. That is bound to take him at least a week, probably rather more. He has amply proved his ability and artistic sensibilities. I only wish he might improve his timeliness and sense of urgency. Still, while he takes his time, I can finalise my own ideas for the interior decorations.'

There is an old saying that it never rains but it pours. That now proved equally true of the amount of information reaching Adam about Frederick Dalston. After a long period of drought, it started to arrive in a flood. Indeed, it was rather more than he could assimilate all at once.

Later that same day, his wife received a response from Charles Scudamore in Holt. After the usual pleasantries and some amusement that he had received two nearly identical messages from both his aunt and Adam, he turned to the meat of what he had to say. It seemed that a report had been spreading around the legal community of the county concerning Frederick Dalston. It was said that he had consulted several lawyers about a rather unusual problem relating to the laws of inheritance. Charles didn't know what responses Frederick had received, but he felt the nature of the problem itself was certainly worthy of Adam's attention. Unfortunately, it was rather too complex to explain properly on paper. Various business matters would require him to remain in Holt for at least another week. If Adam could be prepared to wait a little, he and his wife would visit them in Aylsham. Then he could explain everything in person. Since he and Sophia also had some important news they wished to share, it would suit them very well to make a visit at that time.

Adam and his wife sat down at once to write letters to Sir Henry Barnes, Ruth and Charles making the necessary arrangements in each case. They would leave for Norwich on Friday, arriving before noon. That would give them time to settle themselves and recover from the journey before visiting Adam's mother and Ruth the following morning. Adam called for his groom, William, to inform him that he needed to have the carriage and horses ready at that time. Lady Alice wrote to the housekeeper in Norwich forewarning her of their imminent arrival. They could not at this stage be precise about how long they would stay in Norwich, since that would depend on what they discovered when they arrived. However, they would certainly leave in good time to entertain Charles and Sophia at the beginning of the following week.

Adam had never visited their Norwich property before. It had belonged to Sir Daniel Fouchard, Lady Alice's first husband. Since it had not been part of the original Fouchard family estate — Sir Daniel had purchased it himself — he had been free to bequeath ownership to his widow, together with a mass of other properties and investments that he had built up over the years. Legally, all this was now Adam's, though he was careful to acknowledge that it was really his wife's property and thus was only his by virtue of their marriage. The only thing he knew about the house itself was that it stood in Colegate, not far from the Octagon Chapel, and that they employed a housekeeper to look after the place when they were not in residence.

You may imagine his surprise when they arrived on the Friday at a substantial, modern house of two stories and seven bays, with steps up to the front door. The whole house was built of fine brickwork, with ashlar stone on the corners and around the windows and doors. Even from the outside, you could tell it was the home of a wealthy man. Amongst the other houses on that part of the street — all of them substantial buildings and most of them instructed in the modern style — it stood out like a thoroughbred horse in a paddock full of ponies.

On entering, Adam was dumbstruck to be greeted by a line of staff, consisting of the housekeeper, the cook, a parlour maid, a kitchen maid, a scullery maid, a footman and a groom. Would he ever become used to living on this scale of munificence? He knew Sir Daniel Fouchard had been an extremely wealthy man but he had not realised that he was able to afford to live in such luxurious accommodation wherever he went.

'A groom?' Adam said to his wife after the welcomes were over and they had retired to the parlour to drink a cup of coffee together.

'Of course,' she replied. 'Surely you did not expect to have to walk around the city, especially in bad weather. There are no stables attached to the house itself. You would not expect that. The horses are stabled at a livery further up Magdalen Street, where there is also space for our carriage. The groom sees all is kept ready for use whenever we wish.'

Adam was silenced. It was going to take him a long time to become accustomed to the kind of life his new wife had been used to since at least her first marriage and probably before that. Then another thought occurred to him.

'Do we also have a London house?' he asked.

'Of course not,' his wife replied. 'We rent one, with the necessary servants, whenever we need it. The cost of a permanent London home would be impossible to justify, unless you intend to live there for a substantial part of every year. You aren't thinking of going into politics, are you?'

'Heaven forfend!' Adam said fervently. 'I can't imagine suffering a worse fate.'

'That's good,' his wife replied. 'I like the fact that we will live in the country for most of our time, and I would hate to be left in Aylsham while you pursued a political career in the capital. This Norwich house will be useful to us. I'm sure of that. It will avoid any need to seek to stay with friends or relatives, let alone risk a dubious room in some hostelry. Unless you would prefer to stay with your mother?'

'Definitely not!' Adam said. 'I would be like some exotic beast to be exhibited to all her friends. This house if infinitely preferable. I'm just unused to living on such a scale. Now, I suggest we take this afternoon to rest after our journey, then go to see Ruth and my mother tomorrow, as we agreed.'

'I think that will be best," Lady Alice replied. 'I'll write Ruth a note and tell the housekeeper to see that it is delivered immediately.'

3

When Adam's father died, his elder brother Giles inherited Trundon Hall and its estate. It was not Mrs Bascom's way to impose herself on her son and his family. She thought it better to allow them to establish themselves in their new lives without feeling she was peering over their shoulders. Therefore, she took her widow's dower and used it to rent a house near the cathedral in Norwich. Now she spent her time socialising with a considerable number of well-born ladies of her own age. Most of them were widows, several had never married and few probably had husbands somewhere, though they rarely, if ever, appeared. All had sufficient wealth in their own right to be able to avoid the pitfalls of being dependent on some reluctant male relative for a home in their old age. After some time, Mrs Bascom had found living on her own — save naturally for the servants — did not suit her, so she engaged a younger woman, equally well-born but considerably more impecunious, as her companion. That arrangement had proved to be a great success until her companion, Miss Sophia LaSalle, took it into her head to marry Charles Scudamore, Lady Alice's nephew.

Even then, Mrs Bascom had not been compelled to return to a lonely state. Charles's twin sister, Ruth, needed somewhere to live.

She and Charles had been alternately living at their parents' home in London and staying with their aunt at her home at Mossterton Hall in Norfolk. When she too was widowed at the extremely early age of twenty-two by a few days, Lady Alice decided that Mossterton Hall was far too large for her. She therefore agreed with the heir to the entailed estate, one of her husband's nephews, to give up her life interest in the Hall and the income it provided, in return for a substantial immediate cash payment. That left Ruth with nowhere to live. Lady Alice had, of course, solved her own accommodation problem by accepting Adam's proposal of marriage. Ruth did not want to return to her parents in London, so an arrangement was made allowing her to move in with Mrs Bascom as joint tenant of the Norwich house. The arrangement had proved to suit both of them. Mrs Bascom's regular outgoings were reduced by a significant amount, allowing her to spend a little more on the fashionable clothes she needed to stay level with her wealthier friends. Ruth gained her independence, along with excellent opportunities to enhance her growing reputation as a botanical artist. Living in Norwich granted her easy access to several fine libraries. It also gave her the chance to attend a number of relevant lectures given by botanists and scientists with national reputations. Thanks to these and the connections she had made through other members of the audience, she had already been approached to provide the illustrations for a book on the flora of Norfolk. There was also talk of an exhibition of her work to be undertaken by the Norwich Naturalists and Botanical History Society. She might yet marry but, if not, her future seemed assured.

The house where these two ladies lived was within the area known as Cathedral Close; a wide swathe of gardens and properties surrounding Norwich's magnificent mediaeval cathedral. Most of the dwellings were allocated to various church dignitaries but a few of them could be rented from the Dean and Chapter, provided you were judged to be suitable. Adam would have walked the few hundred yards from their house in Colegate to the Close but Lady Alice would have none of it.

'The horses could do with some employment,' she said firmly, 'as could the groom. Besides, I should hate to spoil these shoes by walking in the mud and filth of the street.'

When Adam attempted to argue the point, she settled the matter with a question which admitted only one answer.

'What would your mother think if her son, the baronet, was seen to arrive at her house on foot? She would never forgive you for damaging her status amongst the ladies of the city in such a way. We will take the carriage. I have already instructed the groom to have it ready on the half hour.'

They rode the four hundred yards and clattered up to Mrs Bascom's door in fine style.

For Adam, accustomed to the modest buildings of Aylsham, the two great gatehouses, which provided the only entry to the Close from the area of the city known as Tombland, acted like castle towers, protecting the clerical elite from the noise, bustle and stench of the city. Once past their high-arched entries, all was calmness and serenity.

The houses between the entrance towers and the cathedral were grand affairs of three- and four-stories of red brick and pale stonework. Across an open space, perhaps fifty yards in width, lay the cathedral itself, its huge spire seeming to reach into the clouds. Once there had been a monastery to serve the cathedral. Now the inhabitants of these houses fulfilled the same duties so that it remained as it had always been, an enclosed and protected world of its own.

The Close had another entry as well. A road lined with neat, mostly Tudor dwellings ran down past the bishop's imposing palace and the grey stone, mediaeval grandeur of the Great Hospital. There was even a short roadway to one side with a few still more modest dwellings and a tavern. After that, the road became a path which led through open land towards the river beyond, crossed here by a stone bridge of venerable age known as the Bishop's Bridge.

Mrs Bascom and Ruth occupied one of the houses between the grandeur of the canons' houses and the entrance to the bishop's palace. They were rented to certain gentry households or occupied by lowlier cathedral servants, such as the organist and master of the choristers. It was not as fine a mansion as the one Adam now owned, thanks to his marriage, but grand enough and well supplied with congenial neighbours across the Close, including the Archdeacon's family and families of the other canons. The bishop's wife too was one of the more distinguished members of the circle of Mrs Bascom's acquaintance. Two of the minor canons of the cathedral, along with the master of the choristers, were ardent naturalists; all more than willing to assist Ruth with the studies necessary to pursue her chosen artistic career. Between them, they could muster a good deal of botanical knowledge, including a strong interest in wild orchids. The precentor, thanks to a long-term friendship with Mr Robert Masham of Stratton Strawless Hall, was well on the way to becoming an expert in arboriculture. Thus, Mrs Basham and Ruth now found almost all they needed within the Close itself, while the houses of most of the other wealthy residents of the city were nearby, the majority being found from Tombland down into Magdalen Street and Colegate and thence into Pottergate.

The two ladies were naturally eager to hear about Lady Alice's plans for the extensions and improvements to Wrigsby Hall. All Adam wanted to learn was what they had discovered about Frederick Dalston. As usual, it being three against one, the wishes of the ladies carried the day. Adam was beginning to discover that, unless you are a tyrant of the most disagreeable kind, the phrase "master in your own house" meant very little in practical terms. You could fight to get your own way and live a miserable life or you could accept the way things were and maintain a calm and pleasant atmosphere. It did not take him long to make his choice. More than an hour passed, therefore, before the conversation between the four of them reached the point where there was any mention of Frederick Dalston. Indeed, when such a mention did arise, Adam was lost in wool-gathering and almost missed it.

'There was a great deal of gossip stirred up by that young Frederick Dalston's death, wasn't there, Ruth?' Mrs Bascom said. 'There weren't many who expressed any great surprise that his life had ended in violence.'

'Given his behaviour, someone was almost bound to try to harm him eventually,' Ruth agreed. 'His reputation as a seducer of respectable women was well known to everyone. The fellow was a very worst type of womaniser.'

'I suppose all the mothers feared for their daughters' good names,' Lady Alice said. 'I can't imagine any respectable family would have countenanced a marriage between this Mr Dalston and any of the daughters of the house, however ill-favoured and lacking in accomplishments.'

Mrs Bascom agreed. 'It would be a callous parent who condemned their daughter to a marriage which was likely to prove unhappy from the start. No one could have imagined that Frederick Dalston would ever be faithful, despite his marriage vows and whatever he professed before the wedding took place.'

'Sadly, he was not alone in that respect,' Ruth said. 'A good many men are equally lacking in restraint and moral sense. Perhaps it's fortunate most are content with seducing the servant girls, regrettable though that is in itself.'

'True,' Mrs Bascom said, 'though the girls themselves are often not without a share of blame. Some hope to benefit by a dalliance with either their master or one of his sons.'

'If so, most are soon cruelly deceived,' Ruth countered. 'It is more usual for such poor women to find themselves cast off when they are found to be expecting a child. Thrown out into the street without a reference to fend for themselves.'

Lady Alice intervened to bring the conversation back on track. 'From what I have heard, Frederick Dalston was no longer content to confine himself to servant girls, however willing. Rumour has it his targets of late were respectable young women.'

'Or even their mothers,' Ruth added. 'If the reports are true, several wives — some approaching middle age — also succumbed to the man's charms.'

'Was it simply a case of taking his pleasures then walking away without a backward glance?' Lady Alice asked. 'Was he a rake of that kind?'

'As far as we can tell,' Mrs Bascom said, lowering her voice and leaning forwards as if sharing a great secret, 'that was not what he did at all. He was after money, as well as the pleasures of the flesh. Once a woman's reputation was likely to be ruined, he would offer to draw a veil of silence and secrecy over the whole affair, in return for a suitable payment.'

'That's blackmail!' Adam said loudly. He had been silent for so long that the rest jumped at the sound of his voice.

'It sounds very much like it,' Lady Alice said. 'What a despicable wretch! Did anyone pay?'

'It seems likely that some of them did,' Mrs Bascom replied. 'Take his latest conquest — if you can call it that. It happened less than a month or so ago. The story that the family have been attempting to spread about sounds to me as if it was created by Frederick Dalston — and backed up by him — as a result of a suitable payment. They have apparently told their friends and acquaintances that while their daughter had acted foolishly, she had not actually been ... spoiled.'

'Lost her virginity, you mean,' Ruth had no time for euphemisms. 'I very much doubt that it's true. Didn't she elope with Dalston?'

'She did,' Mrs Bascom said, 'but they only got as far as King's Lynn before the girl's brothers caught up with them. I heard the two were waiting there to take passage on a ship to Scotland.'

'And was that on the same day that they left?' Ruth asked.

'The day after.'

'There you are then. I doubt they spent the night in separate rooms or chastely discussing the works of Shakespeare.'

'What did these brothers do when they caught up with them?' Adam interrupted.

'There are two stories about that,' his mother said. 'One holds that Dalston saw them approaching, jumped on a horse that had been left nearby and so escaped. The other recounts that he offered to agree that he and the girl had not actually engaged in carnal intercourse, but only in return for a payment of five hundred pounds. If that was refused, he would proclaim to the world that he had enjoyed her favours multiple times, both before they set out and during the night before they were apprehended.'

'I imagine that was a good deal closer to the truth,' Ruth said quietly. 'How old was she? Seventeen? Eighteen? A man like Dalston would have had very little difficulty in convincing a girl of that age, especially one with a romantic turn of mind, that giving into his demands would be a proof of her love, and that she couldn't prove that too many times.'

'Did he have no regard at all for the girl's feelings?' Lady Alice asked. "Was he really prepared to treat her simply as a commodity whose good name was to be bought and sold?'

'Apparently so,' Mrs Bascom replied. 'At least that is how the gossip has it. You must always make allowances for those who like to embellish a tale as they pass it on.'

'What Mrs Bascom had just said would certainly fit with what a number of my acquaintances have told me,' Ruth added. 'Only yesterday, during my visit to the circulating library, two of them told me that Frederick Dalston was obsessed with making money by whatever means. They were both in a position to know because they have brothers who moved in the same circles as Dalston. In speaking to me, they were quite clear that Frederick Dalston had become notorious, not just as a womaniser but for his attempts to make money by that means. Not only that, it seems he has had a hand in several other schemes, all of them dubious, one or two probably illegal, and every one designed to yield quick returns. It was becoming clear, these ladies told me, that he was not a person to be trusted in any sphere of life. If what they said is correct — and I have no reason to doubt it — you'll need to look beyond angry fathers and wronged husbands, Adam. I imagine there are a great many other people in this city with excellent reasons to rejoice at the news of Dalston's death.'

'I still find it difficult to believe that the young man was entirely evil,' Lady Alice said. 'Has no one suggested anything which might serve to portray his actions in a less harsh light?'

'Rumour rarely seeks for explanations other than the obvious, my dear,' Mrs Bascom said. 'Reasons and excuses spoil a good story. Those who deal in gossip like their villains to be entirely black.'

'I have met no one who has offered anything that might be seen to put a different complexion on Frederick Dalston and his actions,' Ruth said. 'There is nothing to suggest any mitigating circumstances relating to what he has been doing. If he is not entirely evil, he is making a very good pretence of being so.'

'That may be so,' Adam said. 'Yet those who know they are really damned in the eyes of the world sometimes decide they have nothing to lose by behaving exactly as others expect. Especially if they can find an advantage by doing so. It may be that what you have been able to discover so far represents only the very worst side of Dalston's character and that appearing as a thoroughgoing villain benefited him in some way. For example, if you wish to extort money by threats, it will help if people believe you will carry them out if they do not pay you. A merciful blackmailer is a contradiction in terms. What isn't at all clear is why he was so fixated on money.'

❦

THE NEXT DAY PROVED FRUSTRATING. LADY ALICE DEPARTED BY carriage to visit a number of tradesmen known to her who might be able to supply the cloth she wanted for the curtains and upholstery at Wrigsby Hall. After that, she told her husband, she hoped to be able to view some carpets for the new rooms. If not, she would do that on another occasion.

Adam also went out, on foot this time, in search of information rather than furnishing materials. He was hoping to discover more about that part of Frederick Dalston's life when he wasn't engaged in a relentless pursuit of women. Surely, he must have done other things as well, if only to give himself time to rest. There was also the matter of money. Had Frederick still relied principally on his father? If so, was that insufficient in some way? His father had said he'd refused to discharge any further debts incurred by Frederick. He hadn't said he'd denied him all funds. Most elder sons had no need to seek out additional resources, save to pay their gambling debts from time to time. Adam tried to reason it through. If William Dalston held firm, there would be a scandal, which would finally put paid to any chances of his son marrying well and thus adding to the family's wealth and land holdings. If he paid, Frederick would know that any future threats meant nothing. Since, by all accounts, it would take a direct visit from the Archangel Gabriel to persuade that young man to repent his ways, there must have been some other reason for the young man to want to raise money in a hurry.

That made sense so far. If Frederick had some other reason to have a pressing need for money, what was it? Did it have any bearing on his murder? That was the sticking point. It was in pursuit of answers to that problem Adam had now set out, determined to use any means he could think of to achieve his purpose.

Adam's first call was at the office of his banker, Edward Malvers. Luckily, the man was available and more than willing to talk to such an excellent and well-respected customer. That's to say he was eager to talk about the chance of new business for him. As soon as Adam began to ask about Frederick Dalston, Malvers proved just as reticent as Adam had expected. At first, he would only say that he had no direct knowledge of the young man, having never done any business with him. After that, he added that he found mere gossip distasteful — a statement Adam strongly doubted. In his experience, those who made their living in the financial markets relied on listening to gossip to discover opportunities to enhance their profits or impending problems that they should avoid.

Adam tried another approach.

'Speaking as a knowledgeable adviser in such matters,' he said, 'would you be willing to say that Frederick Dalston was the kind of person to whom a prudent businessman should be willing to offer credit?'

That put the banker in an obvious quandary. For a start, he was not a man willing to ever give a direct answer to a direct question — unless it was to make an outright refusal to give someone a loan. He grunted, fussed with his sleeves and fiddled with the papers on his desk. Adam waited.

Finally, when it became obvious that delaying tactics were wasted, Malvers was forced to admit that he would not be comfortable in recommending such a course of action.

'You see, Sir Adam,' he said, 'Mr. Frederick Dalston had ... um ... a certain reputation, let us say. It was known at one time that he owed considerable amounts of money to a number of traders in the city. There were also other ... matters ... concerning his character. These were ... how shall I put it? ... things of a less savoury nature.'

'Did he settle his debts?'

'All were eventually discharged, I believe, whether by Dalston himself or by his father I could not say with certainty.'

This supported the general notion that Frederick Dalston had severe and recurring money troubles of late. Adam already knew that. Since the debts had been paid off, they could not account for the young man's continuing drive to raise money by any means available to him.

Finding Malvers unable or unwilling to provide any further information, Adam left at that point and returned to the house in Colegate. He was glad of a chance for a further walk. It allowed him to puzzle and fret over who else might be able to provide him with useful information. All that he had discovered so far was either hopelessly vague, like the banker's innuendos and evasions, or solely concerned with Dalston's past seductions. Even in those cases, there had been no firm evidence of a specific person known to be hell-bent on taking revenge. There still might be one, or even several, but, if there were, they had kept their intentions from becoming known. Adam was left with no way of putting a name to anyone bent on inflicting punishment for a daughter's or a sister's ruin.

The walk home took him between twenty and twenty-five minutes, during which time he reviewed his meagre list of possible informants again and again. Damnation! He could not think of a single one likely to give him anything different from what he had already. Then, as he raised the knocker on his front door to summon the butler to let him in, a more useful line of investigation came to his mind. Why had Frederick shifted his interest in recent weeks from seeing vulnerable women purely as a source of sexual gratification to using them as the means for blackmail. Surely it must be due to his overwhelming need for money. Damn! Damn again! He was back at the same question. Why? Adam didn't believe it was to pay off gambling debts. Young "blades" like Frederick Dalston spent a good deal of their time in gaming clubs, often indulging in betting for high stakes. Most lost. Some of them heavily. That kind of behaviour had been going on for decades, if not centuries. Their fathers must have expected this period of wild behaviour, if only because they had acted that way themselves at the same age. William Dalston could well have been just such a young fellow before settling down to manage the family lands. Maybe that was why he had treated his elder son with such tolerance. Indeed, he might have continued doing so for some years yet, had the Kessingfield estate produced sufficient money to allow it.

Adam handed his stick, hat and coat to the butler and went at once to the room which served as a library. There, for what felt like the ninety-ninth time, he went over all the evidence he had collected yet again. It was as he had thought; no one had suggested Frederick Dalston's behaviour at the gaming tables was unusually rash or unusually unlucky. True, he had been excluded from a group for cheating, or trying to, but this seemed to have occurred recently, after his need to raise unusual amounts of money had already become established. No one had suggested gambling was especially significant in the long list of Frederick Dalston's vices.

Adam swore to himself again. He was getting nowhere. Until he could set down in his mind some specific alternative topics which needed to be researched, he was like a poorly-trained boxer — reduced to throwing out punches in all directions in the hope of hitting a vital spot, if only by chance.

ADAM SPENT A TROUBLED NIGHT WITH VERY LITTLE SLEEP AND WOKE in a truly foul mood. Rather than inflict himself on his wife over breakfast, he drank some coffee and ate one or two warm rolls then went out to try to walk off his bad temper. Crossing the Fye Bridge, he entered The Cathedral Close, passed across the West End of the colossal mediaeval church, turned down towards the Bishop's Bridge and thus into the streets beyond. Such houses as there were here were widely scattered, since the city had only just begun to extend itself beyond its mediaeval walls in this direction. After wandering for a while amongst trees and hedgerows and along muddy roads, he retraced his steps, recrossed the river and turned right towards the Cow Tower. Once it had served to block the river by means of a chain, preventing any hostile vessels from making their way within the walls of the city. Now it was an empty, partly ruined shell; a haunt of bats and owls, which served only to mark the beginning of that part of the river where barges and wherries bringing goods from Great Yarmouth and the sea beyond could tie up. After that, his way passed along by the wharves and warehouses, back to Fye Bridge and from there to his home.

The moment he arrived, the butler informed him that Lady Alice had left to look at more carpets and, after that, at possible sources of new furniture. He was to advise his master that, on her return, she would be entertaining a number of lady friends to tea. His presence would not be not required.

Adam could have removed himself to another room in the house. It was more than large enough. Instead, he went out again, wandering aimlessly about the city, stopping in a coffeehouse for a while and browsing in a bookshop, then walking on again, his head bowed and his mind somewhere else. He kept hoping that some answers might pop into his mind to the questions that bothered him so much. Either that, or he would suddenly hit upon an idea that would suggest a course for future action.

Why had Frederick moved from seducing servants to praying on the daughters of the well-born and then to extortion? Was it simply a way of making money? If so, why did he need to act in that way? Were there no better, more reputable ways of raising funds than by threatening to ruin respectable girls? What was he spending his money on that meant he constantly needed so much more? It didn't seem to be gambling within the city. Did he frequent the local racecourses? Did he travel to Newmarket and fritter his money away in extravagant bets on slow horses? Was he a denizen of some high-stakes gambling club elsewhere that Adam had not yet learned about? Surely, if any of these ways of losing large amounts of money had been typical of the man, someone would have said so already? If they were not, however did he spend his time? How was he throwing all this extra money away? All anyone had told Adam so far was that Frederick Dalston was a danger to women and was always heavily in debt to local shopkeepers and traders. If young men were now being murdered for vices such as these, the families of the aristocracy and gentry would very soon be made up entirely of daughters.

It looked as if Adam would finally return home in an even blacker mood than before, but fate intervened to save his wife and servants from having that inflicted upon them. When he arrived, he found a note waiting for him from Sir Henry Barnes. Edward Barnes had returned home earlier than had been expected. He and his brother William would, therefore, present themselves at Adam's house at eleven o'clock the next morning, provided that would be convenient. Naturally it was, and Adam sent a note to that effect straightaway via a servant. Perhaps the brothers would be able to tell him something that would at last set his investigation on the correct path.

4

A dam had asked to meet Sir Henry's sons at his house in Colegate. There they would not fear that their father, or one of the servants, would be able to overhear what they said to him. He would also be on his own that morning. His wife would be out for the greater part of the day engaged in yet more visiting and shopping. He had also instructed his own servants to stay well clear. When James and Edward Barnes arrived promptly at ten o'clock as agreed, the butler at once ushered them in to the library where Adam was waiting for them.

Adam was struck by the contrast in appearance between the brothers. You had to look quite closely before you could see a resemblance to their father in either of them. James, the elder of the two, was tall and slim. He moved and spoke slowly as if he was concerned to demonstrate a deep attachment to stability, whatever Adam might have heard to the contrary. Edward, three years younger and at least a head shorter, was already showing distinct signs of the genial, roly-poly figure he would doubtless attain by middle age. Where James was stately and reserved, Edward was bursting with pent-up energy. He was impulsive whereas his brother seemed cautious, talkative where his brother's natural reticence came to the fore.

It was Edward who stepped forward to introduce them both. James remained a step behind, contented to nod his head in acknowledgement, staring somewhere into the far distance. An odd pair at first sight, Adam said to himself, whose lives might soon diverge onto separate paths, however close they might be to one another nowadays.

Adam had spent some time before they arrived deciding what his approach to them should be. After the usual opening pleasantries, therefore, he hastened to assure the pair that anything they told him would be kept entirely confidential. He would most definitely not be reporting it back to their father. James acknowledged this promise with a gentle inclination of his head.

Edward, on the other hand, grinned cheerfully. 'Damned decent of you, Sir Adam, to make that promise,' he said, his voice as loud and cheerful as his expression. 'Naturally we wouldn't want our father to know too much about what we get up to when we're away from the old family seat. Not that it's so very dreadful, you understand. My brother there is the daring one. I'm usually too timid to venture far off the path of virtue. Don't be fooled by his funereal manner. That's just a face he puts on when it suits him. You'd think butter wouldn't melt in his mouth, wouldn't you? It wouldn't, but only because he would have spat it out and used it to make some pal of his slip and end up arse over tip.'

'Really, Edward,' James said, in a tone that would have served for a nursemaid admonishing a naughty infant. 'You do come out with such nonsense! Don't believe him, sir. Neither of us are much given to dangerous escapades. We are here because the group we tend to associate with happened to, at one time, include a number of young men addicted to wild adventures. Frederick Dalston was one of them.'

'We called him "Oily" Dalston,' Edward added. 'Mostly because he was thick and slippery. Always full of wild schemes, none of which were fully considered before he launched into them. The poor fellow's life was a long series of self-inflicted disasters.'

'The inevitable consequence of matching impulsiveness with a notable lack of intellect,' James pronounced gravely. 'He was cursed with a temperament guaranteed to lead him to a bad end.'

'Oily didn't much like my brother,' Edward interposed. 'James was too fond of pointing out the glaring flaws in all his mad-brained schemes.'

'He thought I looked down on him because our family's estates are more extensive than his. If I did look down on him, it was because he was stupidly impulsive. Mostly, I gave him very little thought.'

'That was something else unfortunate about Oily, sir,' Edward said. 'He managed to fall out with almost everyone after a while. People came to realise he wasn't to be relied on. He seemed to believe everyone was impatient to see him come to grief. He could do that for himself. He sounded arrogant and brash, but he was unbelievably sensitive to the slightest suggestion of disdain. As my brother said, most people did their best to ignore him.'

'If no one in your group liked Frederick Dalston,' Adam asked, 'how did he come to be a member in the first place? Even more importantly, how did he remain a member?'

'He simply pushed his way in at the start,' Edward said. 'No one knew much about him, so there seemed no reason to make any objection. As for your second question, Oily could be utterly charming when it suited him. He also had a rare gift for making people laugh. It took a little while for the real person behind the mask to become clear.'

'I think what finally turned many of us against him,' James added, 'was the way he kept boasting about all his female conquests. For a time, that was virtually the sole topic of his conversation. Some people found it amusing. Most of us dismissed it as a mixture of fantasy and exaggeration. When we found out it was true, the man's behaviour took on a far more distasteful aspect. A good many of us have sisters, you understand.'

James Barnes gave his opinion with the air of a judge pronouncing a sentence of death, while his brother nodded enthusiastically in agreement.

'Recently, the fellow had become obsessed with money,' his brother added. 'We heard much less about his women and far too much about his attempts at money-making schemes. Damned boring, I called it!'

'Do you know what caused the change?' Adam asked. 'I've heard the same thing from other people, but no one has been able to suggest a convincing reason.'

There was a lengthy pause at that point while the brothers looked at one another, seeming to communicate with nothing but a series of slight changes in expression. Finally, Edward spoke again.

'There is one thing, I suppose. He told us several times he was very unhappy with his life as heir to Kessingfield Hall,' he said slowly, now sounding more like James than himself. 'He once described it as an existence dedicated to trying to stave off boredom while waiting for his father to die.'

'That's a very harsh way of putting it,' Adam exclaimed. 'All eldest sons must find themselves in the same situation, yet most seem content enough.'

There was another lengthy pause before James made a new contribution.

'Frederick considered his long-term situation to be hopeless as well. According to him, the estate was in a poor financial state. He also considered it too small to provide what he considered a suitable income. Much of the land lies near the coast or on the heaths, and there was no capital available to purchase more land. The same was true of the money that would be needed to bring about any significant improvements in the way the current tenants farmed what they had. Basically, it's poor land, suited to little more than keeping a few sheep and a couple of warrens.'

'Are you suggesting all this emphasis on moneymaking was aimed at acquiring more manors and improving the way the estate was being run?' Adam asked. 'The usual way of doing that would be to find an heiress, however far she's past her prime and however unpleasant to look upon. Failing that, there are usually some wealthy merchants eager to sell a daughter in exchange for an alliance with a family with sufficient lands to qualify as gentry.'

'Of course,' his brother chipped in. 'We're not really suggesting that Frederick Dalston was trying to raise money to buy land or improve what his family held, are we, James? I don't believe he would ever have become reconciled to being a country squire. However much land he had, and however good it was, he seemed to hate the very notion. As for finding an heiress or a rich wife, Oily knew only too well that his past — and current — history of seductions made his chances of securing such a marriage unlikely in the extreme. All the conventional ways of acquiring more capital or more acres were ruled out.'

'Couldn't he have changed his ways?' Adam asked. 'Express contrition for his past sins and set out on a new path? If he gave it a few years, people would start to accept he might prove to be an acceptable husband at least. Memories fade quickly. If he wanted to build a life for himself as his father's successor, surely that would have been a sensible course of action?'

There was an even longer pause than before while the two brothers avoided Adam's eyes. Whatever it was they knew, it was plain that they were finding the greatest difficulty in talking about it, despite Adam's assurance that everything they told him would be treated in the strictest of confidence. Finally, Edward looked at his brother, gave a small grimace and began to speak.

'What I'm going to tell you now was told to me in the greatest confidence,' he began, 'so I'm relying on you to treat it in the same way. Just before the point at which he was excluded from our circle entirely, I became almost the last person willing to listen to Oily's woes. It wasn't because I wanted to. I didn't. I just didn't have the heart to refuse. I suppose, much as I disliked the man and deplored his conduct, I felt a kind of pity for him. James thought I was insane.'

'You were insane,' his elder brother said. 'When his behaviour became nothing but an embarrassment, Dalston was expelled and labelled a pariah. I had to work very hard to persuade the others not to exclude you as well.'

'And I'm grateful,' Edward replied. 'But we aren't here to tell Sir Adam about our own ups and downs. He wants to know about Oily and his doings.' He turned to face Adam. 'I'm only breaking my promise to stay silent because it may answer your question and explain why Dalston behaved in the way he did — why he became so obsessed with getting money; it may also help to bring his killer to justice. Anyway, the man's dead, so he can't object.'

Once again, Adam waited, saying nothing.

'Dalston told me there were two reasons why he was never going to become the squire of Kessingfield if he could avoid it. The first one was simple: he hated the countryside. Hated the mud and the noise of the birds and what he saw as the complete stupidity of the villagers. He hated riding, hunting and shooting and all the other things that most country squires spend their time doing. He may have been born in the country, even brought up there, but the only place he was happy was here in the city. The second reason was financial. The estate was already so heavily mortgaged it would be nearly worthless, even if he sold it once it was in his hands. Of course, the moment he talked to a lawyer, he realised even that was denied to him. The estate was entailed, so all he would inherit was a life interest in the income. It would never be his to sell unless some clever lawyers could find a way to break the entail. To his mind, the only thing left was to go somewhere abroad and start again. To find a place where he was not known and where his history could not be held against him. There he might find a rich wife and set himself up in the style he thought he deserved. The trouble was, to make this dream a reality, he needed a large sum of money to act as capital to get started. He also thought he would have to discover a way to avoid his father's executors and creditors tracking him down to make him pay off the debts on the estate.'

'Where did he intend to go?' Adam asked.

'That varied week by week,' Edward replied. 'First it was Barbados, then Jamaica, then our former colonies in North America. He said Canada was too cold and Australia just a penal colony. Once he even suggested he would go and live in Spain. That was typical of Oily. He was deeply attached to the idea, but he couldn't be bothered to look into the practicalities.'

'It seems a very extreme solution,' Adam remarked.

'Oily liked drama,' James said. 'I always thought he should have been an actor. Sadly, he wouldn't have had the patience to learn his lines. The very fact that leaving England forever would have been such a radical solution to his problems rendered it more attractive to him.'

'He was a strange figure,' Edward said. 'In an odd way, Oily had convinced himself his family was to blame for the mess he was in. Later, he went even further and blamed what he called "England's snobbish and corrupt society" — whatever he meant by that. He once told me his younger brother would love to be the squire of Kessingfield in his place and was, therefore, poisoning his father's mind against him, urging him to cut off further funds and find a way to disinherit him altogether. The reality is that his poor brother is the most mild and inoffensive of men. He would never have done such a thing. By the time he was killed, Oily had gone far beyond rationality. He hinted that he knew a means to fulfil his ambitions and deal his family and his country a heavy blow at the same time. The prospect excited him so much, he even reduced his womanising. How long he would have kept that up is debatable. To Oily, the need to chase women was like the need to breathe; he couldn't live without it.'

'When my brother mentioned this to me,' James said in his most magisterial way, 'I dismissed it as more of Dalston's typical wild talk. He always tried to find ways to blame others for the problems he had brought on himself. After I became convinced the fool actually meant what he was saying, I urged my brother to break off all further communication with him at once. In that state of mind, Dalston was capable of any action, however foolish, criminal or even treasonous.'

'You mentioned that Frederick was excluded from your circle recently,' Adam said. 'Why was that? Had everyone decided he was too dangerous?'

'He was caught cheating at the card table,' James said grimly. 'As you can imagine, everybody felt that was perfectly intolerable. We knew he wasn't too scrupulous about ideas for making money, but to cheat his friends — or try to — was beyond the pale.'

'He couldn't even get that right, you know,' Edward added. 'As a card sharp, he was useless.'

'What did he do after that?' Adam asked. 'By the way, how long ago did his exclusion take place?'

'About three months, I suppose,' James replied. 'When what he had done became common knowledge, no respectable group, however wild, would let him in. I lost track of him about then, thank goodness.'

'Did you also lose track of him?' Adam asked Edward.

'Not quite,' the young man said. 'A friend of mine told me Oily had become part of a coterie of young fellows around whom some extremely nasty rumours had spread. According to this gossip, they funded themselves by preying on wealthy, vulnerable women. Once they had wormed their way into some lady's affections, they set out to extract as much as they could, either by way of gifts or by threatening the woman's reputation if she failed to give them whatever they asked for. I believe they were well on the way to becoming notorious.'

At this point, James looked distinctly uncomfortable. 'When I said I'd lost track of Frederick Dalston, I have to admit to misleading you, Sir Adam,' he said. 'I simply didn't want to go on talking about Dalston and his foul ways. That was wrong and I apologise. You asked us to be open with you and I agreed. It's my duty to tell you all I know, and I shall meet that obligation.'

'Please do,' Adam said. 'I'm sure it will prove useful in tracking down the killer, however unpleasant it is to recall a person who would naturally be abhorrent to all decent people.'

This was significantly overstating the situation, but Adam sensed James Barnes needed to be reassured about his own behaviour.

'I heard the same rumours as my brother,' James began, 'but the person who told me knew more than that. According to him, the behaviour of Frederick Dalston and this coterie had soon attracted the attention of the criminal element in our city. They knew these young men were not as hardened to crime as they were but reckless fools ripe to be exploited.

'I knew nothing of this at all,' Edward declared. 'You never mentioned it to me, James.'

'Did you hear the names of any of these criminals?' Adam asked.

'I did hear one name,' James said slowly, 'but you must understand I cannot vouch for the accuracy of what I'm about to tell you. I only recall it because it was such an odd name. More like the name of one of those evangelical ranters than a criminal. The name mentioned was Obadiah Webley.'

Edward started and sucked in a sharp breath.

'You know of this Webley?' Adam said. 'Who is he? What do you know of him?'

'All I can tell you, Sir Adam,' Edward replied, 'is that I have been told he is a person anyone would do well to avoid. A lifelong criminal without morals or conscience, merciless in pursuing profit and personal gain. Also, the kind of man who can provide whatever you want, as long as you are able to pay his price and don't enquire into the means he used to obtain it — or the source from which it came.'

Adam tried to press them both for more details, but it soon became clear they had told him all they knew. He therefore thanked them and let them go.

Adam stayed in the library a while longer, making notes and trying find some kind of pattern in all he now knew. His mind was in such a whirl, however, that he feared becoming confused and missing the truly important points. One thing stood out with extreme clarity: there were more people than he had imagined who might have decided that putting an end to Frederick Dalston's life would free them from their own problems.

SINCE LADY ALICE HAD NOT YET RETURNED, ADAM DECIDED THAT afternoon to take a long walk alone through the city streets. He always found walking to be an excellent way of stimulating his mind when dealing with some difficult problem. The two brothers that morning had painted a different picture of Frederick Dalston from the one he had formed previously in his mind. Less a simple rake and womaniser, more a young man unable to come to terms with his life and responding with anger and bitterness instead of thinking things through carefully.

He began by wandering idly into Cockey Lane and from there towards the fashionable heart of Norwich, the great marketplace. In recent years, the streets around the edge of the market had filled up with those shops which found their customers from amongst the wealthier inhabitants of the city, the countryside round about and even further afield. Shops such as booksellers, vintners and gunsmiths. Indeed, the whole eastern edge of the marketplace, once called the Nethererowe, had earned itself the title of Gentleman's Walk. There you could find John Toll's drapers shop, probably the best in the city — Adam peered through the window to see if he might discover his wife within — together with the leading wine and spirit dealerships, tailors and milliners. In short, everything a wealthy gentleman's family might desire. The inns there were also the main starting points for the mail coaches and other conveyances for major cities such as London, thus ensuring there was no lack of potential customers at any time of the day.

At Saunders Coffee House, also on Gentleman's Row, Adam loitered for a while drinking coffee and reading the copies of the London newspapers. His mind was occupied in sorting out the facts he had been given into a satisfactory representation of the events leading up to Frederick Dalston's death. He had started out assuming that Frederick was simply a typical young profligate: a reckless gambler and womaniser. That had been altogether too simple a picture. He could see that now. Frederick Dalston was many things. According to the Barnes brothers, he could best be understood as the lonely, confused heir to an estate and a role in society he neither wanted nor felt he could tolerate; a man unable to escape a destiny which he viewed with loathing. Others described Frederick as primarily a criminal; an unmitigated scoundrel now seeking to amass wealth by every means open to him, legitimate or otherwise. To these must be added Frederick the radical; the rejected university man now harbouring ideas of political and social revolution not too dissimilar to those expounded by the Levellers and other supporters of "natural rights" in the time of Oliver Cromwell. Which one of these aspects of the man was the one which had brought about his death? Or had it been the combination of them all which finally proved deadly?

Adam left the coffeehouse and moved on through the crowds. The whole area was thronged with people, from the well-dressed wives and families of the city elite to the rough fellows who brought fresh goods to the market stalls. The roadway was clogged with vehicles of all sizes. Spruce phaetons tried to weave a path through the slower traffic and chaises and carriages bore the wealthy away, while others arrived to replace those which had left and disgorged fresh groups of shoppers and idlers. Stagecoaches emerged from the yards behind the main inns and tried to force their way through the mass of smaller vehicles. Lumbering farm wagons, some drawn by oxen, intermingled with people walking to and from the market stores. Once, a small herd of sheep added to the chaos as they were driven from the livestock market beside the castle to the butchers' stalls and shambles on the market's other side. It was a raucous, bewildering, constantly shifting jumble. A prosperous chaos of humanity intent on earning a living or spending what they had earned. Frederick Dalston, it seemed, had loved it. It made Adam's head ache.

How often would Frederick Dalston have idled away his time like this, leering at the prostitutes and looking out for pickpockets and cutpurses? Had he, as a fashionable young man, bought his clothes from the shops on Gentleman's Walk — at least until the unpaid bills mounted and the shopkeepers refused to serve him anymore? Had he loitered in the inns and coffeehouses, then walked westwards, in front of the houses over which the great tower of St Peter Mancroft loomed, to reach the theatre or the entrance to the Chapel Fields? Had he wandered in one or two of the pleasure gardens, his eyes fixed on the young ladies walking there with their chaperones, selecting the one who should be his next victim? Would he give up all of this for the unknown, simply to avoid doing what he had been born to do?

Norwich was the place where all the upper classes of East Anglia came to shop — at least when they weren't in London. A proud city, not quite as prosperous as it had been thirty or fifty years before, yet still a place to visit to see the members of fashionable society and be seen by them. The glory days of the city's cloth-weaving and dyeing trades had begun to pass, but you could still buy the fine worsted "stuffs" which had once made Norwich the nation's largest city save for London. In recent years, the advent of weaving and spinning machines driven by waterwheels had transferred much of the production of woollen cloth to mills along the fast-flowing streams of Yorkshire. The cotton mills of Lancashire had also begun to start producing colourful printed fabric that rivalled the highly decorated Norwich cloth at half the price. Though it was growing lethargic at the century's end, Norwich managed to conceal its decline well enough.

For Frederick Dalston to emigrate to somewhere like the former British colonies in America was a decision more to do with romantic idealism than clear logic. Did he know anything of towns like New York or Boston? How would he, the discontented son of a provincial

English country squire, fare in a country dominated by people of the middling sort — lawyers, businessmen and merchants. People who created their own wealth through enterprise, not people who lived on the rents of their ancestral country estates?

Adam pulled himself up roughly. All that was mere speculation. A sure sign of a man trying to distract himself from facing his failure in finding the murderer of Frederick Dalston, or even getting closer to doing so. It was high time to turn around and return home, then apply himself with renewed dedication to the task in hand.

5

What would turn out to be the most important event of Adam's brief period in Norwich happened in the middle of the afternoon on the day before he and his wife were due to go back to Aylsham. They had been to say their farewells to Mrs Bascom and Ruth and returned only minutes before, when the butler announced that there was a man at the door asking to speak with the master.

'He says his name is Mr Anthony Ross, sir. He has brought a letter of introduction from Sir Percival Wicken.'

Adam got up from the chair in the drawing room, where he and Lady Alice were awaiting the serving of a dish of tea, and turned to his wife.

'I've been expecting to hear from Wicken,' he said. 'It must be almost a week since I wrote to him.' He turned back to the butler. 'Has this man come on horseback? Is he one of the King's Messengers?'

'Not as far as I know,' the butler replied. 'I would say he had walked here.'

'Odd,' Adam said. 'Give me a few moments and then bring the man to me in the library. I'll see him there. Tell the maid to bring her lady-ship's tea here, as arranged. Bring mine to me in the library. She had also better bring an extra dish, in case this Mr Ross would like a drink as well.'

The man whom the butler ushered into the library was in no way like his employer, the elegant, aristocratic Sir Percival Wicken, Permanent Secretary at the Home Department and coordinator of the finest network of spies and agents in the kingdom. Anthony Ross was compact in stature, almost stocky. A neat man soberly dressed. A man with an unassuming manner and forgettable features. Adam thought he looked rather like an attorney from a small town, or perhaps a rural nonconformist minister.

'I believe you have a letter for me, Mr Ross,' Adam said. 'Please hand it to me, then take a seat while I read it. The maid should be here shortly with tea, if you would like to join me in drinking a dish or two.'

'That I would, Sir Adam, and right gladly. It's been a longish walk to get here from my earlier business on the other side of the city.' Adam noticed that Mr Ross spoke well but with a slight trace of a Norfolk accent.

As usual, Wicken's letter was short and to the point. He began by introducing Ross as one of his best agents, describing him as a clever, resourceful and reliable man, with an uncanny ability to move almost unnoticed amongst many different groups of people. He wouldn't normally be willing to loan such a valuable person, even for a short time, but it so happened that Adam's latest investigation might have some important links to something Ross had already been asked to unravel. Ross would explain the details since it's not something Wicken wanted to write down.

'You'd best also ask Ross to explain his background and what he did before being employed by my department,' Wicken wrote. 'It's rather a complicated story and he'll explain it better than I can. Good luck with your investigation. If you are able to bring some clarity to the other problem I've given to Ross at the same time, I'll be extremely grateful to you.'

Adam re-folded the letter and waited for the maid to place the tea things next to him and leave before speaking to Ross again.

'An interesting letter. Sir Percival says that you are best placed to explain your background, Mr Ross. However, before you do that, let me pour you a dish of tea. Would you prefer green tea or bohea?'

'Bohea, if you please, Sir Adam. That'll be a rare treat for me. I don't usually take my refreshment in such an elegant mansion as this one. Oh and please call me simply Ross. That's what I'm used to.'

'Very well, Ross,' Adam said as he handed him the tea. 'How did you come to be working for Sir Percival?'

'It's a long and complicated tale, sir, but I'll do my best to reduce it to the essential points. I was born not far from here in Saxthorpe, the son of a local bricklayer. Sadly, when I was barely five years of age, the smallpox took both my parents and my younger brother, and I was put into the care of the Overseers of the Poor. They apprenticed me to a shoemaker in the next village. The man was a cruel master and the work was hard and uninteresting, so I ran away two years later. Naturally, they caught me and brought me back, and my master punished me severely for what I had done. I waited another two years and ran away again. This time I met a group of travelling actors on the road. They took me in and treated me kindly. I expected my former master to try to hunt me down but nothing happened. I decided he was too lazy to bother, since he could quickly get a new apprentice from the Overseers.

'To help me pay my way, I did all kinds of jobs with the acting group and eventually started to take small parts in their plays. I was never much of an actor, but I did find I had a talent for mimicry. After a short hearing, I could copy someone's voice, along with many of their mannerisms. It's a skill I found extremely useful in my later years. Even today, I find it quite easy to impersonate others. If I need to infiltrate some group planning sedition, I can do so quite easily. So long as I can get the right clothes to wear, few of them will suspect that I am not one of their number.

'I stayed with the actors for ten years, sir, travelling all around the south of England, and would have stayed with them longer had the troop not split apart due to a series of bitter rivalries amongst the actors and a long-running dispute with the manager over unpaid money from benefit nights. At the time when all that came to a head, we were lodged in a village on the edge of London. The manager and his wife simply disappeared one night. They'd run off with the money that the actors said was due to them. That was the end of the troop. The actors drifted away to join other companies and I made my way into the capital in search of fresh employment. There I suffered several months of hardship before I found a position with the Bow Street magistrates' court and became what people call a Bow Street Runner. It was work I loved, but the noise, filth and crowded streets of London weighed on my health and depressed my spirits. I'm a country lad at heart and missed the open fields, the wide skies and the shingle beaches of my native Norfolk. During the course of an investigation, I happened to meet with Sir Percival. He offered me the chance to return to my home county and I took it at once.'

'And how would you describe yourself today?' Adam asked him.

'As a seeker after and collector of information, Sir Adam. Sir Percival gives me my instructions, either by calling me to his office in London or sending me a letter in cipher. I find out what he wants and reply to him in the same manner. Though I say it myself, over the past few years I have collected together the most comprehensive team of informers and spies outside the capital itself. Now Sir Percival has instructed me to place myself and my people entirely at your disposal. You only have to tell me what it is you want me to do.'

Adam realised that Wicken had given him a priceless gift. The trouble was, he had no idea what to do with it. He was stuck with an investigation that was still at the stage of collecting information almost at random. As he had told himself several times in the past few days, what he needed more than anything else was a sense of a specific direction that he could follow. Rather than answer Ross's question directly, therefore, he played for time.

He began by describing the circumstances of Frederick Dalston's death in as much detail as he could recall. From there, he went on to relate most of what he knew about the man's dubious career, first as a seducer of servant girls and then the way in which he had preyed on the innocent daughters of wealthy families. Finally, he rounded off with the vague and unspecified rumours he had picked up, suggesting that Dalston was either already involved with members of the criminal classes in Norwich or had been likely to become so in the period immediately before his murder.

By the time he finished, he was feeling an acute sense of embarrassment. Ross was a professional investigator, whereas he was no more than an amateur who dabbled in the field and had been lucky enough, on several previous occasions, to come upon the answer to a mystery.

'I think you've done uncommonly well, if you don't mind me saying so,' Ross said. 'I assure you I'm not being impertinent. It's what I truly believe. You've made me feel something of a fool by boasting about my team and the different areas and classes in the city they can investigate. The plain truth is that we've never had to deal with people like those you've been speaking to, the country gentry and the aristocracy. If the need ever arose, we would be confounded before we even started. None of those people would be willing to speak to us at all, let alone answer our questions. Yet somehow, you, with no official backing, have been able to persuade wealthy and important people to tell you a good many things that they would normally keep as their most closely-held secrets. Indeed, it was only when you mentioned that the murdered man may have had some dealings with members of the criminal classes that I began to think that I might be of some use to you.'

'You certainly could help me in that regard at least,' Adam said. 'I'm well aware that ordinary people would be quite horrified at the notion of being questioned by a baronet — unless of course I was sitting on the bench as a magistrate and passing judgement on them.'

'The more I think about it, sir, the more I'm convinced that we could make an extremely formidable team between us. You can deal with the upper classes, where I and my people would be viewed with complete disdain, and I can discover what is happening, or what is planned, by those who would hope to profit from naïve and well-born young men tempted to stray into matters of which they have no experience.'

'Very well, Ross. Let me tell you what little I do know — or rather what little I have been told — about Frederick Dalston's possible contacts outside his natural level in society. Two young men who knew him told me he had been talking about going away to start a new life and I don't just mean to another part of this country. He seemed to be thinking of going overseas somewhere. Since his estate is entailed and already heavily mortgaged, he knew that he could never raise the amount of capital he thought he needed to turn his dream into a reality. That was when, these two young men said, that he began to seek ways of raising money quickly and in large amounts. Since he lacked the knowledge or the skill to do this by conventional and respectable means, he was willing to try to bring it about in other ways. For a start, he seemed to have turned his skill of seducing young women into a means of blackmailing their families. He would promise to keep all quiet and agree with whatever excuses they felt were appropriate, in return for receiving a large monetary payment. You'd imagine that this was his idea, but I was told there was a small coterie of young men already using this approach in one way or another. Most of those simply preyed on rich wives or widows, obtaining gifts in return for their company at night. A few had added the idea of genteel blackmail to this, based on the need of such women to avoid compromising their reputation in society. Dalston's contribution seems to have been to forget the idea of gifts and concentrate entirely on blackmailing vulnerable families by seducing their marriageable daughters.'

'A most disreputable, even wicked approach, sir. Did any of these families pay what he asked?'

'I don't know for certain, but I suspect that some of them did. How many families were approached in this way, I have no idea, since the activity depended almost entirely on the family wishing to make certain the disgrace of their daughter never came to light. Thanks to this attitude, even finding them was next to impossible.'

Ross nodded his head. 'Yes, I see that that would make it particularly difficult for you. However, you did mention contacts with known criminals ...'

'I did,' Adam said,' but in connection with what activity I really don't know. I suspect Dalston either couldn't obtain enough money by extortion or he found the process was too slow. That's when he started to work on other schemes. I gather he wasn't the only one with that idea either. The trouble was that none of these young fellows could turn their plans into a practical scheme. That's how they drew the attention of real criminals to their activities. Their clumsy attempts interfered with the settled arrangements and territories of existing villains.'

'I probably know something of most of those rogues, Sir Adam. Are there any whose names have been mentioned to you?'

'All I have is a single name: Obadiah Webley.'

'Webley! That's bad, sir, very bad. I've had my eye on Obadiah Webley for some time, but he's an extremely slippery customer and I've never been able to turn my suspicions into the kind of evidence needed to bring him to court.'

'You've heard of him then?' Adam said. 'All my informant could tell me was that he was a man to be avoided at all costs.'

'He is that indeed, sir, and more. He calls himself a commission agent. In practice, what that means is a promoter of dubious, usually criminal, business propositions and get-rich-quick schemes. Anybody foolish enough to be drawn into Webley's activities will soon come to regret it.'

He was about to launch into further detail when Adam stopped him, explaining he was already confused enough by all the information he had amassed in the past week and didn't need any more.

'Why don't you see what you can discover about any specific contacts between Frederick Dalston and this man Webley?' he told Ross. 'I'll need to take some time to see if I can perceive any patterns in the information I have already. If I can, they may help to point us in some more definite direction. I suggest you come to see me in Aylsham in a week's time, when you can tell me what you have discovered, and I will tell you what may have occurred to me in the meantime. Perhaps then, given time and space to pay proper attention to the facts we have, we can formulate a clearer set of tasks for you going forward.'

Ross agreed to this arrangement, thanked Adam again for the splendid tea and took his leave. Adam stayed where he was for a while, still trying to assimilate what Ross had told him. Despite the man's kind words, he was still annoyed with himself for not being able to give Ross clear instructions straight away. What with spending time with his mother and Ruth, being paraded before several of his mother's friends and being introduced to a number of Lady Alice's acquaintances, he had little or no time to sit quietly and think through the implications of what he had learned.

He had just risen to return to the drawing-room and Lady Alice when he realised he had omitted to ask Ross how he could contact him, should he need to do so before next week. He really was losing his touch!

❦

WHEN ADAM AND HIS WIFE SAT TOGETHER AFTER DINNER THAT night, they took care to discuss only inconsequential matters. Adam had already given Lady Alice a full account of his meeting with Ross and what had been decided about future progress. For her part, Lady Alice curbed her enthusiasm for talk of renovation and re-furnishings, knowing that her husband was quite content to leave all to her and had little interest in such matters. In truth, she was feeling rather pleased with herself. She had discovered that she had quite a talent for hard bargaining. That made her hopeful that the eventual cost of the furnishings for their new house would be significantly below the amount she and Adam had agreed upon. All in all, her visit to Norwich looked to have been a considerable success. She was, therefore, delighted that this mystery concerning the death of Frederick Dalston had come along to occupy his mind so fully. Adam was not the kind of man to be happy to be idle, so she had worried that giving up his medical practice would upset him more than it had. The fact that he was willing to discuss his investigation with her so openly, and — even better — allow her to take some part in considering the implications of what he had found, was enormously satisfying. Lady Alice might be small and delicate in appearance, but she was a tough-minded, resourceful and intelligent woman, happiest when she was busily occupied with matters of some importance.

❦

THAT NIGHT, ADAM DREAMED AGAIN OF THE MURDER. IT WAS AS IF his sleeping mind couldn't let go of the problem. Instead, it turned it around and around and, in the manner of dreams, produced notions that strayed well beyond the obvious or conventional ways the world works.

At the start of this dream, all was much as before. Only when the murderer stepped clear into the road to come up close behind the rider were things different.

It was a woman!

To free her arms to be able to use her weapon, the woman had thrown back her cloak, revealing her true gender. A tall woman, perhaps somewhat unusually so, well-built and sturdy too. Adam's sleeping mind labelled her as being of the female warrior type of legend. A virago. The kind of domineering, violent-tempered female who might be found running an inn where criminal types met to drink. Someone capable of dealing with brawling or drunken fellows and tossing them outside into the gutter.

This time, the attacker was on foot. She darted forward and raised a long, narrow-bladed dagger above her head, before plunging it into the rider's back with all the strength in that formidable arm.

There was another change in the pattern of the dream after the rider slumped forward and fell off his horse. This time one of his feet remained caught up in its stirrup. The woman tried to get the rider's foot out of the stirrup, but the horse, spooked by the sudden loss of its rider, spun around against the weight of the corpse and tried to make off. In doing so, the beast dragged the body onto the edge of the road, where its foot slipped out of the stirrup and the corpse was left amongst the rough grass while the horse cantered off somewhere into the wood.

That was when Adam woke up.

He lay still for a while, musing on the picture the dream had conjured up for him. What if Frederick Dalston's killer had been a woman? Not one of those he had seduced. They would be far too gentle to resort to violence to take their revenge on him. But couldn't it have been a woman from amongst the criminal classes? Perhaps someone whose territory Dalston had blundered into, causing her to fear his ham-fisted actions, would draw the attention of the authorities and cause them to look at her activities as well? That kind of woman might well be angered enough to try to put a stop to Dalston's interference for good. Violence would probably come naturally to her as well. Was that what his dream had been trying to tell him?

There was also the weapon this fantasy woman had used: something like the stiletto used by Italian brigands. Wasn't that kind of dagger a popular weapon of criminals and assassins everywhere? It certainly might have produced the kind of wound Harrison Henshaw had described. Both ideas — the woman and the weapon — might be worth considering further, despite their unusual source.

⚜

DURING THE SHORT JOURNEY BACK TO AYLSHAM THE NEXT DAY, both Adam and his wife sat in silence in the carriage. They had decided to leave early in the morning, when the roads would be least busy with traffic and the herds of sheep and cattle that were driven daily to the markets in Norwich should already have reached their destination. What Adam was thinking about his wife had no idea, but she found herself pondering several matters concerned with Frederick Dalston's murder. After all, he had probably passed along this road — or at least part of it — on his last journey.

That was it! Now she knew what had been bothering her ever since she had heard about the young man's death.

'About Frederick Dalston,' she said aloud. 'Why was he killed in such a remote country area, not far from his family home? Most of his time was spent in Norwich and most of his enemies, from what you tell me, were there as well. Is that not odd?'

Adam turned and looked at his wife in surprise. 'I hadn't thought about it,' he said. 'Now you mention it though, it does seem rather peculiar.'

'Do you know if any of those wild young bucks that he went about with, or any of those poor young women he seduced, had family homes in the same area? If you found one who did, that might prove to be a useful pointer to who was most likely to have committed the crime.'

'That's an excellent thought. On the other hand, the murderer might simply have followed Dalston that night, reasoning that killing him where they did would serve to divert attention away from Norwich altogether.'

'I suppose so.' Lady Alice was a little cast down at how easily her husband had suggested an alternative explanation. 'I suppose you have looked in some detail into the matter of who it was amongst these women that Dalston had wronged most recently? You have told me little about them, save a general observation that Dalston was a confirmed and cruel womaniser, who had shifted from abusing helpless servants to focusing on rich young women whose families could be blackmailed. Was there any woman whom he had treated especially badly? Might there be a husband, a father or some brothers impatient to take their revenge as a result? If so, where do they live? Was it anywhere near the site of the killing?'

'You are a wonder to me, my dear,' Adam said. 'For hours, even days, at a time, you appear to occupy your mind solely with domestic matters. Then you put your finger on a series of points in an investigation that I am supposed to be fully occupied with and have simply missed. I have no idea how you do it.'

'It may be because I am not involved in all the other detail,' his wife replied, 'and because by the time you tell me what you have discovered you have already sorted and simplified it. It is, therefore, easier for me to take it all in and spot any questions that have yet to be resolved. Do not give me too much credit, I beg you. I could never undertake this kind of investigation on my own. I am simply happy to be able to help you from time to time. Too many men assume their wives are feeble-minded and must confine their interests to household management, looking decorative and indulging in gossip. It is my immense privilege to have married someone who does not subscribe to such foolish beliefs.'

'Now you give me too much credit,' Adam replied. 'I hope I will always understand my limitations and delight in the ability of others to help me where I fall short.'

'I know you find it useful to discuss your progress, husband,' Lady Alice continued. 'You will now have several opportunities to do so in the coming days. My nephew, Charles, and his new wife will join us tomorrow. While I bore Sophia with all my ideas for our new house, you may more profitably discuss your investigation with Charles. Then, once they have left, it might prove useful to talk everything over with your friend the apothecary once more. I know he has been of great assistance to you in the past.'

'You are quite right in your suggestions,' Adam said. 'Indeed, if you recall, Charles wrote that he is coming to bring me some specific information he has picked up about Frederick Dalston. It is not purely a social visit, though I know both of us will be delighted to see Charles and Sofia again.'

Lady Alice smiled at him and they both relapsed into silence.

Perhaps five minutes later, as they were passing the Fox Inn at Hevingham, Adam spoke again.

'It might also have been a woman. The murderer, I mean.'

'A woman? Surely, from what you told me of the power needed to strike in the way Dr Henshaw described to you, a woman would be too feeble.'

'Not necessarily, my dear. Not every woman is as delicate as you are — though I imagine even you are not nearly as weak in muscular strength as many might imagine. Add to that the powerful emotions which must have surrounded the murder, together with a woman somewhat taller and more muscular than most, I think it would be possible. One of the criminal classes, maybe. Someone inured to hard work from childhood.'

'I cannot imagine how you arrived at that idea,' Lady Alice said, 'but I am willing to admit you could be right.'

'It was partly something Ross said. I'd heard from the Barnes brothers that Frederick Dalston and a new group of cronies — or at least some of them — were beginning to dabble in the kinds of money-making activities usually reserved for hardened criminals. I was also told that this had attracted the attention of genuine criminals who saw in these silly young men ample opportunities for profit. What if others saw them as a threat? The kind of bumbling fools who would soon attract the attention of the constables to whatever they were doing. Once the constables got involved, that might easily draw established criminals into their net.'

'It is certainly another avenue which might be worth exploring,' his wife replied. 'How you would do it, I have no idea.'

'I shall write to Ross as soon as we reach home,' Adam said. 'He and his men, he told me, are well used to dealing with professional criminals. He can add it to the tasks before him.'

❧ 6 ❧

'I feel I need to apologise for my wife, uncle,' Charles Scudamore said to Adam. 'She might at least have allowed us a few moments to leave your hall and settle down somewhere else before blurting out the news that we are expecting our first child.'

'You know, I find it hard to get used to you calling me uncle,' Adam said.

'But you are my uncle now,' Charles replied. 'We're part of the same family.'

'I know and the fact pleases me enormously. It still sounds odd. And there's nothing to apologise for. I can quite understand how excited Sophia is. Becoming a mother is important to any woman. Your aunt and I have already told you how delighted we are.'

'I expect you will be joining me on the verge of fatherhood very soon,' Charles replied. 'Then my wife and I will be able to congratulate you.'

'These things don't run to a strict timetable, you know. Besides, you were married a little before us.'

The two of them had left their womenfolk deep in discussion of feminine matters and come out to take a walk on what was proving to be rather a nice day. At that moment, they were walking along the edge of Aylsham's large open marketplace, currently filled with stalls and booths selling everything from fresh greens to bags of flour and pieces of cheese. Many of the citizens of the town were thronging around the stalls, happily engaged in bargaining for the best prices. After they had passed along the edge of the market, Adam intended to turn to the right and take Charles down the hill to the outskirts of the town to show him Wrigsby Hall, at least from the outside. Presently the house was tightly locked awaiting the attention of an army of builders and decorators.

Marriage, setting up his practice and impending fatherhood had matured Charles considerably. He looked every inch the young lawyer. He was neatly and conservatively dressed in a dark-blue coat, the edges trimmed with gold braid, and linen breeches with black shoes. On his head, he wore a felt hat over his natural hair. Wigs had fallen out of fashion a while ago, though some physicians still wore them — something which Adam himself had never done.

The noise in the marketplace was too loud to allow for comfortable talk, so Adam waited until they had passed in front of the Black Boys Inn and turned to the right onto the road towards Blickling, before Charles started their conversation on another tack.

'I have heard some rumours amongst the legal community about Frederick Dalston,' he began. 'Strange rumours, though perhaps not quite so unexpected if what my aunt mentioned in her letter about the young man being desperate for money is true.'

'That's certainly true,' Adam replied. 'What are these rumours saying about him?'

'That he's been consulting different lawyers on the subject of finding some way to renounce his position as the heir and the next inheritor of the Kessingfield Hall estate,' Charles said. 'It really is a most eccentric thing to wish to do. Difficult as well. Perhaps even impossible. You understand that holding an estate in entail means it must pass to the next direct male heir, if one exists. If not, it passes to the nearest in line. The current holder — that would be Dalston's father — holds only a life interest in the income, together with the right to live there. Generally speaking, the life holder can also raise mortgages on the estate, if he wishes to. What he cannot do is sell it or interfere with the right of succession.'

'That was Frederick Dalston's problem, I was told,' Adam replied. 'He knew the entail prevented his father from selling. The estate was already quite heavily mortgaged, and the land was poor. No lender would be willing to advance yet more money without some evidence it would be repaid in a timely fashion. His father was struggling to meet the interest costs as it was. That left little or no income available to invest in any kind of improvements to the land. His only hope of extracting more cash would be if his father could sell everything. If that meant he would no longer inherit automatically, so be it. He planned to go abroad and start a new life. I've been told that the estate is not run particularly well and that the rents from the existing tenants do not provide the family with more than a barely adequate living. Since capital would be needed to help willing tenants improve their agricultural methods, there seems little chance of bringing that about in the foreseeable future either.'

'Now it makes sense. It would still be difficult to achieve though, even if his father agreed to the arrangement.'

'But can't an entail sometimes be broken?' Adam asked.

'A well-written entail is very difficult to interfere with. What's more, I have never heard of an heir seeking to break an entail while his father is alive and in residence. I'm no expert, but I can't see how it could be done. His father would have to be the one who would do it, as well as convince the executors and trustees appointed by the original Will, or their successors, to support him. Under an entail, a trust is set up to hold the actual ownership of the land with trustees to make sure that the wishes of the original person making the bequest are honoured. Would they agree to breaking the entail, simply because an heir did not wish to inherit the estate? I doubt it. Would his father have agreed to ask them?'

'Almost certainly not, I imagine, since it would leave him and the other members of the family almost destitute. Still, if you were going to try to bring such a change about, how would you go about it?'

'You'd need an expert in the law of inheritance to answer that, uncle,' Charles replied. 'Even then any legal path is likely to be expensive and tortuous, probably involving the Court of Chancery. Cases argued there can take many years to resolve and absorb vast amounts of money in fees to lawyers.'

'From what I have heard,' Adam said, 'the need for money would rule Frederick Dalston out from trying it himself. Would he have been prepared to maybe force his father to beggar himself and his brother and sister by taking it on? That's an open question. It appeared he had very little concern for others. However, he was also in an enormous hurry. If legal action would be slow, it would have been unlikely to appeal to him.'

'Why didn't he want to inherit? With some care and hard work, even a somewhat unproductive estate can be made to yield substantially higher returns.'

'I've been told he had no taste for the life of a landed gentleman,' Adam said, 'and scorned the sort of income Kessingfield could return, even if it were substantially improved. Instead he wanted to emigrate somewhere — precisely where seemed to vary from week to week — where he could take up a different life. Perhaps he wanted to be a brewer as his grandfather was. If he went abroad with enough money to his name, he would have been able to marry a wealthy woman. That's something that was no longer open to him in this country, thanks to his various exploits with the fair sex. What's perfectly clear is that, however you think about it, this dream of his required him to amass a significant amount of capital either before he left or very soon afterwards.'

'Do you know if he approached his father with this mad idea?' Charles asked.

'The simple answer is that I do not. His father had certainly been paying off his debts and had to take out mortgages on the estate to do so. I doubt that he could have made the young man any swift monetary payment, even one in lieu of his inheritance.'

'I gather from what you've been saying that there is a younger brother,' Charles said. 'Do you know what he thinks about this?'

'I do not. What I have been told is that Frederick reckoned his brother would make a far better squire than he ever would. I don't think we can take that as a compliment, especially given the fact that I understand he was also heard to describe his brother as a "dull, conscientious nonentity, organised to a fault". It sounds to me as if there was little love lost between the two brothers. I cannot imagine the younger one being eager to gain control of an estate that was heavily mortgaged, poorly run and unable to raise enough capital to make any significant changes. At least with Frederick dead, his father and brother have a better chance of putting things right.'

'What I don't understand,' Charles said, 'is why this Frederick Dalston didn't simply find a way of amassing the money he needed, then disappear, head for America, or wherever else he had decided upon, and change his name after arrival. After seven years, he would be presumed dead and the inheritance, whatever there was of it, would pass to his younger brother.'

'That would have been simpler, but for two facts. His money-making schemes — even those which worked, as most did not — weren't going to yield enough to satisfy him in the time he seemed to have had available. He couldn't leave because he didn't have the money he thought he required. I was also told he was afraid his father's creditors would start to hound him any day to pay off the debts on the estate. I know that legally he wouldn't have been liable, but that has never yet prevented a frustrated creditor from trying to retrieve his money from any family member who appears to have some.'

'What did he do then? Assuming there was time to make a start before he was killed?

'He turned to crime. But that is another story and we are almost there.'

They were now at the bottom of the hill that led from the town and had reached the place where the driveway to Wrigsby Hall began. Fortunately, it was not a lengthy driveway, so the house was clearly visible from the road itself. They would not have to walk up the drive, in order to see it. Unless, that is, Charles wanted to see it from all sides. Adam was rather glad to discover that was not the case.

'It's a remarkably handsome house,' Charles said. 'Quite a large one too by the look of it. Far larger than mine in Holt.'

Charles now lived in a substantial town house in Bull Street seven bays in width, three stories and attics above. He could make a good estimate of any building's size from the most casual observance. All he had to do was compare it with the dimensions of his own.

'Are those stables to the right of the main building?'

'They are,' Adam replied, 'and fine ones too. There is space for three carriages, stabling for at least half a dozen horses, as well as accommodation for the grooms, a tack room with space for a hay store above and all the other paraphernalia needed. There is certainly no need to alter or extend on that side.'

'What is it my aunt wishes to do?'

'Make some alterations to the accommodation inside to add a morning room and extend the dining room. She also wishes to move the kitchen and other domestic services into a new service courtyard at the rear of the house. After that, she plans to add a new wing on the left-hand side as we look at it, housing a large drawing room and a smaller private room on the ground floor and new bedrooms above. She also wants to do a good deal of redecoration, change many of the curtains and add some extra furniture.'

'That will turn it into a grand mansion. One to rival Blickling Hall, which I believe must stand almost next door.'

'It does. The two estates border one another along one side, though the Blickling estate is the larger by some little way. As for constructing a grand mansion, that's what she's used to and that's what she believes our status requires. You know what she's like when she sets her mind on something.'

'I do indeed. I think you're very wise to let her have her own way from the start.'

'She knew I would,' Adam said, 'especially after the disappointment she had when her dower house proved unsuitable for alteration. Are you and your wife happy with your accommodation in Holt?'

'Very happy. Sophia thinks it will be quite large enough to last us many years, unless our family grows so large — and my legal practice so valuable — that we can afford something larger.'

Despite being pressed to stay longer, Charles and Sophia left on the afternoon of the day after they had arrived, since Charles had business that he needed to attend to at an agreed time. They promised to return to spend longer with their aunt and uncle just as soon as they could.

⊗⊷⊗

Next day, Adam went to see his friend Peter, the apothecary, exactly as his wife had recommended. Despite protesting that he was a busy man who needed to make a living and who had no time to sit and listen to long and complicated stories, Peter did just that. It took Adam some time to tell him everything that he had discovered while he was in Norwich.

At the end, Peter shook his head and gave a groan. 'It seems to me that you have amassed a remarkable number of new facts but are still not much further forward. Let's take the areas you've been exploring one at a time, shall we? I'll start with Frederick Dalston's womanising. From what you have said, you have yet to find that he had made anyone a sufficiently bitter enemy through these actions for them to wish to see him dead. As for using this approach as a way of raising a large amount of money quickly, that's plain nonsense. The man was either extremely irresponsible or never stopped to think through a course of action before starting on it.'

'Probably both were true, from what I've heard,' Adam said. 'Frederick Dalston's whole life has been filled with ill-thought-out or even stupid actions, all entered into on the spur of the moment. He was rash and impulsive. Everyone I've spoken with agrees on that. He also never showed much sign of great intelligence.'

'The other young men you mentioned — those who are also extorting money from lonely wives in return for paying them attention — are much more likely to succeed. They have probably committed adultery many times but nothing worse in the eyes of the law. Reprehensible, but not illegal. If it were, there would be no judges left outside gaol for a start.'

'They cannot all be deceiving their wives,' Adam said.

'Most of them, I imagine. However, that's hardly relevant. What isn't is this. The amounts these hired lovers will manage to gain in this way probably does little more than keep them in fine clothes. On the other hand, Dalston might have been able to extort several hundred pounds in exchange for keeping quiet about daughters losing their maidenheads, though it's not a trick that can be repeated very often. However good you are at seduction, it will take a good deal of time before you can persuade some young woman to get into bed with you. How did he meet all these young women? The daughters of the wealthy and well-to-do aren't to be found wandering around in the city on their own, are they? If they aren't with a family member, they'll have someone else on hand to act as chaperone. Ruining some of these young women might have bolstered Dalston's arrogance and delight in making sexual conquests, but I very much doubt that it would have worked as a way of amassing a significant amount of capital. Don't you agree?'

Adam nodded his head. He realised now that he'd been so appalled by what he'd been told that he'd not taken the time to think it through himself. If he had, he would have realised long before that the only way to make any progress in this respect would be to track down someone angry enough to take vengeance on Frederick Dalston; not for demanding money, but simply for the fact that he had deliberately set out to ruin some young woman's life. So far, he had found nothing to point him to such a person.

'Next we'll take Dalston's gambling,' Peter continued. 'It takes a great deal of practice, together with skill and natural talent, for someone to make a living as a professional gambler. If Dalston had wanted to cheat and not be caught, he'd have needed to practice and hone the necessary skills thoroughly before trying them out. Only a madman tries to amass a fortune by genuine gambling, however high the stakes might be. If you won a very large sum of money once — almost certainly by chance — you would need enormous strength of character to walk away at that point and hang onto your gains. Most gamblers are convinced that the next turn of the card will produce another large win so they wager a good part of what they've already won. Of course, it never does — or almost never. In the long term, all gamblers lose money, especially impulsive amateurs like Frederick Dalston. Even if he hadn't been caught cheating and banned from all the gambling clubs in the city, he would never have made enough money that way to fulfil his dreams.'

Peter was well into his stride and enjoying himself immensely by this stage. For the most part, his own life was quiet and conventional — save for his weakness for taking young widows as mistresses. Even there, he had assured Adam many times, he never enjoyed any woman's favours unless she was a willing partner in their romps. Taking some part in Adam's cases, even at second hand, was a considerable treat.

'That leaves us with some form of swindle,' he continued. 'Would Dalston have been able to plan and execute a successful fraud likely to net him thousands of pounds and allow him to walk away with it afterwards? I very much doubt it from what you've told me of him. That may be when this man Webley came on the scene. From the little you've told me, he sounds to be the exact opposite to Dalston: a cunning, professional criminal with plenty of experience behind him. If I had to take a bet on it, my belief would be that Frederick Dalston first tried seduction and gambling and found they didn't work — or didn't work quickly enough. Then, having made a mess of being a criminal on his own, he turned to Webley to help him plan and carry out some kind of grand swindle instead. If he was foolish enough to involve a man like — what did you call him? Obadiah Webley — in his schemes, he could well have ended by being swindled himself. What a marvellous name for a villain. Obadiah Webley.'

'All you say is true,' Adam said, 'yet none of it helps me know what to do next. I've already asked Ross to see what he can discover about any link between Dalston and Webley. If that's what occupied Dalston's time over the few weeks before his death, it will be entirely up to Ross to investigate it. I can see no way in which I could be involved myself. I am now thinking that I can set gambling aside as providing the cause of the murder. It's possible that somebody became so incensed at being cheated they decided Dalston had to die, but there's no evidence to support that idea whatsoever. Despite what you say, I'm not ready to ignore Dalston's womanising as the source of a killer. Even if you're right — as I am sure you are — it would be a very poor way of amassing a fortune, playing with people's emotions is extremely dangerous in its own right. You can never be quite sure when you might you push someone too far and they decide they'll never be happy until they can see your dead body lying at their feet.

'It's been extremely useful talking all this over with you, Lassimer. Despite what I just said, I do think it has helped me see a way to proceed. I'll leave Ross to look into matters concerning Webley, and any other links to the criminal community, while I concentrate my own efforts on looking for a murderer motivated by a profound sense of being wronged. Whether that might be by injuries done to his women-folk or by the personal affront occasioned by being cheated out of significant sums of money by a fool like Frederick Dalston, hardly matters. I just need to look for traces of someone whose hatred and anger boiled over enough to impel him to violent action.'

'I hate to cause you more trouble, my friend,' Peter said, smiling to show that he meant it, 'but I've just thought of something else that you and Ross could well feel is worth investigating. What if Frederick Dalston and his schemes trespassed on an area one of the smuggling gangs are convinced is their own private domain? They don't just confine themselves to bringing in contraband, you know. There's money to be made from controlling the ways such merchandise is sold and to whom. If any of the merchants they used was being cheated by Dalston and Webley, they would be extremely angry. Angry enough to seek to do him harm and perhaps even to kill him? It's quite likely. He doesn't sound to have been a very perceptive kind of person. Even if the gangs tried first to warn him off in less violent ways, he might simply have missed their meaning. They'd be bound to interpret such continued intrusion on their territory as a deliberate refusal to keep away from what was theirs. From that point, it's quite likely they would assume the only means of blocking him from any future inter-ference would be murder. The principal smuggling gangs are well known to be violent men who will stop at nothing if they feel threatened.'

Adam sighed loudly. 'I thought coming to talk with you would make me feel better,' he said. 'Now I can see that I was wrong. All you are sending me away with is yet another set of puzzles to present to Ross. Dealing with criminals has to be his business, not mine. I'd send him a message to get in touch with me as soon as possible, if only I knew how to do so. Damnation! Why on earth didn't I remember to ask about that?'

❧

LUCKILY, FOR ADAM'S PEACE OF MIND, ROSS SENT HIM A MESSAGE. IT arrived later that afternoon. In it, he apologised for forgetting to explain how messages could reach him. Given his work for Wicken, it was important he should not be easily identifiable; nor should it become known who was making contact with him. Messages should, therefore, be addressed to Jonas Stainer at The Bakery, Rampant Horse Street, Norwich and, in Sir Adam's case, only be signed with the single word "Thomas". If at all possible, their content should be confined to requests to meet, since all confidential information was best exchanged personally. He was willing to come to Sir Adam's home at any time required, day or night.

Adam pulled a face at this elaborate playacting but supposed that it was necessary. After all, he had no idea what kind of work Ross might be involved in for the bulk of his time. He knew Wicken kept a close eye on all kinds of subversive groups, as well as spies and agents working for the country's enemies. Doubtless they would be happy to discover a man like Ross and put an end to him.

Adam's message was therefore simple. He wanted a meeting within the next few days.

In the meantime, he considered Peter Lassimer's summary of possible courses of action and could find no flaws in it. He explained it to his wife and she agreed. Furthermore, to his great surprise, she suggested he should leave it to her, Ruth and his mother to delve further into Frederick's last amorous adventures. That kind of thing matters greatly to respectable women, she told him, and they will have been quick to pass on a warning to their friends. Anyone badly hurt by Frederick Dalston may also have sought comfort and support. Besides, she added, women will tell another woman things they would never repeat to a man, especially to a stranger.

Adam could only agree.

'You realise that gives me very little to do?' he said to her. 'Any investigation of felons or criminal gangs is best left to Ross. You, Ruth and my mother will be exploring what Dalston may have been up to amongst the women of Norwich. We have already more or less ruled out the likelihood that Dalston's murder had anything to do with his gambling. There's nothing left for me.'

'Nonsense,' she said. 'The best thing you can do is to go and talk with Frederick Dalston's father again. I'm sure he will be wondering what progress you have made. You can also take the opportunity to see what explanation he might offer for his son's sudden, urgent need for money. Oh, and while you're there, see if he knows the reason why his son was on that particular road on that specific night. If he wasn't going to Kessingfield Hall, where was he going? Is there anyone else living nearby whom he might be visiting?'

Her husband pulled a face. 'I was hoping to avoid having to talk to William Dalston again for as long as I could,' he said. 'What am I to tell him? That I have so far discovered only a string of wicked deeds and crimes that would make Satan blush? That his son was a selfish, heartless brute, who preyed on innocent women and sought to extort money from their families? That he cheated at the card tables until he was banned from all the gambling clubs in the city? The poor man is already deeply upset by his son's murder. Explaining just what an unmitigated scoundrel the fellow was is not going to make him feel any better, is it?'

Lady Alice patted him on the arm. 'Don't be so dramatic,' she said. 'All you have to tell him is that you have so far not been able to identify any particular person or group with a serious enough grudge against his son to have wanted to kill him. On the other hand, as he will no doubt be well aware, his son's behaviour was such as to make him a significant number of enemies. Something like that. I'm sure you'll find the right words when the time comes.'

dam had never been to Kessingfield Hall before. It wasn't that far away from Aylsham but, by the time Adam's carriage had travelled perhaps a mile or a mile-and-a-half from the turn-pike to Cromer, he was already beginning to feel he must be entering a different county. He presumed much of this land was part of the Dalston estate. As he looked at it from the carriage window, it was obvious at once that the land was poor and the soil thin. Since Adam was now the owner of an estate, he was schooling himself to look at the land from the point of view of how productive it would be for useful crops. All the actual farming of his lands would be done by tenants, of course, but the rent they could be charged was linked to how productive the land could be. At present, he was leaving every-thing to his land agent to manage. The man seemed to be conscien-tious and able, yet how would he know whether the land agent was doing a good job if he took no interest in farming? Unlike his elder brother, Adam hadn't been raised expecting involvement in estate management. It was high time he learned.

They had set out from Aylsham along the turnpike road, which was full of traffic at this hour of the day. Aside from farmers on horseback, with their wives sometimes riding behind them, there were carts and brewery drays, carriages of all sizes from four-in-hand to the light-weight phaetons, people on foot and flocks of sheep or herds of cattle going to market. Once they were held up for some time behind a cart which had lost a wheel and now lay on its side, with its load of hay thrown off the road into a hedge beyond.

The contrast when they turned off to follow the country lane to Kessingfield was striking. Within half a mile, they were alone, with no vehicle, horse or pedestrian in sight. Such solitude made Adam nervous, even in broad daylight. The busy turnpikes were no place for highway robbers until the traffic thinned as the sun set. You were as safe there as anywhere on England's roads. Even so, most of the wealthier travellers made sure to carry some means to defend them-selves, should the worst happen. Adam knew William, the groom, always kept a loaded shotgun beside him on the driving seat. That would usually be enough. Today, however, for what reason he could not now recall, Adam had put a bag with a brace of loaded pistols on the seat beside him. Seeing the deserted road and empty fields around, he was very glad that he had.

As the carriage tipped and swayed its way along the narrow, rutted roadway, Adam leant as close to the window as he could and peered out at the fields. To his amazement, one or two of the fields were still divided into thin strips in the old mediaeval style. He could hardly believe his eyes. Nearly the whole of Norfolk had been suitably enclosed and divided into orderly farms long ago. This must be a curi-ously remote area, if not in distance then in the attitudes of the people who lived here. No wonder the estate yielded a meagre income if much of it was farmed in this outmoded manner.

A few miserable-looking sheep were grazing one area and a few scrawny cattle another. Aside from the tracts of heathland, fit only for rabbits, the soil everywhere looked poor and sandy. What it needed was a plentiful application of marl, along with large flocks of sheep to enrich the land with their droppings. After that, a rotation which included turnips and clover would put some strength back into the soil. He had already heard that Frederick Dalston was telling people the estate in its present form would never be worth owning. It was clear that he was correct.

The road wound on for three or four miles before passing a set of gates. This must be the entrance to the Hall itself. From here, Adam reckoned the sea would be barely two miles distant as the crow flew. The bulk of the land on the seaward side could only be a mixture of heath and sand dunes; an ideal spot for the smugglers to land their contraband, far from the prying eyes of the Revenue men. Not much use for farming.

The carriage turned down the drive, which was hardly in any better condition than the road they had been travelling on. As usual, the driveway wound its way between an avenue of trees. Not the majestic limes which marked the approaches to most grand houses, but a thin line of pines and holm oaks, all leaning away from the direction of the sea, and most gnarled and stunted by the poor soil and the incessant wind. When the house itself came into view, it proved to be very different from Adam's expectations. It stood within a moat — where the water came from, he could not imagine — and was roughly rectangular in shape, two stories high and constructed of deep red-coloured bricks. The windows were small and divided by brick mullions. The walls were decorated with a low parapet and crenellations; the roof above then steeply pitched and covered with pantiles. The drive approached the house on the left side where there was a shallow, three storey wing, its window larger than the others and the gable end crow-stepped in the Dutch manner. At the right-hand corner of the building you could see a kind of tower, as if the building had once been a castle, though Adam was certain that was not the case. A projecting, oriel window, constructed of freestone with mullions in the manner of a church occupied the lower two stories of this tower.

Adam's carriage passed along this edge of the building and swung round to the left to approach what appeared to be a mock castle gatehouse flanked by two octagonal towers, their tops extravagantly decorated with crow-stepped battlements. Here a stone-arched bridge led across the moat to gates under the tower. Visitors were clearly expected to drive over this bridge, through the gates and come to a halt in the courtyard inside.

How large the house might be was difficult to estimate. There was no sign of other buildings, save for some stables away to the left, so

Adam guessed all the kitchens and other domestic offices must occupy at least one wing of the inner courtyard, if not more. If that was the case, the house itself would be considerably smaller than it looked from the outside. The place had probably been built in the time of Good Queen Bess or even earlier and had not been extended or modernised since then. In fact, when he thought about it, he realised any extension would be impossible beyond the boundaries set by the moat surrounding the building. As it stood, the place conveyed the impression that you had somehow gone back in time and should expect to see men-at-arms in chainmail manning the battlements. What on earth had possessed the current owner's father to purchase it defied logic. He'd been a highly successful brewer and maltster by all accounts. Surely, he could have found a better house and estate in which to found his dynasty?

William Dalston had obviously heard the carriage as it passed over the bridge, through the open gates and came to a halt in the courtyard. Adam was surprised to see that he had come outside to welcome his visitor. Maybe he couldn't afford to employ a butler, or none could be found to come to this isolated spot? There was another house fairly close by, together with the parish church, but whatever village had been here had been reduced to a small cluster of humble cottages, probably housing estate workers.

It was clear from his appearance that the death of his son was weighing upon William Dalston heavily. His face was pale and there were dark smudges under his eyes, indicative of poor sleep. Still, he welcomed Adam heartily enough and led him through a decorated doorway into a hall which obviously stood, at least in part, under the tower that Adam had observed as he drove up. They did not stop there, however, but passed on through a small library and into an even smaller room which Dalston must use as a kind of study. It was dominated by a large desk, with three easy chairs arranged in front of the desk; one for Dalston himself, one for Adam and the third for the other man who had risen on Adam's entrance.

A single glance was enough to confirm that this was a clergyman. He was dressed all in black with the neat white stock and pair of fluttering bands at his throat that more traditional clergyman wore. He also had an old-fashioned, slightly grimy wig on his head. Dalston introduced him as The Reverend Simon Geddy, Rector of Kessingfield and a family friend of long-standing.

After they had seated themselves, exchanged the normal pleasantries and tasted some second-rate punch brought in by an elderly maidservant, Dalston got down to business.

'Tell me, Sir Adam,' he said. 'How does your investigation proceed? Do you think you are any nearer to finding who it was that murdered my son?'

Adam, as he had decided previously, tried to summarise his findings as painlessly as he could.

'I'm afraid that I have discovered that your son's lifestyle in Norwich had generated him many enemies,' he began. 'So numerous indeed that he must have found himself being shunned by reputable people. However, I have, as yet, not been able to identify any particular individual or group bearing a grudge that appears severe enough to have led to his murder. These are early days, and I have a number of other areas of investigation open to me ...'

At this point he was interrupted by the rector. The man's voice had clearly been schooled by giving sermons calculated to keep a somnolent congregation from sleeping. His voice was loud — far too loud for such a small room — and severe in tone.

What did I tell you?' he said, directing his comment to William Dalston. 'Your son had become totally abandoned, entirely given over to evil works and riotous living. He has brought this death upon himself, for he was surely not raised in that way. Put him out of your mind, my friend. I have said all along that the kind of investigation you have asked Sir Adam to undertake is neither necessary nor useful. Frederick's death was but the first stage in the Lord's judgement upon him.'

Adam expected Mr Dalston to respond angrily to this statement. Instead, he merely sighed. When he answered his voice was heavily tinged with weariness, as if he had suffered this kind of statement many times in the past few weeks.

'I cannot simply step aside with no attempt to bring the murderer to justice,' he said. 'Whatever he did, Frederick was my son. I did not disown him in life, and I will not do so in death. Murder is a crime against man and God. It's forbidden in the Ten Commandments. It should not be left unpunished.'

'Vengeance is mine, saith the Lord. I will repay,' Geddy said, his voice just as loud as before. 'What is man's justice compared with the justice of God? Frederick must already be standing before the Judgement Seat. His murderer too must stand there someday. Then he will answer for his crime, not before.'

'Peace, Simon,' Dalston said. 'Let Sir Adam continue so that I may hear what he has to say.'

'Whatever he says is of no matter,' Geddy persisted. 'That young man was intent on bringing the whole family to ruin. He would have blighted the futures of both your other children, had he been able to continue. I have told you several times already that his death was the just reward for his actions. These investigations can only result in yet more revelations of wickedness. It will bring disgrace and shame on the name of Dalston.'

Adam was appalled by Geddy's behaviour. Surely a parson and an old family friend should be seeking to bring comfort and solace to a bereaved father? How could he be urging him to forget his errant son and tell Adam to cease any further investigations? There was also the matter of his blatant discourtesy in addressing all his remarks to William Dalston and ignoring Adam himself entirely. It was not to be tolerated. It was already clear that he would get no useful information unless he could stop these continual, self-righteous interruptions.

'Mr Geddy,' he said firmly. 'I would be grateful if you would leave me alone with Mr Dalston. I have come here to talk with him. I find your interruptions both unhelpful and discourteous.'

Mr Dalston looked at Adam in surprise. It seemed as if few people were willing to confront Geddy rather than seek to placate him as he had done.

'Please do as Sir Adam asks,' he said. 'I am well aware of your views on this subject. Now I wish to hear what Sir Adam has to say and hear it without interruption or commentary.' He spoke in a mild voice, yet in a tone that implied a command, not a request.

Mr Geddy appeared physically to swell with the fury growing

within him. His face became an ugly, mottled, reddish colour. His breathing grew shallow and laboured. He raised his hands and clenched his fists. All in all, he gave every indication that he wanted more than anything to set upon Adam and drive him from the house, had that been possible.

'The mighty of this earth are filled with pride!' he cried. That remark was directed at Adam himself. 'The Lord does not look at the things people look at. People see only the outward appearance, but the Lord sees the heart within. Through insolence comes nothing but strife. Wisdom is with those who receive counsel.'

Finding Adam completely unmoved by this outburst and William Dalston prepared to support him, Geddy rose, strode across the room and left, making sure the door banged shut behind him.

'I shall suffer for that for many days ahead,' Mr Dalston said. 'Even so, it had to be done. I lacked the courage to do it, so I am grateful to you, Sir Adam, for doing it on my behalf. Do not think too badly of our rector. He grows old and set in his ways. He was my tutor for a time, then tutor to both my sons before I sent Frederick to the university. I could not afford to do the same for George, I am ashamed to say. His brother had already begun to consume too much of the estate's income. Frederick's behaviour has wounded Simon Geddy deeply, though he will not admit it. I am sure he believes that he has failed; that Frederick's waywardness was in some way linked to his past failure to give the young man a proper moral compass by which to direct his life. It is his guilt and sense of inadequacy that drives him to make these wild statements. Deep down, I am sure he doesn't really mean it.'

Whether he meant it or not, Adam thought to himself, is not something that concerns me. If this pompous, demanding, tradition-alist clergyman had been my tutor, I'm sure that I too would have been tempted to rebel. Naturally, he said none of this aloud. It was time to move on and try to forget Geddy's intemperate outbursts.

'I do have one important question for you, Mr Dalston,' he said. 'I understand your son had been living almost entirely in Norwich for some time. It is, therefore, to that city I have been primarily directing my investigation. However, my experience tells me it is not unknown for crimes of this kind to have their origin in some past event. Something that would have taken place when he still lived with you here. Some people hold grudges and meditate on them for many years before turning to violent action to ease the emotions boiling inside them. I imagine that your son must have had friends and contacts closer to his home during his childhood and youth. Unless he has lived in Norwich for longer than I have assumed, the murderer we are looking for either lives, or has lived, somewhere nearby.'

'Frederick was still spending the bulk of his time here at his home until he went up to Oxford,' Mr Dalston replied. 'When he returned, he began spending a good deal of his time in Norwich. That was five years ago. Before long, I was forced to tell him I was no longer able to keep paying the debts he incurred through gambling. That was when he flew into a rage and vowed to make his own way in the world, initially by living in Norwich full-time. Since then, I do not know how he has been funding himself — you may be able to answer that — but his demands to me for money lessened, at least until very recently.'

'Then they began again?'

'Only once. Not that long before his death he came to me again for funds.'

'And how did you respond that time?'

'I repeated my former statement. I told him that unless he amended his style of life, there would be no more money available. I have already been forced to take out several mortgages on the estate, thanks to his previous demands. This is not rich land, sir, as I'm sure you will have seen as you drove here. The local people, poor souls, scrape a living through their small holdings of land in the common fields and the few beasts they are able to keep there as well. Some also go fishing for crabs, lobsters and anything else they can catch close to the shore. None of them own boats capable of sailing far away from land. The waters along this coast are dangerous, Sir Adam, as I'm sure you know. The beaches and cliffs are continually washed away by winter storms, leaving a shifting pattern of reefs and sand banks under the waves. The smugglers seem to be able to find their way through but every winter storm sees one or two other vessels wrecked offshore. If you were to make your way down to see what passes for a fisherman's village, you would see that almost every building, as well as all the fences, have been constructed in large part using the driftwood that comes ashore from those wrecks. I have been urged to apply to enclose this land, Sir Adam, and I know that it would improve the rents I could charge. However, I do not have the heart to turn the villagers off their meagre strips or prevent them from keeping a few sheep or a cow. If I were to do so, most of them would be forced to turn to Poor Relief or starve. Frederick thought I was mad. His younger brother says he understands my reasons, but I have little doubt that when he inherits this estate, as he now will, the land will be enclosed within a very short time.'

Adam felt glad that the land of his new estate had been enclosed long before he bought it. He wouldn't want to be the cause of anybody being put out of their cottage or forced to seek Poor Relief. At once he made a mental note to instruct his land agent to be certain the wages his tenants were offered would always be slightly above those offered by the estates round about. That way they could have the pick of the workers, as well as the comfort of knowing that they would have no complaint against their employer.

'I could see as I arrived that the land around here is not naturally endowed with rich soil,' Adam said, being as tactful as he thought he could be. 'However, there must be some good land, because I know that there are a number of estates in this area where the owners are wealthy.'

'That will be in the river valleys and floodplains, especially by the Bure,' Mr Dalston said. 'That's always where you find the richest land and the deepest soil.'

'Given that there are quite a number of your neighbours who are prosperous, I imagine your sons and their sons would have been natural companions and playmates.'

'Yes, that was so. Generally speaking, we are on excellent terms with all our neighbours. However, when I say "we", I mean everyone except Frederick nowadays. It would have been true of him as well until a few years ago. Once he had returned from the short time he was allowed to spend at the university, it was clear his character had changed out of all recognition. At times he could be charming, at other times wild and erratic, and then morose and withdrawn. You never knew what to expect from minute to minute. Needless to say, he went from being a welcome visitor amongst our neighbours to being someone most of them preferred to avoid if they could. For example, he used to go hunting and riding with the eldest son of a nearby family, a delightful young man called Philip Vickers. I don't know what Frederick did, but he caused some kind of upset and was abruptly told he was not welcome there anymore. Recently, I have heard that Mr Vickers was telling anyone who would listen that Frederick was a blackguard who deserved to be shot. Sadly, the Vickers family cut all contact with me as well when they banned Frederick from their house. I have, therefore, been unable to discover what it is that he did to them.'

'Do you think they would speak to me?' Adam asked. 'It would be helpful to understand what your son did to cause them to act in that way. With no obvious people to suspect for his murder, the only way I will be able to uncover the person who did it will be to know what matters might have turned someone into a deadly enemy. Few people murder at random, Mr Dalston. The majority always have a reason, even if it seems trivial or nonsensical to everybody else.'

'I really have no idea. You'll have to ask them. Just don't tell them that I have sent you.'

'Going back to this change in your son's character,' Adam said. 'Do you have any idea what might have been the reason?'

William Dalston paused for a while. It was plain he was racking his brains in the attempt to come up with an answer.

'Do you know,' he said, 'until now it has never occurred to me to ask that question? I clearly should have done but I was too busy at the time trying to cope with the chaos that Frederick caused everywhere he went. I never stopped to try to understand what might lie behind the change in his behaviour. To be honest, I still don't know the answer.'

'Perhaps we can work it out between us,' Adam said. 'When did you notice this change had begun?'

'That's easy. It was when he returned home, having been expelled from Oxford college. I think the decision made him so furious he became intolerant of any kind of authority or restraint.'

'Why did they expel him?'

'They never explained in detail. All they would tell me was that his behaviour was having a bad effect on the other undergraduates. Frederick wouldn't explain either. The only hint I could get came via a friend I had who was a fellow of another Oxford college. He said the gossip was that Frederick had been smuggling various women of the town into the college so that they could entertain — I think that's the correct euphemism — his friends. If that was correct, I can well see that the college authorities had to take action. Still, it was harsh to expel him at once and say he could never return. I suppose they felt they were left with no alternative.'

'But Frederick couldn't see that?'

'Not at all. I was always somewhat easy-going with him as a father. He grew up without any experience of living under firm discipline. When he encountered it, he refused to accept that it could be necessary. He saw those who tried to impose such discipline on him as tyrants. Perhaps, because of that, he didn't try to find ways to evade the rules, he simply ignored them. When that got him into serious trouble, as it was bound to sooner or later, he responded with violent anger.'

'Yet you had never treated him in that way,' Adam said. 'Why, then, should he turn against you and your friends?'

'I think he somehow became infected with the kind of radical ideas he believed could justify his anger. Like the ones promulgated by that wretched fellow Thomas Paine. As a result, he saw anyone who was a member of the classes who rule this country, locally and nationally, as being similar to the Master and fellows of his college. They had expelled him without giving him a second chance. That treatment somehow turned him against the existing laws and customs of his own country as well. Now I think about it, that could also explain some of the other changes in him at the same time.'

'What changes were those?' Adam asked. 'From all that you have told me so far, I wouldn't have expected your son to have changed to such an extent. For him to claim to believe in the arguments of Tom Paine and his demands for the overthrow of the monarchy and the ruling elite seems incredible. He might have been angry, but he had no cause to blame people he had never met. If he wanted a second chance, why didn't he take it when he returned. Why not show everyone that the people at Oxford were wrong about him?'

'You might have thought that's what he would have done, mightn't you? All I can say is that he didn't. As well as directing his anger towards political matters, such as the way the country is ruled or wealth is distributed, he turned it towards those amongst whom he had been born and brought up. He even professed to dislike the countryside itself. He began to say he hated anywhere outside the streets of a busy city like Norwich or London. Such places were too quiet, too dull, too lacking in any kind of entertainment. Rural people were all ignorant peasants, he said, and the local gentry greedy fools, who lived off others' toil and lacked either intellect and or sensibility. Before he went to Oxford, he used to enjoy country pursuits. He went riding and hunted foxes and we went out together shooting pheasants and partridge in the season. He even sat beside me when I spent time fishing in the moat. All that stopped. He now swore he hated horses and that hunting and fishing were boring pursuits, fit only for idiots. Not long before he left this house for the last time, he told me that when he thought of becoming squire of Kessingfield, it made him want to vomit.'

'I imagine none of this endeared him to anyone in this neighbourhood.'

'Certainly not to the gentry! As for the rest, he made it so abundantly clear that he despised them, none of them would as much as give him the time of day. Do you know if he was happier in Norwich?'

'That I cannot say,' Adam replied. 'He certainly had friends and acquaintances there. Or rather, when I say friends that may be overstating the situation. The few I have been able to speak with told me that he had more or less forced himself into their groups at the start, only to fall out with them over one thing or another fairly soon afterwards. I'm very sorry to have to tell you that, if the impression I have picked up is correct, almost nobody liked him.'

'Not even women? Ever since he was quite young, he had a knack for charming his way into ladies' affections. Did that not continue?'

'Yes, that continued. Not generally, I would say, and certainly not amongst many of the respectable wives and mothers. They had encountered men like him before and saw him as a danger. Even so, if he set his sights on a woman — and generally it would be a young and innocent one — he nearly always appeared to succeed.'

'He hadn't changed in every respect, then?'

'No, not in every respect. Unfortunately, those women who fell for him soon discovered their mistake.'

'He treated them badly?'

'Not in any physical sense. He simply tired of them quickly, cast them aside and moved onto the next one.'

Adam decided that he must continue to withhold his knowledge of how Frederick Dalston had turned to blackmail. Telling the young man's father could do no good and would cause him a considerable amount of pain. He very much doubted the families concerned would wish Dalston's activities to become common knowledge either. If he kept some matters to himself, there was no reason why William Dalston should ever learn how low his eldest son had sunk in his endless quest for money.'

At this point, Adam decided there was no more useful information likely to be gained from Mr Dalston. The man looked tired and drained. Adam didn't have the heart to press him any further. He therefore thanked his host, promised to get in touch with him again should he discover anything new and made his way back to his carriage. It had been a dispiriting morning and he was sure the journey home amongst those hungry fields would do nothing to raise his spirits. Not until he was once again back on the Cromer turnpike could he look around and take his normal pleasure in the fields and skies of his home county.

After they had travelled maybe four miles, Adam realised he had made a major mistake. He still didn't know whether or not Frederick's younger brother — George, wasn't it? — had any part to play in this tragedy. He couldn't even remember how old he was or how he spent his time. Damnation! He should have asked if he could speak with the young man before he left Kessingfield Hall.

He couldn't turn back now. It would take at least twenty minutes to find somewhere to turn the carriage around and then drive back to the

Hall. Besides, there was no guarantee that he would find George there when he arrived. It was just as likely that he would meet up with the rector and be subjected to another barrage of muddled quotations from the Bible. No, on second thoughts, it would be much better to see if young George could come to talk with him at his house in Aylsham. That would get him away from the rector's reach and provide a venue where no one, including Mr Dalston himself, could be tempted to listen in.

Did George really want so badly to be squire that he might have been tempted to remove his brother as an obstacle to his ambitions? Younger brothers usually found themselves forced to earn their own living with little help from the rest of the family; especially if, as he suspected it was in this case, the income from the estate had already been put under severe strain by the demands of the elder brother. Thanks to the English system of primogeniture, the eldest male child always inherited the estate together with the vast bulk of any cash that might be available. Adam should know. He was a younger brother himself.

The system of entail, which was also commonly implied to family estates, insured that any children other than the eldest could not expect to inherit more than could be made available from funds not deemed to be part of the estate itself. In essence, the person who set up the entail bequeathed the estate and its associated funds into a trust, giving each successive descendant a life interest in the income, but no ability to sell any of the lands. As a way of keeping the family's wealth together it was superb. Unfortunately, the "winner takes all" aspect of the system meant all the children other than the eldest might end up dependent on money from their mother or a female grandparent. He himself had only been able to complete his medical training thanks to the generosity of an uncle who died intestate.

William Dalston's father, the brewer, had clearly imagined that by the purchase of Kessingfield he would be able to found a dynasty of landowners. If so, it had been a poor choice as it stood, probably made by a man who knew little or nothing about the land and only measured its worth in acres. Then, to confound his descendants still further, he had left it in entail, so they would be unable to sell the land once they discovered its failings. He could not have known that, by doing so, he would set in place the sequence of events that would later end in murder.

Adam sighed. However distasteful it was to imagine one brother murdering another to gain the inheritance, the practice had a very long history. It went back to Cain and Abel, if the Bible was to be believed. There was no doubt about it. He would have to find a way to question George Dalston as soon as he could.

Still, some of what he had learned was useful. The next step must be to try to identify the members of the coterie of young tearabouts that Frederick had turned to after his maladroit efforts at card-sharping had persuaded his former friends to shun his company. He would write to Ross that very day and request another meeting.

❧ 8 ❧

Ross responded with remarkable promptness to Adam's summons, arriving at about ten o'clock two mornings later. Between then and his trip to Kessingfield Hall, his sleep had been mercifully free of dreams about Frederick's death. Maybe his sleeping mind had disclosed everything it wished already. Only on that very morning, as he lay in a state somewhere between sleep and wakefulness, had one or two images arisen to set his thoughts off once more. He had seen — if that is the word — the killer go to where Frederick had fallen face down, then sit on his back, lift a dagger high in the air with both hands clasped around it and plunge it into the prone man's back. In another set of fleeting images, the killer had stood over the fallen man and thrust his dagger downwards, putting both his strength and his weight behind the blow. Man or woman? He hadn't been able to see.

Adam certainly wasn't going to share these 'revelations' with Ross, however. Wicken's man would probably decide he'd lost his mind if he did. Still, they weren't things he could simply ignore. If his sleeping mind was working on his behalf to solve the question of the manner of Dalston's death, he'd be grateful for the assistance.

Once they were seated in Adam's library and Ross had refreshed himself after his journey, Adam began by describing how he had spent his time since their last meeting and what he had discovered as a result. Ross sat in silence throughout, apparently stunned by what he was hearing. At the end, he expressed himself as totally amazed. Wicken, he said, had told him Adam had a flair for unravelling mysteries but, he said, experiencing it for himself had taken his breath away.

He was particularly impressed by the summary of areas for investigation which Adam and Lady Alice had drawn up between them. He also agreed about a possible response by a criminal gang, some group whose territory Frederick Dalston had blundered into. It was, Ross said, an idea well worth following up.

'There are plenty of such gangs in Norwich,' he said, 'though most of them are small. I don't think those would be likely to resort to such violent action as murder. What may be relevant is this. Some of the smuggling gangs don't restrict themselves to handling contraband. They'll turn their hands to anything that they think can make money. As I expect you know, those gangs are large, well-organised and entirely without scruples when it comes to getting their own way. If young Dalston had done something to enrage a gang of that kind they would certainly have dealt with him ruthlessly, especially if he had ignored attempts to warn him off.'

'We know he was naïve and impetuous,' Adam replied. 'Just the kind of fellow to think of a money-making idea and rush into it without any preliminary investigations. Since he was also arrogant, he might well have seen any warnings as being beneath his notice. Can you look into that?'

'Most willingly, Sir Adam. I'll get my informants onto it right away.'

'One other thing. I'm interested in the young men I'm told Frederick associated with after he was blackballed by his previous set. I was told they dabbled in various petty crimes. They might have set him on his way to more serious ones — ones that might have attracted the notice of the gangs you mentioned. Can you look into who they were and what they did? Now, tell me what you have discovered since we talked last.'

'Before we do that — since I have discovered little enough

compared to you — I'd like to talk a little about the plan of action you and your wife have drawn up, if I may,' Ross began. 'As regards Dalston's history of praying on vulnerable young women, the suggestion that this should be left to the ladies to explore strikes me as quite correct, although I have to say I was stunned when you mentioned the willingness of your wife, your mother and your wife's niece to get involved in this way. I always thought well-born, respectable women had no interest in anything save fashion, novels and gossip. I can see now that I was sorely misled.'

'If it makes you feel any better, I can assure you that those three ladies are quite exceptional in many ways,' Adam replied. 'All the same, there's no doubt that they are best placed to persuade other ladies to talk about things which are bound to be embarrassing. I think we should leave them to it. I'll let you know if they come up with anything.'

'I'm not sure that we should ignore the possibility that Dalston's death was due to someone taking vengeance on him for cheating at the gambling tables,' Ross said. 'You mentioned that after the group of young bucks excluded Dalston, the one which included the Barnes brothers, word of his guilt would have gone around very swiftly. After that, none of the other gambling clubs which attract wealthy members would be willing to allow him through the door.'

'It was for that reason I thought that we could now ignore that area of investigation. Where would he go to venture his money in the hope of producing a large win?'

'If you focus on the gentry and members of the upper classes — and I would include the rich merchant families in that — there isn't anywhere,' Ross replied. 'However, there are other options. I know of a number of back-street gambling dens where the stakes are high and a good deal of money changes hands. The kind of characters who congregate there are a long way from the sort of people Frederick Dalston would have been used to dealing with. They're also the kind of places which attract professional card-sharpers. Those devils would have emptied Dalston's purse within days, believe me. Still, so long as he had money and was willing to gamble it away, I suspect dens of that kind would have welcomed him with open arms. If he tried to cheat them though, he wouldn't stay alive for long. The one thing that doesn't fit with that picture is the place and manner of young Dalston's death. The penalty for cheating amongst those ruffians would be to end up in the River Wensum with your throat cut, not stabbed to death on a lonely road, miles from the city itself.'

'I see your point,' Adam agreed. His mind had gone back at once to his dream of a tall, strong woman as the killer. 'Perhaps we shouldn't altogether rule out the idea of an aggrieved gambler as our murderer, though I too cannot easily understand why that person would not simply have waited for Frederick Dalston in some dark place in a narrow alley and put an end to him there. That's another area for you to explore, I think. I hope you don't mind being asked to undertake so much of this investigation?'

'Not at all, sir. That's what Sir Percival Wicken sent me here to do. There's no way that you could, or should, deal with habitual criminals and the other scum of the city. What might be most useful in your case would be to explore the reason why young Dalston was so obsessed with making as much money as possible in a very short time. I haven't discovered nearly as much as you have since we last spoke, but one thing I have been told by several of my sources is that Dalston tried to extort money from some of the stallholders at the market. He got together a gang of hired thugs who threatened to damage or destroy their stalls if they refused to pay.'

'Isn't that exactly the kind of thing that would have infuriated one or more established criminal enterprises?' Adam said.

'It must have done,' Ross said, 'but, if what I've heard is true, Dalston had the good sense to back off after they threatened to strip him naked and throw him into one of the carts that collected night-soil.'

Despite his best efforts, Adam couldn't stop himself from laughing out loud, while Ross joined in.

'I wonder if such a potentially "revealing" experience would have convinced him to stay away from areas of society in which he had little or no personal experience?' he said, when they had both recovered their composure. 'Everything we know about Dalston suggests he never persisted with anything that caused him too much trouble. If the attempt on the stallholders was fairly recent, it might explain why he turned instead to trying to extort money by seducing well-born young women. That activity would return him to dealing with the kind of people he would have found familiar.'

'I'll try to find out exactly when the business with the stallholders happened,' Ross said. 'I've also picked up further traces of a possible arrangement between Frederick Dalston and Obadiah Webley. At this stage, it's nothing but hints and whispers; nothing very tangible but enough to encourage me to probe further. Webley's a confirmed villain and confidence trickster but, on the outside, he poses as a cultured man of business. If he contacted Dalston in some way, as I believe he did, the young man would easily be taken in by this outward show of respectability. From the other man's point of view, Webley would quickly confirm Dalston's naïveté and lack of caution. After that, it would be a small matter to convince Dalston he could help him achieve his aims, while planning to use this foolish gentleman's gullibility for his own ends. It would be typical of Webley to come up with a plan whereby he could walk away a good deal richer, while Dalston bore all the blame.'

'Do you have any suspicions of what such a plan might be? This might be an area we can both investigate. It sounds as if Webley would want to focus on the wealthiest citizens of Norwich, if he could, seeing Dalston as his point of entry. I know quite a few of those and can find out about quite a few more. What type of crime do you think Webley would suggest they might get involved in?'

'Based on Webley's past history, some sort of commercial or financial fraud would be my bet, the larger the better.'

'Yes,' Adam said eagerly. 'That would be it! I've come across several wealthy people who would question and cross-question the butcher who supplies their household with meat over every item on his bill, then happily venture hundreds — even thousands — of pounds on the basis of a talk with a friend of a friend and a simple handshake.'

'I've set my sources searching for more situations where Dalston might be trying to make large returns quickly,' Ross added. 'I've also spoken with some of my Brothers in the Craft. Between them, they'll know almost everything that takes place in the city, if it pertains to commerce or finance. Fraud is something they abhor. Helping to root it out will certainly appeal to them.'

'You're a Freemason?' Adam asked in surprise.

'And I already know you are not,' Ross said, smiling. 'I was received into a lodge in London some years ago now. They knew I was a Runner, but they accepted me nonetheless. When I moved to Norwich, I transferred to a lodge here. They know my true name, of course, but not what I do — at least, not my real occupation. It can be a lonely life, Sir Adam, as I'm sure you understand. The Craft offers me fellowship and the chance to improve myself. I would never involve them in the particular work I do for Sir Percival. What I'm doing for you is different. Many of my Brothers are merchants, traders and bankers. Others range from shopkeepers to master craftsmen. It would be wrong not to warn them if someone is setting out to commit some scheme to defraud.'

'I thought those who are Freemasons kept the fact secret?'

'That is true, generally speaking. However, I'm sure you can be trusted not to tell others.' Ross was smiling again. 'Now, both of us have much to do and, unless there is more for you to tell me now, I will take my leave and go about my business.'

After Ross had left, Adam took paper and pen and wrote two further letters. He felt it was critical to word the first of them correctly, so he took his time over its composition. It was directed to Mr Vickers senior, the former close friend of the Dalston family that William Dalston had told him about. Adam would normally have been quite open about the reason why he wanted to arrange a meeting. He certainly wasn't going to lie, that wouldn't be right, but he had to respect what William Dalston had told him; saying he was working on Mr Dalston's behalf would probably result in an immediate refusal. He therefore decided to mix truth — the fact that he was interested in Frederick Dalston's death — with what he hoped would be a plausible fiction, given the general state of alarm about the possibility of a French invasion. He knew it was weak, but it was the best he could think of on the spur of the moment.

After thinking as hard as he could and rejecting several approaches as either too mendacious or too straightforward, Adam finally put pen to paper. What he wrote was this.

"I HAVE BEEN ASKED BY THE RELEVANT AUTHORITIES (HE LEFT THEIR nature unspecified) *to use my local knowledge to assist them in making preparations against a possible sudden attack by our French enemies. As I'm sure you are well aware, it is no great distance to the ports of the Low Countries and northern France. It is also impossible to defend every single part of the coast fully. Our army and navy are already stretched to the limit. Therefore, they wish to discover which particular points might best be watched, using the limited resources available. Since the coast of Norfolk is much used by smugglers, it is obvious that it would make a good place to land a raid by hostile forces.*

"It has also come to their notice that the son of a local gentleman has recently been murdered while out riding not too far from the boundaries of your estate. I have spoken with the unfortunate man's father and he informed me that your son, Philip, was for some time a close friend of the murdered man. He was also a welcome guest of yourself and your family. I am, therefore, making bold to request to speak with you and your son. It is possible that the murdered man was seen in some way as a threat to those hoping to make an armed landing on this coast. Why that should be is far from clear. I am hoping that you might be able to tell me something from the young man's past that might have a bearing on his murder.

"Please be assured that anything you may be willing to tell me will be treated with the greatest confidentiality. If, as a result of talking with you and your son, I'm able to inform those in London that you are able to tell them nothing of relevance, you will not be bothered in the future."

THIS WAS A BLATANT STRETCHING OF THE TRUTH, BUT IT WAS ONLY by playing on the general public fears and appealing to the man's patriotism that Adam believed he could persuade him to agree to be questioned. By mentioning "those in London", he hoped also that he would suggest these enquiries had a degree of official backing and should be taken seriously. Given Wicken's suggestion that Adam's interest in the death of Frederick Dalston in some way overlapped with his own concerns about activities along the coast, there was even a slight degree of truth in this fiction.

When he had finished writing to Mr Vickers, he breathed a sigh of relief and turned to the other note: this time to George Dalston. Here he could be quite open about his intentions, saying that he had some questions to ask him about his brother and the relationship between them. He then gave both letters to William, his groom, and asked him to deliver them early next morning.

A dam had been delighted to receive a speedy reply from Mr Vickers, in which he expressed himself more than willing to cooperate in any way possible. Perhaps Sir Adam might be able to call on Thursday morning at about eleven? Since that was the very next day, Adam hastened to send back a note confirming the arrangement. This was progress at a speed he relished.

Mr Vickers's family home was considerably more modern than Kessingfield Hall. Adam guessed that it had been built less than a century ago. However, it too was built using similar deep red bricks, the windows edged with pale freestone and the roof covered with orange pantiles. In this eastern part of Norfolk, you could see the strong Dutch influence on building styles everywhere. Ships from the Netherlands, arriving empty to load up with barley and malt, used either bricks or tiles as ballast on their outward journey. These were unloaded to make way for the cargo of grain and sold to be used as building materials. The appearance of Mr Vickers's house, with its curved gables at either end of the main building, might as easily have been observed in the countryside around Rotterdam or Amsterdam as here in Norfolk.

Seven bays, Adam noticed, and two stories with attics lit by dormers behind the parapet. A good, substantial property, though not exceptional. What looked like well-built stables alongside a courtyard must hold the kitchen and other domestic offices. The drive was lined with tall limes and well-kept, unlike that at Kessingfield. The pastures of what must be the Home Farm alongside the driveway held a large flock of sheep with their lambs, together with some fine red-coated cattle. Along the way, Adam had also noted the land around must have been properly enclosed many years ago, since the hedges between the fields were grown thick and tall. Now the earth everywhere showed green shoots of what was probably either barley or wheat. This land bore all the signs of a well-tended, flourishing estate, likely to yield excellent rents. It might be close to Kessingfield in distance, but it was worlds away in the way it was being managed.

Mr Vickers himself looked as unassuming and comfortable as the house that he inhabited. There was a cheerful look to his face as Adam was shown into the library, where he had obviously been waiting for his guest to arrive. He was a man of perhaps slightly below the average height, yet of considerably more than average girth. Not a fat man, he would doubtless claim, but merely one who enjoyed his food and the contents of what was most likely an excellent, well-stocked cellar. His welcome seemed warm and genuine, though Adam detected some apprehension behind it. He decided, therefore, that it would be best if he confessed to his mild deception right at the start.

'I am sorry to say that I have come here under somewhat false pretences,' he began, 'and your kindness in receiving me may not last once I explain my true reason for calling. Everything I said in my letter was the truth. However, only part of it is linked to the real reason for asking to speak with you and your son. The principal purpose of my investigation is to discover the identity of the murderer of Frederick Dalston. I am not the only person who feels that the explanation accepted by the coroner and the local magistrate falls a good deal short of reality. There is much more to this death than a bungled highway robbery. I should also confess that Mr William Dalston has asked me to help him prepare a suitable prosecution. Let me tell you what I told him. I am only willing to investigate this case if I am allowed to do so independently. Any conclusion I reach will be totally impartial and based only on the facts I am able to unearth.'

'Why did you feel unable to tell me this in your letter?'

'Because Mr Dalston warned me that if I told you at the start of my connection to him, you would refuse to see me.'

'What he told you is wrong, Sir Adam,' Mr Vickers replied. 'No one regrets more than I do the breach that has come between our two families. I certainly bear no ill will towards William Dalston, his son George or his daughter. In terminating the friendship that had existed between us previously, I did only what I felt I was compelled to do under the circumstances.'

'I gather Frederick Dalston used to be a welcome guest in this house, as well as a particular friend of your son.' Adam was mightily relieved that Mr Vickers had not asked him to leave on the instant. However, he had still not openly agreed to assist. 'I suspect it was Frederick Dalston's behaviour that was the direct cause of the breach between your two families.'

'That is correct. After his return from Oxford in disgrace, there was a marked change for the worse in that young man's behaviour.'

'I imagine that the immediate cause of the breach had to do with your daughter,' Adam said quietly. 'Is that the case?'

Mr Vickers reared back as if he had been struck in the face. He lost all his colour and seemed to be struggling to get his breath.

'How the devil did you know?' he gasped. 'I knew that accursed blackguard would never keep what he had done secret. What is he telling people? I am sure it will be a long way from the truth of the matter.'

'I simply guessed,' Adam said, 'based mostly on the knowledge I have gained of Frederick Dalston's behaviour over the past year or so. Please, do not be alarmed. So far as I know, Frederick Dalston spoke to nobody at all about you or your family, on this matter or any other. I have not shared my guess with anyone, nor will I. You may be assured that everything we say to one another will be kept in the strictest confidence. The details of this sorry affair are strictly my concern and only for the purpose of understanding who might have had a sufficient grievance to carry out this killing.'

'If you guessed, Sir Adam, others may do so as well. I told my son at the time to watch his tongue! For a time, the young fool went about threatening to take revenge on Dalston. Please do not hold that against him. He was not even here at the time that Frederick Dalston was killed. I'd sent him to stay with good friends of ours who live near Colchester. They have a son too and he and Philip have known one another since childhood. They also have three daughters, the eldest a year or so older than Philip, one of roughly the same age and one about two years younger. It has long been the dearest wish of both our families that my son should form a sufficient attachment to one of these young women for it to result in matrimony. Philip set out for Colchester about ten days before Frederick was killed. He has not yet returned.'

'Thank you for telling me that, Mr Vickers,' Adam said. 'I can see that your son is entirely innocent in this matter. I am relieved to be able to cross him off my list. However, purely for my own information — and in the strictest confidence, as I have already said — I would be grateful if you could confirm what I believe must have taken place between Frederick Dalston and your daughter. In the other case I know about, Dalston won over the affections of an innocent young woman and persuaded her to elope with him. He took care not to proceed too far away so that the pursuers might easily come upon them. Unfortunately, he took equal care to deflower the woman. After that, he told her distraught family that he could be persuaded to claim he had never touched her in that way provided they paid him the large sum of money that he demanded.'

'Did they do so?'

'Yes, I believe they did.'

'Perhaps I should have done so as well,' Vickers said, 'though that is of little consolation. As I told you earlier, Frederick Dalston used to be the close friend and hunting partner of my son, Philip. All went well until he returned from Oxford, having been sent down for some kind of immoral behaviour; I can now imagine what that might have been. My son and I were both shocked, but Frederick seemed to be his normal, charming self and we were willing to forgive him on the strength of the close friendship that had developed over many years between his family and ours.'

'And then? Something must have changed.'

'You were right in guessing that Frederick Dalston set out to ruin my daughter, Amelia, in the same way. We didn't notice it at first. By the time we realised what was going on, he had convinced her that she was in love with him. We tried to persuade her that this was a mere adolescent infatuation, but it was to no avail. It seemed that he had already told her others would stand in the way of their love, due to what he called his unjustified reputation. The silly child believed him rather than us."

'What happened next?'

'They eloped and he abandoned her at King's Lynn, rushing back here to demand money for his silence. It seems they had stopped at an inn there for the night. She believed he was taking her to Scotland where they could be married, since she was below the age at which he could marry without my consent in England. He tried first to charm her into allowing him to possess her fully, supposedly as a token of their love. She refused, I'm glad to say, and demanded the innkeeper give her a separate room.'

'But that was not the end of the matter?'

'It was not. When he judged she must have fallen asleep, Frederick tried to break into her room and take her by force. Perhaps she had anticipated such an event, for she had done her best to block the doorway. The wretch managed to break through all the same.'

'He raped her?'

'No, thank God. She fought and screamed, making so much noise both several servants and the innkeeper came to see what the matter was. Frederick tried to claim he'd gone to her room because he'd heard her screams and suspected she was having a nightmare. She accused him of trying to assault her. Caught between the two of them, the innkeeper ordered Frederick to return to his room and set a servant to keep watch on him.'

'He stayed there?'

'For a time. The servant fell asleep, of course. When he awoke, Frederick's door was open and there was no sign of him inside. He called his master and they rushed to the room where my daughter was sleeping but found her quite safe. They realised Frederick had crept out in the night and left, leaving the bill for the two rooms and the meal they had eaten unpaid.'

'That was when he came to demand money for his silence?'

'It was. Foolishly, he told me where my daughter could be found, as well as the lie that she had willingly allowed him to sleep with her as husband and wife. Then he demanded money for keeping the whole affair secret. As you can imagine, his words threw my mind into turmoil. I called Philip and sent him post haste to King's Lynn. There he found his sister safe but overwhelmed with shame and fury. I think she was, if anything, more angry with herself for falling victim to Frederick's fraud than with the one who had tricked her. Philip brought her back here and she told me the whole story.'

At this point, Mr Vickers paused. It was clear that bringing up the memory of these events was causing him significant pain. Adam hated to have to persuade him to continue, but he needed to be absolutely clear whether there were any significant differences between what had happened to Amelia Vickers and her family and what Dalston had done in the previous case.

'What did you do about Frederick Dalston's demand?' Adam asked softly.

'His demand? He said that he would keep silent about deflowering my daughter if I paid him five hundred pounds. He also promised to remain silent about the elopement as a whole. So far as we knew, no one else was aware at that time of what had happened. The rogue even went so far as to point out that if Amelia stayed silent and we stayed silent as well, he was the only person who could make my daughter's shame public knowledge. If that happened, her future matrimonial prospects naturally would be ruined.'

'Did you pay him?'

'Pay him? Of course, I didn't! I knew my daughter. However much she had believed herself to be in love, I was sure she would never have agreed to allow him to deflower her until they were properly and legally married. I spat in his face, cursed him soundly and told him to go to the devil, which was where he belonged. Since he is now dead, I imagine that is where he is today. I hope he rots in Hell for ever!'

⚜

THAT WAS THE AFTERNOON WHEN THE MAGISTRATE WHO SHOULD have been investigating Frederick Dalston's murder, Mr Stephen Palfrey, arrived at Adam's house and asked to speak with him. Adam had his own suspicions about the reason for this visit. They proved to be entirely correct. Mr Palfrey demanded to know why Adam was interfering in an affair that was none of his business. He had already done all that was required of him in placing the usual advertisements offering a reward for information that could lead to a prosecution. No one had come forward. That meant there were no witnesses and nothing to suggest that the death had not been as a result of a failed attempt at robbery. That had been the conclusion he had reached at the start; nothing had happened since then to change his mind. The coroner agreed with him, as would any sensible person. There was no call for Sir Adam to get involved in any way.

Adam listened to this harangue calmly, amusing himself by observing the way in which Mr Palfrey gained greater courage the further he proceeded. When he had finished, the man waited for Adam's response — and presumably his humble acceptance of the rebuke — with his expression showing the confidence he felt.

After allowing the subsequent silence on his part to drag itself out until Mr Palfrey was looking distinctly unsettled, Adam responded calmly that he was acting on behalf of the dead man's family. They had every right to bring a prosecution if they wished. He had also been asked to look into the affair by "certain highly-placed persons in London".

His words, mild though they were, caused the magistrate to deflate like a punctured balloon. Instead of looking smugly confident, he now wore the expression of a man who had walked into a room expecting to find a cat and had found himself facing a ravenous tiger instead. The poor fellow was plainly terrified.

'What on earth persuaded you it was a robbery?' Adam asked, his voice as gentle as before. 'Nothing was taken even though the dead man was carrying a purse full of money and wearing expensive rings on two fingers. Not only that, I have been told the corpse was neatly laid out, hands crossed over his chest, as if already prepared for the coffin. Where in that are there signs of a robber being interrupted and fleeing in haste before he could be apprehended?'

Palfrey looked dreadful. His face was now chalk-white. His eyes bulged as if someone had him by the throat and was throttling him. Still Adam pressed on.

'Let us turn to the matter of the death-wound, sir. Frederick Dalston was riding a horse, yet he was killed with a single thrust from a narrow blade, driven home so fiercely that it almost pierced his body from side to side. If you were sitting on a horse yourself, could you thrust a sword into someone that hard? If you were on foot, it would have been impossible to drive any blade home at the correct angle. And if you had pulled the man off his horse, surely he would have tried to defend himself?'

For a moment, Palfrey was plainly unable to speak. Then he managed to stutter a reply.

'I ... um ... err ... well ... I see ... But what if the robbers had knocked Dalston unconscious first, then attacked him?'

'How? With a blow to the jaw? That would have left bruises. By striking him over the head with a cudgel? That too would have left unmistakable signs. None were present. I have spoken with the doctor who examined the body. He tells me the coroner would not allow him to raise such matters during the inquest and that you made no attempt to speak with him afterwards.'

At this point, Adam began to worry whether Mr Palfrey might not actually faint away from fear. Here was a man who had jumped to a convenient solution to save himself trouble. Now, he realised, far too late; what an incompetent fool he had revealed himself to be.

'Are you ... I mean, are you going to report all of this to the authorities in London? Are you going to report me to the Lord Lieutenant of the county?' Mr Palfrey stammered. 'If you do, it will cost me my position. I beg of you ... I have no experience of serious crime ... none whatsoever ... this is the first murder I have been forced to deal with. I didn't know ... I did the best I could.'

Given another moment or so, the wretched man would be on his knees begging for mercy.

'I haven't yet made up my mind,' Adam said coldly. 'You may not have any experience of dealing with murders, but your approach in this case was not even worthy of the words "skimpy and superficial". If you keep out of my way from now on, I may decide to give you another chance. If you do not, the plain negligence of which you are guilty will be reported to the Lord Lieutenant, as well as to the Home Department in London.'

However sorry Adam felt for a man so plainly out of his depth, it would not serve justice in the future if he continued along his present path.

Later, Lady Alice asked her husband who the "little man strutting around like a bantam cock" had been and laughed when Adam told her what had happened.

'What do you intend to do?' she said. 'I can't help feeling rather sorry for the wretched fellow.'

'I assure you, my dear, I have no intention of causing him any further trouble, just as long as he keeps out of my way and amends his ways. It certainly did no harm to puncture his pride in the way I did. My hope is that he has learned an important lesson and will cut no corners in the future.'

৩৫৩

THE NEXT DAY, AT AROUND NOON, GEORGE DALSTON ARRIVED IN response to Adam's summons. He looked to be perhaps two or maybe three years younger than his brother. Aside from that, he was a younger version of his father. There was the same rotund figure, the same round face and cheerful expression, even his voice sounded similar. The only obvious difference was that he seemed, if anything, far more strained and wretched than his father had been. What the reason for this might be was something Adam would have to discover.

Adam ushered him into his library and former consulting room.

There they partook of coffee and exchanged the normal pleasantries before getting down to business. It might have been a difficult conversation, but to Adam's relief George Dalston declared himself entirely willing to answer any questions that were put to him.

Adam opened by asking him about his relationship with his brother. According to George, he and his brother had had a very close relationship — that was, until Frederick went to Oxford. They walked in the estate together and Frederick spent time teaching his younger brother how to shoot and how to ride. That all changed when Frederick returned home after being sent down, expelled, from his college. He refused to continue their walks together and told George that riding and shooting, let alone fishing, were only fit activities for those without any spark of intellect or originality. When George refused to agree with him and persisted in spending time outdoors on the estate, Frederick started to make fun of him. He called him "Farmer George" and "my rustic little brother". It hurt. Soon George had begun to avoid Frederick's company whenever he could.

'How do you feel now that you are heir to the estate?' Adam asked.

'At first, I hardly thought about it,' George replied. 'My brother's death was such a terrible shock. When it finally occurred to me that I was next in line, I suppose I felt a mixture of guilt and excitement. I never expected to face the prospect of becoming squire. The fact that it had happened due to my brother meeting his death far too soon made me feel somewhat guilty about the prospect. On the other hand, I love the estate. I love being here with the sweeping expanses of heath and marsh, the distant sound of the surf on the beach and the immense Norfolk skies, full of towering clouds. I like hearing the geese flying overhead in the winter and the skylarks over the summer pastures. I used to lie in bed at night and cry at the prospect of being forced to leave it someday to earn my living. Now that never need happen, I cannot help feeling excited — if that isn't a terrible thing to admit in all the circumstances.'

'Not at all,' Adam said. 'My own brother felt much the same way. He had the advantage of being the elder one, so we always knew he would inherit our family estate in due time. I was the one who had to leave to take up a profession.'

'There wasn't enough money left after securing my brother's educa-tion to pay for me to go to the university in my turn. When he threw his opportunity away, I couldn't help feeling resentful, I suppose. You see, I could probably have gone to the university after all, only Fred-erick began piling up enormous debts on all sides and my father felt that he had to discharge them for the sake of the family's honour. Once again, my brother's needs, and later his wild actions, had denied me my chance. I had to settle on becoming a lawyer. Even then, there was no prospect of paying for articles with a leading partnership in Norwich or London. My father did his best, but all he could manage was to find a place for me with a partnership in North Walsham. I'm halfway through the third year of my articles and only at home now because of my brother's death.'

'Will you return and complete your training?' Adam asked.

'I very much doubt it,' George said. 'My father is in sore need of help and support. Besides, I hope to convince him to let me assume the business of running the estate. I think I just have enough legal knowledge to be able to serve as land agent as well, provided we use someone qualified to check and approve the leases and other legal documents I will need to draw up. I have been reading a good deal about the practical side of estate management too.'

You could hear the pride and enthusiasm in his voice. His brother might not have wanted to manage the family estate, but George radi-ated eagerness for the task.

'The land is poor,' Adam stated.

George was clearly not willing to be discouraged by any reserva-tions concerning Kessingfield.

'Not so poor as it looks. If it was enclosed and we insisted the tenants followed a proper rotation with clover and turnips, we could grow good barley. Maybe wheat as well. All it would take to put some heart into the land is sufficient application of marl and dung. If any tenants refuse to do what we ask — or cannot meet their share of the cost — I will terminate their leases as soon as I can. There will be other better men eager to rent our farms, I assure you.'

'And the cottagers? You father told me he didn't have the heart to take away their strips in the fields and use of the common grazing.'

'My father is too soft-hearted for his own good, Sir Adam. Times have changed and we must all change with them. I will do my best for these people, but the plain fact is that the estate will collapse into bankruptcy if nothing is done to set it on a sound footing. I assure you that any new owner would eject them all without a moment's thought.'

'Turning to the death of your brother, Mr Dalston, have you any idea why he was riding on that road so late at night?'

'Not the slightest one, I'm afraid. He'd know very well that it would be a dangerous thing to do. This is an exceptionally quiet and deserted part of the county — apart from the free traders, of course. The shallow seas close offshore and the sandy beaches make it an ideal part of the coast to beach small craft for unloading. That's why the smugglers' gangs are so active. Frederick would have more sense than to risk tangling with the free traders. Everyone knows they respond furiously if interfered with. If there had been a large shipment of contraband landed at the beach that night, the smuggling gang would be using that road. It's the simplest route to get their goods inland quickly. A lone rider on a good horse was likely to be mistaken for a Revenue Riding Officer.'

'And if he was?'

'They'd drag him off his horse and give him a good beating. They wouldn't shoot him, unless he used his pistol to try to fight back. It's rare for a Riding Officer to lose his life, other than during an attempt by gang members take back confiscated contraband or release their ringleaders from gaol. Then it can easily turn into a fight to the death, with pistols and cutlasses being used on both sides. In all other circumstances, the smugglers avoid causing the Revenue men serious injury. Doing that, let alone ambushing and killing a Riding Officer, would be likely to cause the authorities to send in patrols of dragoons to find the killers. Smugglers don't fight dragoons. They'd be much more likely to go elsewhere to land their contraband until the fuss died down. That would be a severe interference in their activities. No, a Riding Officer on his own might be beaten, but I don't believe he would have been murdered in the way my brother was.'

'You're saying the smugglers frequently use that particular stretch of beach?' Adam said.

'Certainly, it's one of their favourite spots. My father has learned to turn a blind eye on most occasions. You see, if you don't interfere with them, they leave you alone. Only if you cause them trouble do they start to be a dangerous nuisance. One of our neighbours to the south, whose house is really quite close to the sea, did his best to capture a group of smugglers and hand them over to the authorities. He failed, but in revenge they killed half his sheep. They also brought their cutter in close offshore and fired their cannons at his house. The bombardment did a considerable amount of damage, as well as terrifying those inside. Since then, he's left the smuggling gangs well alone, believe me!

'There's another matter. Working for the smugglers to help them land and transport their contraband is often the only way some of the poor fishermen and labourers around here can survive. They can earn more in a single night that way than they can earn in a week of regular work. My father is a kind man, as you may have noticed. Too kind, in many ways. He would hate to think that, by driving off the smugglers, he might bring starvation to the villagers. Because he leaves the free traders to their business, he sometimes finds a few kegs of spirits or a package of tobacco left by his back door. He isn't the only one who acts in that way. The rector enjoys his pipe and a glass of brandy on the quiet. You may be sure he doesn't refuse the occasional gift from the smugglers either.'

By this time, Adam felt certain George could not be involved in any way in his brother's death. Everything about him argued against it. He might have resented Frederick wasting the money spent on him and pushing his brother into second place all the time, but Adam couldn't see him doing anything about it. He might, of course, be proved wrong but, unless substantial evidence arose to suggest that was the case, it was time to cross George off the list of potential suspects. Still, Adam decided on a final question before sending George on his way.

'This is my last question,' Adam said. 'Can you think of anyone living in the locality of Kessingfield Hall who might wish to do your brother any harm?'

'I've asked myself that over and over again,' George said, 'and I can't come up with anyone. Besides, Frederick had been spending all his time in Norwich for more than a year. All that I can think of is this. It's not really evidence, just an oddity. About three weeks ago, I'd been out riding. I was returning home just as the light was fading and I could have sworn I saw my brother riding across a field that forms part of this estate.'

'What was he doing?'

'Heading towards the fishermen's village. Look, I'm not certain it was Frederick. All I'm telling you is that it could have been. Whoever it was, he was too far away for me to call out and riding too fast for there to be any possibility of me catching up with him. I did think of going to the village myself to see if Frederick was there, but it was getting late and I was hungry. I headed for home and convinced myself it was simply a mistake. All I'd really seen was a man, heavily cloaked, riding what looked like a good horse. It was merely that there was something about his build and the way he was riding that reminded me of my brother. Most likely it was a Riding Officer out on his rounds. They don't usually ride across the estate though. They usually keep to the road. Still, this one might have been in a hurry and decided to take a shortcut. As I said, the light was beginning to fail. I'd rather forgotten about it until now.'

❧ 10 ❧

From where he stood, looking out of the window towards Aylsham's marketplace, the sunshine which had greeted Adam when he first awoke had faded. In its stead he could see thin, high cloud streaming in from the direction of the sea. That meant a brisk east wind and a spell of cold weather. A quick glance to his right at the trees surrounding the parish church confirmed that an easterly wind had set in and was bending the tops of the trees, so that they tossed and fretted much like the sea must be doing. A wind like that would search out every crack and crevice around windows and doors, filling the house with bitter drafts.

Adam pulled his quilted silk banyan tighter about him. He'd asked his maid, Hannah, to light the fire in here as soon as she finished serving him his breakfast, but the room was still cold. That damned east wind, he supposed. April in this part of Norfolk could switch from balmy days to cold and miserable ones in a matter of hours. At least he didn't have to go out to visit patients any more on days like this. Given time, the room would grow a little warmer, though he doubted the small grate was adequate for the job of making it truly cosy. It had been a cold winter and the amount of coal he had been forced to buy was almost double the normal amount. He could afford it, but such a heavy expenditure on heating still rankled. He told himself firmly to stop complaining. The poor had no money for coal and little shelter from the wind and the frost. What was a simple inconvenience for him must have brought many real hardship to most of the country folk.

That morning he had taken his breakfast of coffee and warm bread rolls alone. Lady Alice had already retired to her dressing room to get ready to leave in search of more information about Frederick Dalston. Last night, before they retired to bed, she explained that she would be leaving a little earlier than usual to meet with an acquaintance of hers at Briningham Hall. When he protested that the place she was heading for must be five or six miles from Aylsham, and in the opposite direction to Kessingfield, she smiled and told him that the lady she was meeting was a most notorious gossip; the kind who kept a close eye on the activities of members of the gentry over half of Norfolk. He could only hope Lady Alice would know to wrap herself up warmly enough for the journey and that the house where she was going would offer her a warmer room than this one was proving to be.

In a way, Adam was happy at the prospect of being alone for the greater part of the day. He really needed time and space to think. When he'd first taken on this investigation, he'd struggled to find anything that would help him understand Frederick Dalston's death. Now information was coming in thick and fast and he was already feeling somewhat overwhelmed. There was always a point in an investigation when he needed to take time to try and sort through all he had discovered. If he pushed on too quickly, there was a real danger that he would overlook something vital.

Had the day been warmer, Adam would have taken himself outside for a bracing walk. Somehow, the process of walking, regardless of the destination, seemed to allow him to see things with greater clarity. Sadly, on a day like this the bitter wind would cripple any attempts at serious thought. Instead, he would be conscious all the time of his frozen feet and legs. You could wrap yourself in a thick coat and cram a sound hat on your head, but breeches, stockings and leather shoes provided little protection against the cold.

Recognising that these musings about the vagaries of spring weather were merely attempts at procrastination, Adam turned away from the window and settled himself in an upholstered chair, drawing it as close to the fire as he dared. Then he closed his eyes and tried to subject all he knew to some kind of logical analysis.

He began by thinking about the young women on whom Frederick Dalston had preyed. They were innocent victims, of course. Their families were what mattered. He could well imagine their fathers and brothers being moved to bitter anger; the kind of harsh fury that might well breed thoughts of vengeance. But murder was surely altogether too extreme. Yet these people were leading members of polite society, not uncivilised peasants eking out a living in some far-flung valley in the mountains of the Balkans. They might have challenged Frederick to a duel or tried to take a horsewhip to him, but Adam couldn't see any of them creeping about in the dark woods to lie in wait with murder on their minds. To take violent revenge in such a case risked discovery and the whole sorry business becoming public knowledge. Would they be willing to take a gamble of that kind just to relieve their feelings?

No, none of the families he knew about were likely to have turned to murder. It was time to move on. What about someone whom Dalston might have cheated at the gambling tables? Was he correct in ruling that out?

The same considerations that applied to the fathers and brothers of the women Frederick Dalston had wronged held good here too. The young men amongst whom Frederick Dalston had moved in Norwich came from good families. He simply couldn't imagine them deciding to kill.

What about the notion that Dalston might have turned to one of the rough, secretive, back-street drinking dens where men with coarser natures gambled for high stakes? Ruffians like that might well turn to knives to settle scores with one another but in some city back alley, not six or seven miles away in the depths of the countryside. There was also the fact that neither he nor Ross had found any evidence Frederick Dalston had frequented such places. That was another promising idea best set aside.

If Dalston's murderer hadn't come from either of these sources, what did that leave? He knew of one situation in which Dalston had tried his hand at a genuinely criminal enterprise — threatening the traders in the marketplace. That had turned out badly for him. If the young man had learned anything, it would be to stay firmly within his own social class and background.

What about this Obadiah Webley? Had he seen Frederick as a means to inflict some fraudulent scheme on members of the moneyed classes? If he had, it would have shown poor judgement. Young Dalston would have been no use to any plot Webley might have planned in that context. He could point to no past business or financial dealings to give him credibility, and his reputation would have ruined any attempts he made to convince people to put money into schemes he was involved with.

Adam got up and walked back to the window. All his thinking and analysis had done so far was rule out most of the obvious possibilities for finding Dalston's killer. He desperately needed fresh ideas, yet none had presented themselves. For several minutes, he stood looking at the good folk of Aylsham as they scurried about their business and tried to keep out of the wind. The street was wet as well. There must be drizzle or even sleet mixed in with the gusts which were shaking the trees and threatening to upset the few market stalls put up be traders brave — or desperate — enough to offer their goods for sale regardless of the weather. So much for spring!

He turned back to the other side of the room and rang the bell to summon Hannah to bring him some hot coffee. She could also refresh the fire when she came. He'd poked at it once or twice, but his feeble efforts had failed to make it burn any more vigorously.

To add to his frustration, Adam managed to burn the roof of his mouth on the coffee. Hannah's efforts with the fire hadn't been any more effective than his either. Not only was it refusing to produce more than a sullen heat but from time to time gusts of wind had started blowing smoke into the room. What a wretched day! Still, he refused to give up. Instead, he returned to his chair and tried to ignore his discomfort. There were still other possibilities that he needed to review properly. He wondered whether he should suggest to his wife that she stay at home until a warmer day arrived. Still, she would be well wrapped up in the carriage and the houses she would be visiting were probably at least as warm as this one. She might even have already left. He'd been so wrapped up in thought he probably wouldn't have noticed any sound of the door being opened or the carriage drawing up outside. He turned his thoughts back to the damnable, implacable mystery of who killed Frederick Dalston.

What about some kind of involvement with the smuggling gangs or other free traders? Pff! What could Frederick Dalston offer them that they didn't have already? Adam shook his head in frustration. This kind of thought was of no benefit. He could spend hours ruling out a whole series of ways of making money dishonestly, but it would take him no further forward.

You're stuck, Adam told himself angrily. Why don't you just admit it? He got up and rang the bell, intending to ask Hannah to bring him another pot of coffee. It wasn't likely to help him produce any better ideas, but it might help to warm him. She could bring another bucket of coal as well. He'd already nearly emptied the last one she left by the grate, and the room felt almost as cold as it had been when he first came into it.

He had just lifted his hand to ring the bell when Hannah came into the room, bringing him a letter that had arrived with the morning carrier from Norwich. A quick glance at the handwriting revealed that it was from Ross. Adam had insisted they should communicate by letter whenever possible and discard Ross's elaborate codes and ciphers and the like. Coming and going from Aylsham to Norwich took an hour or more in each direction. It was a waste of time. A letter could be sent in the same time while you got on with doing something else. Adam curbed his curiosity and laid the letter on the table while he waited for Hannah to bring the coffee and the coal that he had asked for. Then he let her wield the poker vigorously on the sluggish fire, add fresh coal and use a pair of bellows to stir some flames from its depths. After that he poured himself some coffee and retired once again to the chair, this time taking Ross's letter with him.

HONOURED SIR,

    I write briefly and in haste to acquaint you with two pieces of fresh infor-

mation. *One concerns a possible enterprise set up by Dalston and Webley. I am still trying to obtain the details but can say immediately that it is to do with shipping using the ports of Great Yarmouth and King's Lynn. I will write again the moment I have discovered more.*

The other matter may or may not be relevant. I received warning that a Revenue Riding Officer was stabbed and killed only yesterday in the vicinity of the village of Kessingfield. A poor fisherman has been seized as the likely culprit and will be taken before the magistrate today to be charged with the murder. He is thought to have connections with the smuggling gang which uses that area.

I have despatched one of my best men, James Wulstan, to discover all he can about the event. He will contact you himself when he has a detailed view of the killing and the events surrounding it.

I am, sir, ever your most obedient and humble servant,
Anthony Ross

THE MENTION OF SHIPPING STIRRED A SUDDEN HOPE IN ADAM'S mind. His good friend, Captain Mimms, an elderly retired naval officer and sea captain, had sons who had taken over his successful business as a shipowner. As he recalled, they were based in Great Yarmouth. If anything strange was going on concerning the shipping trade in the German Ocean, they would either already know about it or could soon find out. The thought roused Adam at once from his chair. He took pen and paper to write to Captain Mimms to ask when it would be convenient for him to travel to Mimms's home in Holt to seek his help.

Hannah was summoned yet again and entrusted with the letter, which she was told to give to the carrier first thing the next morning.

That done, he turned his mind to the dealings between Frederick Dalston and Webley which Ross had mentioned. Webley was as cunning as Dalston was naïve. He would surely have been keeping an eye on Frederick Dalston for some time, marking him down as the kind of fool he could exploit. Did he know about Dalston's earlier attempts to get money? Almost certainly. Some at least had been successful, so that money must be stowed away somewhere. Webley would soon ferret out where it was hidden. If Dalston was foolish enough to get involved with Webley, Webley's plan would probably be not just to seize all the profits of any joint enterprise but would also wish to relieve Dalston of whatever money he already had. After that, he would throw Dalston to the wolves, take the cash and leave, while Dalston was still wondering what had happened to him.

So, why would Webley murder Dalston, if his plan was to abandon him and let those he had cheated, or the public hangman, do the job for him? Even more perplexing, if such an enterprise existed, it must still be in operation. Ross would never miss a crowd of furious people, all trying to get their money back from a bewildered Frederick Dalston.

Stuck again.

In the end, after going over the possibilities three or four more times, Adam finally gave it up. He would try to put the whole complication of Frederick Dalston and Obadiah Webley from his mind — if he could — until he at least had a response from Captain Mimms.

To help him further in turning his mind to fresh things, Ross's man, Wulstan, came to the back door at around ten the next morning. At Adam's request, Grove, the butler, brought him straightway to where Adam was seated; not in the library this time, but in the morning room, where he had been lingering over a late breakfast with Lady Alice. Her trip to Briningham had been a disappointment. Her acquaintance there had been full of gossip, but none of any interest. Now she would have left the room for her husband to see his visitor on his own, but Adam motioned her to stay.

Wulstan proved to be a man of unremarkable appearance, just like Ross. He was perhaps thirty years of age, slightly above the average in height, but otherwise possessed of no clearly distinguishing features. He wore the clothes typical of a skilled artisan or a local shopkeeper, with a slouch hat of greyish felt. His speech, when he spoke, was clearly marked by a local accent, yet still clear and assured.

'Mr Ross said as I was to come to you and tell you what I found at Kessingfield, sir. With your permission, I will do as he asked.'

'Please do.'

Wulstan glanced at Lady Alice and looked uncomfortable. 'Some of what I have to describe is not very suitable for genteel ears, sir. I mean about the details of the corpse.'

'Do not worry about offending my sensibility, Mr Wulstan,' Lady Alice said. 'Not all ladies are such shrinking violets as some men believe. A little blood and gore will not bother me at all, I assure you. I am sure you will moderate your description a little anyway.'

'If you insist, your ladyship.'

'I do. Remember that women may well have to deal at some time in their lives with giving birth. That is a messy and bloody business, I am told. That is probably why husbands are usually banned from the confinement. Too many faint at the sight of blood.'

'Please continue as my wife bids you, Wulstan,' Adam said. 'I take it you now have a complete picture of what took place where the Riding Officer was killed.'

'Clear enough, sir, though you may tell me I'm wrong about that. Mr Ross says you're a rare one for seeing things what other folk miss. Anyway, what I was told was as follows.'

He took a deep breath, collected his thoughts and delivered the rest of his speech in the manner of a sergeant reporting to a senior officer.

'After what had happened to your Mr Frederick Dalston, sir, it seems as the Revenue instructed the Riding Officers in that area to go out only in pairs. The day before yesterday, one such pair rode into Kessingfield to look for hidden contraband. Seems like that place is well known as the haunt of smugglers and free traders. According to the Riding Officer that survived, Brent, they split up to search the cottages and outhouses, agreeing to meet again at the same spot when each had finished. When Brent returned, his colleague, Hartwell, was nowhere to be seen. Brent waited, then goes looking for him. He found his body at the edge of the dunes, close to a shack where a man called Narbord lives with his daughter.'

'Is this Narbord a fisherman?' Adam asked.

'No, sir. A poor man as earns what passes for a living by catching eels in the marshes and rivers there about. Brent said he saw Narbord by his shack, trying to wash blood off his shirt and jacket. There was a large knife on the ground beside him, also covered in blood, together with a sack of eels.'

'Do you know what kind of knife it was?'

'They said it had a long blade, sharpened on one side. Something like the knives the fishermen use to slit fish open and scrape out the roe.'

'And it had blood on it?'

'Yes, sir. There was blood all up the blade, I believe.'

'What next?'

'Brent took hold of this Narbord and dragged him to the village constable, shouting to all who could hear that he'd killed a Revenue Officer. The constable sent at once for the coroner and took Narbord into custody, so as he could be taken before the magistrate, like I said.'

'What did Narbord say?'

'From what I was told, not much at all. Seems he was too bewildered by what was happening to him. The villagers say he's not too bright in the head. All anyone heard him say was that he'd been killing eels, which was why there was blood on his knife.'

'Does that make sense to you, Wulstan?' Adam said.

'It does, sir. Eels are right hard to kill, unlike most fish. They don't suffocate out of water for a long time, and you can hit them on the head several times and they'll still wriggle away. Horrible, slimy things! The only way to kill them is to stab a knife into their bodies, just behind the head, then make sure you cut through the backbone.'

'That's what Narbord said he was doing?'

'Yes, sir. Seems when he catches an eel, he does it by tying a ball of rough twine soaked in blood to the end of a fishing line. The eel grabs the ball, thinking it's something good, and its teeth get entangled in the twine. Then you haul it up out of the water and shake it hard over the open mouth of a sack, so it drops inside. You don't take it out to kill it until you get home. It'll be just as lively when you get it out of your bag as it was in the water, even if you've been out several hours.'

'Hmm,' Adam said. 'Here's what I'd like you to do. Where's Narbord now, do you reckon?'

'Probably in the lock-up in Aylsham,' Wulstan replied, 'waiting to be taken to Norwich gaol. The assize isn't for several months yet.'

'Go there and talk to him. Get his side of the story. Then go back to the village and talk with his daughter. After that, come back here and tell me what they say. Will you do that?'

'Most willingly, sir. Mr Ross said I was to carry out any orders you gave me, without asking questions.'

'You can ask all the questions you wish,' Adam said, smiling broadly. 'I'm asking you to do this because what you have been told sounds altogether too neat and straightforward, and I don't trust village constables — or some magistrates — to look at anything other than the obvious. It seems to me there's more to this killing than you've been told so far.'

'Do you think it links with your investigation, sir? I know young Mr Dalston was also stabbed and people think he was mistaken for a Riding Officer on his rounds.'

'Maybe. Until you find out more, I'm going to suspend judgement on that. There are too many inconsistences for my liking.'

'Very good, sir. I'll be on my way. With luck, I should be able to report back to you tomorrow or the next day.'

After Wulstan had left, Adam turned to his wife. 'What do you think of the story as presented, my dear? Was I wrong to ask Ross's man to find out more?'

'Certainly not,' Lady Alice replied. 'People talk about smelling a rat. I could smell a whole nest of them in that tale. For a start, no one bothered to ask this Narbord why he'd killed the Riding Officer — if he had. From what I have read in the newspapers, even smugglers avoid doing that, save in some pitched fight. What did a wretched eel-catcher have to gain by it? If he had killed him, why stand in the open washing off the blood, where anyone could see him? Even a man who's weak in the head must surely see how foolish that would be. And have the knife by his side as well? Nonsense, if you ask me.'

'Exactly my thoughts,' Adam said. 'It sounds more as if the other Riding Officer noticed him and rushed over to arrest him without thinking. Village constables are notorious for their laziness and stupidity. It's hardly surprising that this one passed the whole thing on to the coroner and magistrate as quickly as he could. I wonder who the coroner for that area would be? If, as I suspect, it's our friend Mr Palfrey, the chance to "solve" the case without any appreciable effort might well be too good for him to turn down, even after the rebuke I gave him.'

'I imagine he'd think you could not possibly have any interest in a poor eel-catcher, husband, so he'd be safe this time.'

'If that's right,' Adam said grimly, 'I think he's about to get another painful lesson in what happens when you shirk your duty.'

CAPTAIN MIMMS' REPLY ARRIVED WITH GRATIFYING SPEED. ADAM hadn't been in touch with him since his wedding to Lady Alice, so there had been the possibility that Mimms might not have been at home. However, Adam's luck had held. The letter said Mimms was delighted to be able to be of assistance once again and would look forward to welcoming Adam on the following Tuesday. In the meantime, he would write at once to his sons and ask if they had heard any rumours about criminal activities emanating from Norwich. They managed the family shipping business these days, as Adam knew. If anything untoward was going on, they would be bound to be aware of it.

Wulstan didn't appear the next day, so Adam occupied part of his time in writing to Ross to tell him the instructions he had given to Wulstan and the action he had taken to contact Captain Mimms. He hoped by that means to discover from people involved in shipping themselves what Webley was up to, at least in Great Yarmouth. In the meantime, he suggested that, in addition to exploring the Webley connection further, Ross should try to find out how far advanced Frederick Dalston was with any plan to leave Norwich and start a new life elsewhere.

Adam knew Frederick Dalston had been in a great hurry to enrich himself. He'd tried a number of different approaches to making money in quick succession, all with remarkable unconcern for concealment. It might have been simple arrogance on his part, but it might also have been that he was under some pressure to be gone as quickly as possible. Hiding what he was doing was of very little importance, since he would soon be away and out of anyone's reach.

It was Lady Alice who had planted the question in her husband's mind about the speed with which Frederick Dalston seemed to be rushing into this new criminal career. She had remarked over breakfast that morning that when one approach failed to provide him the money he required, the young man set off instantly in a fresh direction. Nothing suggested he was learning from his mistakes, then making another attempt based on his experience. It might be sheer impatience. Whatever the reason, it ensured every time he embarked on another scheme to raise money, he was forced to do so as a complete beginner.

Her suggestion niggled at the back of Adam's mind. Perhaps Frederick Dalston was indeed suffering from a deadly blend of overconfidence and impatience. Maybe he simply lacked enough determination to try one method fully, before moving on to another. But what if the fellow was under pressure to leave as quickly as possible? If he could discover why that was, Adam might be a good deal closer to making sense of Frederick Dalston's behaviour.

Wulstan returned next morning looking like a dog who had found a large marrowbone with plenty of meat still attached.

'Narbord denies the killing absolutely,' he told Adam. 'Not only that, he claims he hadn't even known the Revenue men were in the village. He'd been out all night in the marshes and had just arrived home when Brent jumped on him. The blood he was trying to clean off his shirt and breeches was eel blood, not human. He tried to explain, but nobody listened. When I told him I was going to talk to his daughter he was delighted. He wasn't worried that she couldn't look after herself. More anxious that she should hear from him that he was innocent.'

'That all makes perfect sense,' Adam told him. 'I suspected early on that there had been a rush to judgement. Now, tell me about Narbord's daughter. What's her name?'

'Nancy, sir. A bold one too, believe me. I'd heard before from the other villagers that she was not a young woman to be trusted too close to your husband. Now I can see why!'

'Why, is it true then?'

'For a start, Nancy Narbord is what you'd call a rustic beauty, sir. Ignore the old, patched clothes and grimy face and hands and you'd see at once she has everything a woman needs to attract men. Her figure is the stuff of dreams. Not only that, she was all too ready to display it fully. She took one look at me and opened the neck of her dress so I could see her magnificent breasts in all their glory. Then she said that, for a shilling, I could feast my hands on her charms as well as my eyes. I gathered afterwards that she adds to her father's meagre earnings by selling her favours to any man she meets who looks as if he could afford to give her a shilling.'

'I hope you didn't succumb to her offer,' Adam said, trying not to laugh.

'Oh no, sir! I was on duty, as you might say. I only tell you to let you know the kind of woman she is.'

'How old would you say Nancy is?'

'Hard to tell, if you know what I mean. Not a girl, that's clear. Not with a figure like that. Not very old either. If I had to guess, I'd say perhaps eighteen or twenty.'

'What did she tell you about what happened?' Adam asked. 'Assuming she'd seen anything at all.'

'She said she'd only come out of the cottage when she heard all the noise. Then she tried to tell the constable her father had only just arrived home, but he brushed her aside saying he'd not trust the word of any harlot over his own eyes.'

'Did she mention Brent, the other Riding Officer?'

'Not at first. Eventually — and rather reluctantly I thought — she admitted he'd been to the village several times before and they'd "cuddled a bit". I think he was a regular customer, but she didn't want to admit it.'

'And the dead man? Hartwell, I recall you called him.'

'There she was more open. She claimed he'd been to see her many times and that he was "sweet on her". Wanted her to marry him, she said, and leave the wretched hovel she lived in. She'd refused only because she didn't feel right about leaving her father. By her account, the man hadn't been quite right in the head since he was out fishing and got caught in a storm. The boom on the sail of his boat swung round violently and hit him on the head, knocking him unconscious. He only survived because he was close enough to shore for the boat to be driven up onto the beach instead of being overturned or smashed on a sandbank. When they brought him home, he'd been in a sort of coma for three days. When he finally woke up, she'd had to teach him to walk again. Even now, she told me, his balance is poor and he slurs his speech. He could never manage on his own.'

For several minutes, Adam sat in silence, his mind considering all Wulstan had told him. Then he told the man to find out at once where Brent was living.

'Go there with all speed,' he said, 'and arrest him. Then take him to Ross. Tell him he should question the man closely, especially on the subject of what happened when he and his colleague first arrived at Kessingfield. He'll probably be told a parcel of lies at first, tell him, so he should ignore those and put Brent under pressure to tell the truth. If I'm right, nearly all Brent said on the day Hartwell died is a series of fabrications. Will you do that?'

'Right away, sir!'

'You can also tell Mr Ross that I'm delighted with all you've done for me.'

A LETTER FROM ROSS ARRIVED THE NEXT DAY, EXPLAINING FIRST that Wulstan had done exactly as he'd been told. Brent was now in custody in the city gaol awaiting what he termed "an intensive and thorough examination". Adam imagined that behind that bland phrase lay one or more sessions likely to cause Brent intense discomfort at the very least — unless he confessed swiftly to save himself from greater agony. Ross looked mild enough on the surface but could doubtless exert substantial pressure, or maybe worse, when questioning a suspect.

Ross went on to write of what else he had discovered so far. It wasn't so much Frederick Dalston's behaviour that seemed odd, but Webley's. Sir Percival Wicken had instructed Ross to keep an eye on Webley for many months now. In all that time, Webley's approach had been to stay in the background and collect steady returns over long periods. Most career criminals did all they could to avoid being caught, but Webley had taken it to extremes. That was what first suggested he was engaged in something in addition to the frauds and extortions they knew about; something where secrecy was imperative. All that had changed. Webley too was trying to amass a large amount of money with little regard to being found out.

Ross was also able to confirm Frederick Dalston had been planning to leave for the New World. Several people had told him Dalston had been enquiring how best to travel from Norwich to either Bristol or Liverpool. If Dalston had planned to make a run for it and leave Webley behind, this behaviour was inexplicable. Webley would hear what he was up to within a matter of hours. Was Webley planning to leave in haste as well?

Adam sat and thought about this. If Webley was trying to leave England quickly and quietly, the obvious answer would be for him to flee to France or the Low Countries. The German Ocean held many privateers and smugglers based in towns like Dunkirk and Rotterdam. They would certainly be willing to whisk him out of the country in return for a suitable payment. Dalston might well be uneasy about taking such a route, since a young English gentleman arriving in France or the Netherlands in possession of a large sum of money might well be seized by the authorities and thrown into gaol as a spy. That is, if the smugglers or the privateers didn't relieve him of his wealth before he even reached the other coast.

Another thought struck him. Before he was involved with Webley, Dalston's tendency to swap from one means of raising money to another could be explained by lack of experience or forethought. He was bumbling about, trying one thing after another, hoping to stumble on a method of combining rich returns with minimum effort. What if it was Webley who was responsible for the haste that had characterised their joint endeavour in Dalston's final days? Might Webley have feared that the other man's maladroit attempts to make money on his own would draw too much attention. Did he dread this might reveal the secret enterprises Ross and Wicken suspected he was engaged in? That would provide a powerful reason for wishing to see Dalston removed.

'Hell and damnation!' Adam said aloud. Fortunately, nobody was present to hear this expression of his total exasperation. Even if they had been, the latest news from Ross was more than enough reason to descend to curses and profanity. It was also a deuced inconvenience. Here he was trying to rule out unnecessary parts in the investigation, while Ross was adding more people with sound reasons for wanting to see Frederick Dalston dead.

❧ 11 ❧

Lady Alice was worried about her husband. The investigation into the murder of Frederick Dalston clearly wasn't going well. She could sense her husband's anxiety. Several times he had only picked at his dinner, before retiring with her to the drawing room. There he sat quiet and withdrawn in his chair. She chided herself for not paying greater attention to this sooner. She'd been so wrapped up in organising the changes to be made to their new property that she'd failed to take sufficient notice of Adam's state of mind. That was definitely going to change. She had lost her first husband to sickness, but he was an old man and not in the best of health when they had married. Adam was young and vigorous — or had been until the last week or so.

She wondered whether the loss of his medical practice was weighing on him. He had been a conscientious and devoted physician until his elevation to the baronetcy had put an end to any possibility of continuing to serve as a local doctor. He still had a number of important appointments which demanded medical knowledge. He was on the Board of Governors of the Norfolk and Norwich Hospital and had retained his position with the Duke of York's household. He still served a number of his most eminent clients in Norfolk. Even so, these demanded relatively little of him compared with his previous work. Perhaps he was simply bored?

She'd encouraged her husband to undertake his current investigation to give him something which would exercise his mind. He'd solved problems like this several times before, and with great success. She knew he was not only capable of carrying things through to their proper conclusion but generally found doing so enjoyable. This time, however, lack of progress appeared to be inducing some kind of melancholia.

There was another matter too. She would like him to come to her bedroom more often and display greater passion when he did. He was always so tired at present. Her kisses and caresses were more likely to send him to sleep than arouse him as they should. Though she tried to set it aside, the news of Sophia's pregnancy had raised worries in her own mind. Lady Alice's first husband had been eager for her to give him an heir, but it had not happened. In his case, it was easy to blame it on Sir Daniel's advanced age and poor state of health. Now she had been married almost as long as Sophia, yet there was still no sign of a child on the way. Perhaps if Adam was more relaxed, he'd be as eager to do his duty as a husband as he had been at the very start of their marriage. If so, her chances of conceiving would surely be much improved. There was no use just worrying about it, she decided. She needed to take some action.

In the short term, she would look for any opportunities to reawaken his ardour. Beyond that, they needed more time to relax and enjoy one another's company, free from the pressures that had weighed on both of them in the last few weeks. She needed to choose her time carefully to tell Adam what she had in mind, otherwise he would dismiss the idea at once on the grounds that he was far too busy. Perhaps she might find an opportune time at the weekend to raise it with him. It would be worth trying.

She had always longed to travel to Italy to see the spectacular scenery of the Alps and the many antiquities and works of art there. Unfortunately, the present war with the revolutionary government in France made this impossible. Nor was there any sign when a settled peace might return. However, several of her friends had told her of the views of modern writers on aesthetics like Reverend William Gilpin. One or two of them had recently visited the Lakes in Cumbria and brought back excited descriptions of the natural beauties to be seen there. She had also heard that the Scottish Highlands offered vistas of similar grandeur to the Alps themselves. She had, therefore, come up with a plan that would offer her the chance to see such places for herself and also provide Adam with the rest and relaxation he so obviously needed.

After dinner that Sunday, she broached the subject with her husband, telling him it was high time they travelled to Hereford to visit her noble relations at Kentchurch Court. They had never met Adam and it was many years since she had seen them herself. She had invited them to the wedding, even though the distance from their home to Norfolk was considerable. When they replied offering their best wishes while stating that it would not be possible for them to attend, she was not surprised. However, if she and Adam were to combine a visit with a diversion on the way to view Tintern Abbey and the Wye Valley, the lengthy time it would take to cross the country might seem more worthwhile. Then, after spending a few days with her relatives, they might travel north to the Lake District and perhaps even into Scotland. Such a trip should not take more than four to six months, which was about the time she'd been advised it would take to make their new home habitable. The house wouldn't be completely finished by then, but it would be sufficiently completed for them to move in and live in reasonable comfort.

To her delight, Adam did not dismiss the idea straightaway; rather he seemed to welcome it, though he grumbled about taking such a long time away from his various commitments. When she hastened to assure him that their trip could be shortened, if necessary, and that it would do him a great deal of good, he agreed to consider it, provided that he could finish his current investigation before they left. Wisely, she decided to leave the matter there.

ON TUESDAY MORNING, WILLIAM BROUGHT THE CARRIAGE ROUND early to take his master to Holt to see Captain Mimms as arranged. The most direct route involved a steep ascent from the place where the road crossed the little River Glaven, then passed through a great area of heathland to the south and east of the town. The carriage might be able to manage the climb with but a single occupant, but it would be difficult, exhausting work for the poor horse. Instead, Adam told William to take the indirect route via Itteringham and Hempstead. That followed more level ground.

The bitter cold of the previous day had been replaced by hazy sunshine and a mild south-westerly wind. On a day like this, the northern hills and valleys of Norfolk looked at their best. The land was surprisingly well wooded, with the many beeches now dressed in pale, goldish green, thus creating a delightful contrast with the dark hollies and the reddish new growth on the oaks. On the heathland, the gorse was covered with a blaze of golden flowers, while damp areas by the roadside held small clumps of primroses and violets. Bees zoomed about everywhere and the songbirds loudly proclaimed their presence from the tops of almost every bush and tree. Adam loved the countryside. These certain signs of the approaching spring ensured this whole trip would be a pleasant one.

By taking the route they did, they approached Holt by passing the former racecourse, now disused since the meetings had moved to Fakenham. Forty or fifty years before, Holt had been crowded with the Norfolk gentry during the regular race meetings. As Adam's father had described it to him, these were important affairs in everyone's social calendars. There would be racing during the day, with large amounts of money changing hands, then dances and dinners each evening, usually at "The Plume of Feathers" or "The King's Head". Wives and daughters dressed in their finest clothes while young, unmarried men prowled around, boasting to one another of their wins or losses, having an eye to the daughters and sizing them up as potential wives, their mothers smiling to encourage some and frowning to send others on their way. Though all that had passed, the little town still managed to hold on to a certain atmosphere of importance. The Petty Sessions and Quarter Sessions were held in the neat Shire Hall in its centre. Regular markets took place in the marketplace. Most of the town now consisted of modern brick houses and shops, thanks to the terrible fire of 1708.

After passing through the marketplace and onto the High Street, Adam's carriage came to a halt on the driveway outside Captain Mimms's house, which lay at the top of the hill that ran down towards the river at Letheringsett and on towards Fakenham beyond. The old man himself came to the doorway to greet his visitor. He must have heard the vehicle pulling up for there he was, his face still showing something of his many years spent staring into salt winds and spray, while strands of white hair peeked out here and there from under the linen cap he wore on his head. A stocky, smiling man. A man confident of himself and proud of the way his young friend Adam Bascom had risen in the world.

'I was delighted when your young relatives chose to settle in our town,' he said to Adam, when they were seated comfortably inside and sharing a welcoming glass of good ale. 'Mr Scudamore is a fine lawyer, I'm told, and his wife has already made it her business to enter fully in society. I believe she also extends a good deal of quiet assistance to the poor of the town. A good many of our local ladies doubtless envy her fine carriage and her fashionable dress. Even so, wife and husband are well liked. Neither tries to lord it over others who have lived here longer. As you know, we have no titled families in the town or nearby, such as yours is now, Sir Adam. Even your brother a few miles off at Trundon Hall is plain Mr Giles Bascom. Yet for all that we manage to maintain a certain civility.'

Adam was quietly amused by Mimms's pride in the place where he now lived. He spoke of it as he had surely spoken of the frigates and ships-of-the-line he had once commanded. All he said was true, yet nearly all the market towns in this part of Norfolk were similar in size and equally dependent on a few wealthier merchants and local squires to provide the uppermost levels in society. The few actual aristocrats, together with the scattering of baronets and knights hereabouts, spent only the summers on their Norfolk estates, returning to London for the winter season. It was a well-established pattern, whether it was fashion and society which drew them or involvement in politics.

'I hope to pay a brief visit to my relatives before I return to Aylsham,' Adam said. He decided not to mention Sophia's pregnancy, in case she had decided not to mention the news publicly for the time being. 'Fortunately, I have seen them very recently, so they will not be disappointed that I will be able to stay for a brief time only. If possible, I wish to be back in Aylsham well before nightfall.'

Captain Mimms merely nodded in response. They both knew it was time to get down to business.

'My sons replied to me with all speed,' he began. 'They're good lads and I'm sure they would have responded as quickly as they could under any circumstances. However, it seems that the question you asked me to pose them struck on a topic of great concern amongst the captains and shipowners at Yarmouth — indeed amongst all those who pass by our coasts. What's worrying them is a steady upsurge in activity by those cursed French privateers who infest the German ocean. According to my sons, over the last month or so, many ships travelling alone have been seized. In the past, the privateers have shied away from attacking large merchant ships, since many of them are heavily armed. Instead, they confined their nuisance to the smaller colliers and similar vessels which make up the bulk of the traffic. All that seems to have changed.'

'Is the navy no longer able to offer protection to ships travelling in convoy?' Adam asked.

'Oh no, that continues just as before. What I'm talking about are ships which travel on their own.

'Why would they do this? Are they not running a considerable risk?'

'Of course, they are, but it's a matter of balancing higher risks against higher rewards. A convoy has to wait until it is assembled, then sail at the speed of the slowest vessel. Since all reach port at the same time, there is usually a temporary glut in whatever the majority of them are carrying: wheat, coal or barley are the most usual cargoes. That drives prices down. If you contrive to arrive on your own, well ahead of the ships coming in convoy, you're likely to get a higher price from the London merchants.'

'I see that,' Adam said. 'What do the insurers think of this?'

'What do you imagine they think? It adds substantially to their risk, so they view it with considerable distaste. Most contracts of insurance actually stipulate that the ship must travel in convoy to be covered. The insurers can't demand all convoys should be protected by naval ships. Not enough of them are available. What they favour, if no naval ships can do the job of protection, is to collect a large number of vessels close together, as many of them armed as possible. A convoy like that will be able to deter or drive off privateers on its own. It's become a kind of contest. Our ships arm themselves and cluster together for protection; the privateers sail in larger and larger vessels, all of them carrying many cannons. A few are even able to engage our frigates in something like an equal contest, damn them!'

'So, any vessels sailing alone are especially vulnerable?'

'Of course. That's why any captain who says from the outset they're going to sail unaccompanied will either be unable to obtain insurance or will have to pay far higher premiums. Some captains simply take their chances, relying on slipping out of port at some unexpected time and travelling as fast as their ship will sail. The more unscrupulous shipowners and captains tell the insurers they intend to travel in convoy, then go it alone, trusting in luck to get them through unscathed. Either approach used to work four times out of five under normal circumstances. The extra profits more than covered paying the occasional ransom to a privateer, while failing to mention it to the insurer.'

'You say "used to work". That implies this practice of trying to arrive ahead of the competition is well-established,' Adam said. 'What has changed?'

'Two things — no, three. First of all, more of the privateers seem to be ignoring the convoys and smaller boats and going after these lone ships. When they find one, they attack at once, however large and well-armed our vessels may be. Secondly, they aren't accepting a ransom to free the ship and cargo. They commandeer everything and take it back to Dunkirk or Rotterdam. There the ship and its cargo are sold, and the crew thrown into some rotten gaol.'

'And the third thing that has changed?' Adam asked.

'That's the worst of all,' Mimms replied. 'The buggers are being tipped off. They know far too often exactly where and when to find the best targets. Privateers will pay a substantial "bounty" for information like that. Some of the captains and shipowners will be brought to bankruptcy if it goes on.'

'I hope your own business hasn't suffered in this way,' Adam said.

'Never fear. My sons have got more sense than to send ships out unprotected. We have some trouble with privateers, of course we do. Everyone does. But we make sure our ships travel in convoy and arm them well.'

'Let me get this straight,' Adam said. 'The privateers are now targeting unprotected vessels, probably because they know when and where to find them. When they seize a vessel, they no long accept a ransom to release it. They take it home to sell instead. Are all of them behaving in this way?'

'No. That's another oddity. Only some of them. Ships coming south from Hull or neighbouring ports don't seem to be experiencing extra problems — unless they put in to Yarmouth or King's Lynn on their way. Small vessels sailing between small ports like Cley, Wells or Blakeney are also unaffected by the change.'

'If so, it must mean that whoever is passing information to the privateers only knows about sailings from Great Yarmouth or King's Lynn — which is where most of the larger vessels must start from. The other ports are too small and their approaches too narrow and silted up. Is that right?'

'It is.'

'Going back to the suggestion that someone is giving information to the privateers about which ships are sailing, when and by which routes,' Adam said, 'what would happen to that person if they were found out?'

Mimms smiled a grim smile and drew a finger across his throat. 'They'd better make as much money as they can, then run for it,' he said. 'Best of all, leave the country. I wouldn't rely on the furious shipowners instigating a prosecution for theft or fraud. They might as easily take direct action and leave the informers in a ditch somewhere with their throats cut.'

Mimms didn't have much to say after that, but Adam left him

feeling well satisfied all the same. What he'd been told might well be the key to the whole mystery surrounding the death of Frederick Dalston.

A brief call at Charles and Sophia's fine property in Bull Street and Adam was heading home.

❦ 1 2 ❦

By the time he and William finally arrived, Adam was tired and
hungry. His wife, however, was not minded to allow their
dinner to be served before he promised to tell her all he had
discovered from the old seafarer. Adam promised to do so as soon as
their meal was ended. She also wanted to know whether Adam had
found time during the day to call on Charles and Sophia. He said he
had and, once again, undertook to tell all after he had eaten. Satisfied,
his wife stepped aside to allow him to go up the stairs to his dressing
room where he could set aside his outdoor clothing. She had spoken to
him on several occasions about getting a valet, but he was still resisting
it. Adam disliked the idea of having somebody fussing over him while
he dressed and undressed, let alone advising him on the correct things
to wear. He preferred to make up his own mind on matters such as
that. He left the coat, jacket and hat which he had worn during the day
on his bed for Hannah to put away. That done, he wrapped himself in
his favourite deep blue quilted banyan, put a matching silk cap on his
head, slippers on his feet and went downstairs to where his wife was
doubtless waiting for him.

They went into the dining room together and took their seats.
After the first course was eaten and the dishes carried away, Adam

decided to deal with the matter of his visit to the Scudamore's house straightaway. There was no need to wait until later. His call could be described quite swiftly while the second part of their meal was being brought to the table.

'I did manage to visit Charles and Sophia as I told you, my dear,' he said, 'though I was not able to stay for long. They were bound to have heard that I had been to Holt to see Captain Mimms and would have thought it deuced rude of me if I did not call on them too. Do you know, this is the first time I have been to their new house in Bull Street? Happily, Charles was not occupied with business and was able to show me around the place. It's really very fine. Quite new — probably less than twenty years old — with seven bays, three stories and attics in the roof. Plenty of room for a growing family.'

'Speaking of family,' Lady Alice said at once, 'how is dear Sophia? Don't tell me you never enquired!'

'Of course, I did! I'm still a doctor, however it might appear on the outside. I'm as interested in her welfare as you are. You may stop worrying. Sophia is very well; a little sickness in the morning, but that is to be expected and will soon pass. Otherwise, she remains hale and hearty.'

Adam's expression must have indicated at that point he was not willing to answer any more questions until he had satisfied the last of his hunger. During the second part of the meal, therefore, neither spoke. Only when he and Lady Alice were seated in their drawing room — he nursing a glass of his favourite cognac and she sipping at a cup of finest Bohea tea — did he keep his promise to tell her what he had learned from Captain Mimms.

As was her habit, his wife listened to him carefully and refrained from asking questions until she was sure he had finished.

'Is that the answer then?' she asked after a suitable pause. 'Was Frederick Dalston involved in passing information to the privateers, then killed by an assassin sent by a group of angry shipowners?'

'On the surface,' Adam replied, 'that would appear to be what happened. It fits almost all of the facts, provides a powerful reason for someone wishing to kill him and offers an entirely plausible reconstruction of events.'

He shook his head and stared off into the far distance. It was not the look of a man who was now in possession of the solution to a complex and difficult puzzle.

'Yet it does not satisfy you, I can see,' his wife said. 'I note you say it fits almost all of the facts. That implies that there are some that this explanation still cannot explain.'

Adam smiled at her. 'I am beginning to realise you can read me like the pages of a book, my dear. You are quite right. I am very far from being satisfied with that explanation. It may be part of what brought Frederick Dalston to his death, but I do not think it is a complete elucidation of the circumstances. On the other hand, the reasons for my dissatisfaction seem somewhat trivial. To take the first point only, it still does not explain why the murder took place when it did.'

'Why do you say that?' Lady Alice replied. 'You told me it was a quiet, deserted piece of road. It would seem to be an ideal place for an assassination. The killer would be unlikely to be disturbed or seen, especially since it was dark.'

'When I left Captain Mimms's house,' Adam explained, 'I felt sure that what he had just told me explained everything. He'd even suggested that the shipowners and captains would be likely to be angry enough to decide to take justice into their own hands — or at least exact revenge. I think the first signs of doubt crept into my mind after I had finished my visit to Charles and Sophia and we were about halfway to Hempstead. It was then that it occurred to me that a quiet assassination on a country road, far from anywhere, would be most unlikely if the killing was the work of furious shipowners. You see, Mimms already knew perfectly well how the business of providing tipoffs to the privateers in return for some kind of share in their takings would work. There was nothing particularly new about it. Others had tried it before. The only unusual aspect, so far as I could gather, was the willingness of the privateers this time to take the risk of concentrating on large, probably well-armed vessels. In order to do so, they had been forced to increase the size and armament of their own ships.'

'So, this must have been planned for some time,' Lady Alice said. 'You can't build larger ships in a matter of a few weeks.'

'True, but I doubt that they would build all from scratch. Remember that Mimms said there was another change in the privateers' approach. Instead of accepting a ransom, then releasing the ship and its cargo, they were taking every ship they seized back to their home ports. Since they were concentrating on large, well-founded vessels, this in itself would provide them with a ready source of suitable ships for future voyages. It also argues for something else. Whoever has been providing the information to allow them to target specific ships with valuable cargoes must be someone whom they trust implicitly. You wouldn't change your whole way of carrying out what you did on the basis of suggestions made by someone who might point you in the wrong direction.'

Lady Alice merely nodded, fascinated by this demonstration of the tortuous ways in which her husband's mind worked.

'By the time we reached Saxthorpe, I was convinced this new information told us a lot about what Frederick Dalston and Obadiah Webley had been involved in recently, but very little about why Dalston had been murdered, especially in the manner and in the place where he was killed. You see, killing an informer has more than one purpose. One is to stop the source of the information and deal out an appropriate punishment. The other is to act as an obvious warning to anyone else who might be tempted to do the same thing, which might seem equally important, if not more so. Killing someone on a lonely country road and leaving his body there would meet the first purpose; it most certainly would not fit the second. You would want as many people as possible to see what happened to informers, even if that meant taking the risk of carrying out the killing and leaving the body in a very public place. Both Dalston and Webley were living in Norwich. Whether Dalston had been set up to take all the blame or not, a prominent place in Norwich would be the obvious site both for his assassination and to leave the body.'

'But you told me before that Dalston had been travelling about widely. Perhaps it proved more important to kill him quickly than to select an ideal place to act as a warning to others. So long as he was still sending information to the privateers, more ships would be at risk.

Best to act quickly and put a stop to him at once, finding him wherever you could.'

Adam smiled at her ruefully. 'Let me make another point. Not only would it take time for the privateers to increase the size and armament of their ships, it would take them a certain amount of sailing time to bear down on the vessel they had chosen — and about which they had been tipped off. If they lurked too openly, or in the same place all the time, the English ships would be able to change course to avoid them. I suspect they are staying well out to sea, so they can set course the moment they get the warning to some place where they hope to ensure an element of surprise.'

'Why does that bother you?'

'How would Dalston and Geddy get in touch with them? Only by sending a vessel to meet with them and pass on the information. Since neither own a boat of any kind, so far as I know, that must mean relying on the smugglers. And how would they communicate with them swiftly enough?'

'Pish! If this increase in privateer attacks is due to their actions, that difficulty must already have been overcome by some means.'

'How easily you pour cold water on my reasoning,' Adam said. 'I told you my reasons for rejecting the obvious were trivial. What you say may very well be correct and I may be wrong.'

'You still aren't convinced, are you?' Lady Alice said. 'Why is that?'

'Intuition? A feeling in my stomach? Call it what you will. I can't afford to ignore what others will see as the most obvious answer. At the same time, I'm not going to give up looking elsewhere. There have been several times in the last few weeks when I thought that the solution to this mystery was firmly within my grasp, only to see new events snatch it from me. Because of relying on the obvious, I have come very close on several occasions to what turned out to be a foolish degree of certainty. I don't intend to make the same mistake again.'

They were silent for several minutes, each one wrapped in their own thoughts. Then Lady Alice changed the subject.

'I also have news for you,' she said. 'Ruth has written to me from Norwich. She wants you to visit her and your mother as soon as you can.'

'But we've not long come back from Norwich and their house,' Adam objected.

'She is well aware of that, my dear, and apologised profusely for asking you to return so soon. Her reason appears to be a powerful one. She writes that she and Mrs Bascom between them have worked out why Frederick Dalston had to be killed. She even says that she thinks they can provide you with a very likely suspect as the murderer.'

Adam groaned. 'Another likely answer!' he said. 'Will it never end? I suppose I shall have to go.'

'Certainly you will, my dear, and I shall go with you. I have contributed a great deal to this investigation and have a right to share in it as much as I can. Don't you think I'm right?'

A swift glance told Adam he would oppose this idea at his peril, so he agreed with her immediately. His only proviso was that the horse needed a day to rest before setting out for Norwich. Since today was Tuesday, they would set out early in the morning on Thursday, probably staying overnight in their house in Norwich before returning. Lady Alice said she would send a message by carrier the next morning to warn the staff at their Norwich house to expect them, along with a note to Ruth saying when they were likely to arrive. Then she put the whole matter of Frederick Dalston firmly aside and began to question Adam in some depth about the decorations and other arrangements in the Scudamores' house in Bull Street.

It was as well that Adam had remained in Aylsham for a day since a fresh letter arrived from Ross.

Honoured Sir,

This afternoon I questioned Brent, The Riding Officer, as you requested. At first, he attempted to tell me the same lies he had told the parish constable, though without much conviction. He must have realised he would not have been arrested if that story had been believed. When I yawned and told him to sing another song, he produced a different version of the events surrounding the death of his colleague, Hartwell.

This time he claimed he knew in advance that Hartwell was sweet on the comely Nancy Narbord and had plans to take her away from her father and the miserable life they lived in that pitiful shack. According to this version of events, as soon as the two Riding Officers reached Kessingfield, Hartwell announced that he planned to spend their time there visiting his lady love. It would be up to Brent to make a cursory search of the village and the dunes round about. He intended to put his time to far better use in Nancy's arms.

Brent, therefore, left him and went about his business. When he returned and found Hartwell's body, his thoughts turned at once to Nancy's father. He claimed it was well known the old man was complacent about his daughter entertaining men in return for payment. However, if Hartwell had succeeded in taking her away, Narbord would have been left alone, unable to fend for himself or earn enough to buy more than the most meagre diet. If Narbord had discovered Hartwell's plans — as Brent believed he most probably had — for him to return and find Hartwell in his daughter's bed might have been too much to tolerate. That was why Brent went at once to Narbord's shack. When he saw the old man outside attempting to wash blood off his clothes, his worst fears were confirmed and he dragged the villain away to the constable at once.

I could see Brent was mightily pleased with this new invention. When I dismissed it with contempt and told him to tell me the truth instead, his dismay was comic. For a while, he swore it was the truth, though it was to no avail. I think it was at that point he finally understood what was facing him. I was willing to continue to question him again and again until I was satisfied I had the truth, however long that might take. After one last attempt to persist with this pretty tale, he gave in and confessed to killing Hartwell himself.

The two of them had ridden to the village as in the last tale, but from then on all was different. It wasn't Hartwell who planned to enjoy young Nancy's favours while leaving his colleague to do all the work, it was Brent. Until that moment, he claimed, he'd had no notion that Hartwell was in love with the girl and hoped she would follow him to a better life. He only realised the truth when Hartwell threatened him with violence. He swore he would break his neck if he didn't leave Nancy alone and get on with the job they had come to undertake. Worse, at that precise time, Brent had been boasting of the number of previous occasions on which he'd come to Kessingfield to pay his shilling and bed the eel-

catcher's pretty daughter. To make matters worse again, he had added several colourful descriptions of her undoubted charms, while using a series of obscene epithets to illustrate how he viewed her and her behaviour.

That proved too much for Hartwell. What started with insults and threats, soon progressed to fisticuffs, then a violent struggle between them with no holds barred. Hartwell drew a knife and Brent did the same. But where Hartwell's lunge missed its target, Brent's aim proved true. In a moment, Hartwell lay at his feet, gasping out his life with Brent's dagger deep in his chest.

Faced with a dead body in need of explanation, Brent looked around wildly for some means of disposing of the evidence of what he had done. It was while he was searching that he saw Narbord washing blood off his clothes. The rest we already know.

I have handed Brent over the to the magistrate and he will be sentenced at the next assize.

Once again, Sir Adam, you have managed to penetrate a mass of lies to uncover a criminal act the rest of us would probably have missed. My admiration for you is yet greater than it was before.

I am, sir, your most obedient and humble servant,
Anthony Ross

AFTER DINNER THAT EVENING, ADAM SHOWED HIS WIFE ROSS's letter.

'You were quite right to be suspicious of what you were told at first, husband,' she said. 'Hartwell was killed as a result of a sordid quarrel over a girl of the loosest morals. What a wretched way to die! When Brent's knife struck home, it not only took away his colleague's life, it deprived that worthless girl of what might have been her only hope of escape from misery and prostitution. At least you have saved an innocent man from the gallows. For the rest, I can only feel it proved a sordid affair of lust and violence.'

'Don't forget love, my dear. Love can be as powerful as hate in leading to violence,' Adam replied. 'When nature endowed such a poor girl with remarkable beauty, it did her no favours. Men were certain to fight over her, though she tried to make the best of what she had by selling to any who could pay her price.'

'Will Brent hang?'

'I doubt it. What he did was not premeditated. He will more likely face a charge of manslaughter. His eventual confession will also tell in his favour with the judge. If the jury believe him when he says Hartwell was the first to draw a knife, I expect he'll be sentenced to a short spell in goal. Then the best he can hope for is that there are none amongst his fellow prisoners in custody through the efforts of Riding Officers like he had been. If there are, he may expect a severe beating — or worse.'

⚶

WHEN ADAM AND LADY ALICE ARRIVED AT THE HOUSE IN THE Cathedral Close, shared by Mrs Bascom and Ruth Scudamore, the atmosphere of excitement exhibited by both ladies was almost strong enough to touch. The normal welcoming pleasantries were carried out in full, naturally, even though the time since their last visit was brief. If they were performed rather more perfunctorily than usual, no one objected. Both ladies were bursting to tell what they had discovered.

'Dear Ruth has most kindly allowed me to go first,' Mrs Bascom said, 'though this should not be taken to mean that what I have to tell you is more important than the news she has. Since we could not both speak at once, and to interrupt one another would be most confusing, we agreed to handle things in this manner.'

'Very sensible,' Adam muttered. He'd experienced his mother in full flow before and doubted that anyone could squeeze a word in edgeways, let alone interrupt her to speak themselves. 'Please tell us what you have learned. I will ask questions along the way, if there is anything that I don't understand.'

That earned Adam a hard look meant to dissuade him from doing any such thing. He smiled happily in return, thus passing the signal that he was no longer a child and would do as he wished.

'As you know,' Mrs Bascom began, 'it is my practice to invite groups of my friends to the house to take afternoon tea. For the most part, these are regular occasions and the same people attend almost every time. Naturally, I tried to see what they could tell me but found them very disappointing. Frederick Dalston's escapades were already old news. They agreed that he had been something of a terror amongst the servant classes, before transferring his attention to better-born young women. One or two notable scandals had followed but, of late, his name was no longer raised where wives and mothers met to socialise. It seems his rate of success with his seductions had declined. Maybe all the frantic womanising had started to lose its appeal. Perhaps the younger ladies of the city had become wary of his superficial charms. After that, there was nothing more I could discover from them. Nothing which might indicate a reason for the man's death.'

'I have found much the same thing when talking to my acquaintances in the city,' Lady Alice said. 'They all knew of the man and heartily disapproved of his way of life but told me most of the scandals associated with his name had taken place months previously.'

'Fortunately,' Mrs Bascom continued, 'I had a lucky encounter whilst visiting the circulating library. There I happened to meet Miss Georgina Wetherby. She is not a close acquaintance of mine, for I find her a rather dry woman with a particularly puritanical outlook on life. Not the sort of person likely to be a useful source of gossip.'

'I think I've met her myself,' Lady Alice said at that point. 'Isn't her father some sort of dissenting minister associated with the Octagon Chapel? Many of the most prominent families in the city attend worship there, don't they? I have heard it is noted as much for the high intellectual standards of its ministers as the wealth of the merchant families who support it.'

'So I believe,' Mrs Bascom said in a tight voice. She didn't dare to rebuke anyone possessing an aristocratic background of the kind Lady Alice could boast, but her interruptions were becoming unwelcome.

'The nub of the matter is that Miss Wetherby proved only too willing to talk about Frederick Dalston. It seems that she had recently been courted by a young man from a suitably wealthy and respectable family. Marriage had not yet been mentioned, but she had the strongest hopes that her status as a spinster would soon be brought to an end. I think it is only fair to mention that Miss Wetherby, while still young, is not a particularly handsome woman. She has a large nose and a very prominent squared jaw. Her eyes, though undoubtedly blue, could best be described as pale and watery. Nor does she have an elegant figure. I have heard her described as scrawny, which is unkind though not too far from the truth. On the other hand, her father is an extremely wealthy cloth merchant and she is his only surviving child. Given that advantage, you would have expected to find her surrounded by suitors. Sadly, if her appearance is something they would happily overlook, given the likely size of her inheritance, her astringent nature and fiercely moralistic attitudes have so far proved effective barriers to any relationship of a romantic nature.'

'Indeed, Mrs Bascom, to my mind you have supplied an admirable description of the woman.' Lady Alice appeared determined to interrupt whenever she wished. 'All you have omitted to say is that Miss Wetherby is a little past her prime. That, as well as her looks and character, may explain why she has so far failed to benefit from her family's increasingly frantic efforts to find her a husband.'

'That's true,' Mrs Bascom said with a sigh. Her son was clearly on his best behaviour, but his wife was beginning to presume on her patience. 'On this occasion, as I was saying, I had the greatest difficulty in stemming the torrent of bitter denunciations of men in general, and Frederick Dalston in particular, with which she assaulted me.'

She hurried on before anyone could interrupt her yet again. 'It seems she had at last been courted by this young man and was quite determined not to let him escape. You can imagine her dismay when she discovered her beau was being sent by his father to undertake a lengthy course of study at the Warrington Academy — a noted educational institution amongst the Presbyterians and independent congregations, and the source of many of their ministers. When she tackled him on the subject, all he would tell her was that he had been discovered to be one of a coterie of young men, which included a certain Frederick Dalston, and that Dalston himself had been engaging in actions of a highly reprehensible and immoral nature. When she pressed him further, he assured her he had taken no part in Dalston's wickedness. Nevertheless, his father had been sufficiently appalled to find a way of removing him from Norwich for the foreseeable future.'

'The only other thing he told her was that if she wished to know more, she should ask the Helston family,' Ruth said, clearly eager to urge Mrs Bascom on towards the main point of the story.

'I was just coming to that, my dear,' Mrs Bascom said in a frigid voice. 'All these interruptions are delaying the story and not adding to anyone's understanding.'

Ruth directed a wicked grin at her aunt, which fortunately Mrs Bascom missed. Adam frowned at the pair of them. He knew his mother of old. Teasing her was rarely productive, though it had not stopped him and his brother from trying and often receiving a severe lecture as a result.

'To cut a long story short,' Mrs Bascom said heavily, 'Miss Wetherby was angry enough to do as he said. She approached one of the Helston sisters and asked her about Dalston. At first the other woman was reluctant to talk about him. That made Miss Wetherby suspicious, so she persisted until the tale of the disaster that had befallen the Helston family came out. Frederick Dalston had contrived to have a number of clandestine meetings with Kitty Helston, the youngest and prettiest of the three sisters. Being both headstrong and bored with the confines of a life hedged in by the constraints of Presbyterian respectability, Kitty Helston proved to be sadly susceptible to Dalston's methods. He soon convinced the young woman he was in love with her and she with him. Blinded by infatuation, the silly girl believed Dalston when he said he would contrive for the two of them to elope. He would wait for her in secret the following evening at a place in the Chapel Field Gardens. All she had to do was devise a way to slip away from whoever was acting as her chaperone and join him there. Then he would explain his whole plan for their elopement and subsequent marriage. Blinded by passion and excitement, she agreed. You can well imagine the rest. They met together and he led her deep into one of the shrubberies "for better concealment" he said. After that he took advantage of her naïveté to have his way with her, whether with her agreement or by force hardly mattered. His pleasure taken, he left her alone to consider what she had done and hurried off to find her father. He told Mr Helston what had transpired and demanded a substantial sum of money to keep the whole matter quiet and prevent his daughter from being hopelessly compromised.'

'Did Mr Helston pay?' Adam asked.

'He did not. His response to Dalston's extortion was to call his servants and have the man thrown into the street. Unfortunately, he came to regret his display of temper before many days had passed. Dalston began to spread the tale of what had taken place amongst his friends, telling them that he was vastly amused by the credulity of girls from dissenting families. Their vaunted morality, he declared, could be breached by little more than a warm glance and a few convenient lies. After that, news of what had happened spread all around Norwich. Poor Kitty was ruined and the family so shamed that they have now arranged to leave the city altogether and retire to a place where their disgrace is not known.'

'What an arrogant, unprincipled rogue that Frederick Dalston was!' Lady Alice said angrily. 'To ruin an innocent young woman like that as a means of making money. It makes my blood boil!'

'That's not quite the end of the matter either,' Mrs Bascom said, 'though what follows serves only to explain why Miss Wetherby was quite so bitter in her denunciations. To that poor woman's intense discomfort, Miss Helston added that her own beau who, she had believed, was on the brink of asking her father for her hand in marriage, was now to be sent away for an indefinite period of time, merely because he was suspected of having made too close an acquaintance of Frederick Dalston. When Miss Wetherby enquired the name of the young man, he turned out to be the very same person who had led Miss Wetherby to believe that he was about to propose to her!'

'No wonder she was so annoyed,' Adam said quietly, 'though if she had thought about it rationally, she might have come to believe she had had a narrow escape. The fellow's only interest in women clearly lay in the size of their likely inheritance. No man like that would take his marriage vows seriously once the money was in his hand.'

'That's hardly the point, Adam,' his mother chided him. 'His behaviour must have been entirely reprehensible, whichever of the two he had married. The more so since he is now apparently set to become a minister of some nonconformist church. However, let me finish what I have to say, before you start passing judgement on the people involved.

'Having heard all that Miss Wetherby had to tell me, I set out for home, only to encounter the Dean's wife — a lady well known to keep a close eye on the morals of the city as a whole. She is always ready to pass caustic comments on those who fall short of the standards she espouses, especially nonconformists. She told me, in the strictest of confidence, of course, that she knew of two other cases in the past six months where Frederick Dalston had carried out exactly the same act of trickery. In both cases, she believed, the families had paid what he demanded. One came to light when the father demanded his daughter should at once marry a distant and elderly relative, whose delight at having a pretty, young wife would more than overcome any scruples he might have when he discovered she had already been deflowered. The young woman refused and her father drove her from his house. I believe she is now wed to a previous acquaintance, who had thought himself too insignificant to obtain her family's consent to a marriage. It's said the two are more than content with the arrangement.'

'How did the other case mentioned by the Dean's wife come to be known?' Adam asked.

'That is indeed a sad story,' his mother said. 'That young woman was so ashamed of her conduct that she drowned herself in the river. Her family tried to pass this off as an unfortunate accident, but I gather her two brothers were so incensed by her fate they uttered public threats to send Dalston to Hell, if only they could manage to lay their hands on him.'

Adam took a few moments to reflect on what he'd just been told. He could not break his promise and tell others that he had heard of precisely the same behaviour in yet another instance. Still, all of it fitted the same pattern of a man ready to make money without regard to morality or other people's feelings. If the brothers of the girl who drowned herself were out for his blood, that might explain why Dalston hadn't been seen around his usual haunts in Norwich for a week or more before he met his end. He'd probably feel safer the further he was from places where others might expect him to be.

Now it was Ruth's turn to reveal what she had discovered. She began by explaining that, while Mrs Bascom had gone to the circulating library or spent time with her usual circle of friends, she had concentrated on visiting what she described as a number of younger habitués of the various bluestocking groups in the city. Many of them were openly contemptuous of the way in which families traded their daughters' futures for social advancement or additional lands. That did not, however, prevent them from displaying a keen interest in such proceedings. As Mrs Bascom had already explained, Frederick Dalston was no longer the central topic of conversation. Even so, they were happy enough to tell Ruth what they knew. Mostly it was a repetition of what she had heard elsewhere, but occasionally something different and important arose.

'Before I tell you what that was,' she said to Adam, 'I want to suggest you may well have received a rather one-sided view of Frederick Dalston up till now. Most of the ladies I have been talking with are below the age of thirty-five years, some barely twenty-five or even younger. To that extent, they mirror the age of the men amongst whom Dalston has been spending his time. Indeed, many of those young men are likely to be the brothers of the ladies I was talking with. Two things I heard on many occasions in the past week or so may be relevant to your enquiries.

'Amongst the younger set generally, Frederick Dalston was perceived as wild, certainly, but also as a rebel against the many restrictions placed on the young by the customs of English polite society. He did what many would like to do, if they possessed the requisite courage. Like them, he said he felt trapped by the expectations of his family; only he was prepared to break out while they felt powerless to change the fate laid out before them. There's no doubt a young man like that can often exercise a powerful attraction to the opposite sex. That may go a long way to explaining why he seemed to find it so easy to obtain victims for his seductions and subsequent attempts at extortion.

'The other thing that many of them told me was that Frederick Dalston was excellent company. He was possessed of a biting, often outrageous wit. This he deployed against targets ranging from the established church to the pompous, gout-ridden merchants who dominate the mayor's court and the Common Council. He could reduce a room full of tipsy young men to hysterical laughter in a matter of moments. His more telling witticisms would be remembered and repeated time after time. Many of his fellows might be wary of him as a person, but his presence at their gatherings was known to ensure a memorable evening.'

Adam agreed this offered him a very different picture of Frederick Dalston from the one he had been getting. It also helped to explain why many of the older people in the city, especially the parents of marriageable daughters, viewed him as being such a danger. They didn't just object to what they saw as his wickedness; they feared the fact that he made such wickedness seem attractive.

'You're right that this presents something of a contrast to what I have been told by those who are probably the parents or grandparents of the young people you have just mentioned,' he said. 'It's useful and important information yet it leaves me with a number of questions. If those amongst whom he moved found his presence so congenial, what possessed him to turn against the class in society of which they were members? And why did he need so much money? It's true he'd been excluded from most of the gambling clubs, but if that meant he could no longer win money there it also meant he could no longer lose it.'

'I'm afraid I can't help you answer either of those questions,' Ruth said. 'What I can tell you is that several of those I spoke with suggested that Frederick Dalston's behaviour had changed in recent weeks — and certainly not for the better. They said he seemed more urgent, more driven. It was as if the time available to him for some project was running out, without him yet being close to achieving what he desired. That might also explain the events I am now about to relate.'

Ruth's second story began with meeting two young ladies, both daughters of wealthy merchants. Their fathers, unlike many of the gentry, had been willing to invest in the education of their daughters and encouraged them in their scientific interests. The two came to a small exhibition of Ruth's botanical drawings set up in the house of a friend. There they sought her out to express their delight and fascination with the detail her drawings had been able to reveal. Naturally, the conversation passed on to sharing ideas and observations on botanical matters and the sisters had become two of Ruth's firmest and most valued friends. As sources of information for Adam's investigation, they had proved invaluable. They had sharp eyes and lively minds. Even better, they had three brothers between them, none older than forty. It was these brothers who had brought home information about an event which had taken place barely two days before Frederick Dalston's murder.

It concerned one of those evenings of drunken hilarity mentioned earlier. Frederick Dalston had been in a particularly wild and outrageous mood. So much so that some of those present had begged him to cease so that they could recover their breath and ease the pain in their sides.

'About halfway through the evening,' Ruth continued, 'a young man called Leonard Hamilton joined the group in a highly excited state. He had just returned from a racing meeting at Newbury at which he had placed two very large wagers at outrageously long odds. To his amazement and joy, both horses romped home at the head of the field. He had come home some £300 richer.'

'And he had the money with him, I suppose,' Adam said.

'He did and dipped into it to buy drinks for everyone present in celebration of his good fortune. Indeed, he bought many rounds of drinks, becoming steadily more inebriated himself in the process. By about 12:30 am, the room was nearly empty. At least, it was nearly empty of those people who were still conscious. Several young men had passed out and were stretched along settles or lay on the floor, completely unaware of what was going on around them. Others had left in small groups, leaning on one another to prevent themselves from falling over. By 12:45 am, according to the steward who was serving the drinks, only Frederick Dalston and Leonard Hamilton were still drinking, though Hamilton's speech was almost incoherent and he was sprawled in a chair, unable to rise. Frederick Dalston, on the other hand, appeared to be quite sober. He had a drink in his hand it was true, but he rarely raised it to his lips and when he did it seemed to be more for show than to allow him to swallow anything.'

'I'm not altogether surprised,' Adam said. 'From what others have told me, Dalston was not a great drinker himself, even if those amongst whom he moved were.'

'As it approached 1:00 am, the steward decided to declare the evening over. He had been serving drinks for more than six hours and was desperate to get to his own bed. He said he would serve no more drinks. The two young men should take themselves home — if they were able to do so. He needed to blow out the candles and lock up for the night. He would clear everything else up in the morning. Leonard Hamilton was not in a state to either agree or disagree, but Dalston told the steward he might leave straight away. He, Dalston, would see all the candles were doused and the room locked. Then he would take Mr Hamilton home to his rooms, since he was unable to walk unaided.'

'The steward agreed to this?' Adam asked.

'He did. He was very tired and other members of the club had helped him out in this way before. He checked to see that Leonard Hamilton was still conscious, got his coat and hat and left them to it.'

'Did Dalston do as he had promised?'

'Apparently, he did. When he awoke next day, Leonard Hamilton's memory of events was naturally hazy. However, he was undoubtedly in his own rooms, so someone had taken him there. According to his story, he had a vague memory of being almost carried along the street to where he was lodging. He must have passed out the moment he was inside. When he awoke next day, he was fully clothed and lying sprawled across his bed.'

Adam sighed. 'I imagine you're going to tell me he had been robbed,' he said. 'He felt for his purse, checked it and discovered it was empty.'

'That is correct,' Ruth said. 'Mr Hamilton swore that he must have had at least £250 in his purse when he was helped back to his rooms. Some of the other club members questioned the steward the next day and he told them the charge for all the drinks that Mr Hamilton had bought came to £42 — an amazing sum. Hamilton had given him the money, in sovereigns and half sovereigns, counting them out slowly and with the greatest difficulty given his state at the time. The steward could see a great deal more money in Hamilton's purse at that point but swore he'd never touched the purse himself, nor taken more than was due to him.

'Hamilton swore Dalston had robbed him and said that he was

determined to get his money back. His friends urged him to bring a prosecution against Dalston for theft, but Hamilton merely laughed. He reminded them that nobody else had been present in the club after the steward had left, nor did he personally have a memory of encountering anybody on his way home. If he tried to bring a prosecution, it would simply be his word against Dalston's. Instead, he swore he was going to catch up with Frederick Dalston and claim his money back. If Dalston refused to hand it over, he was going to kill him.'

'You say that you were told that all this happened only two days before Dalston's murder. Is that correct?' Adam said.

'Two or three days at the most,' Ruth replied. 'The young ladies I spoke with were not quite sure of the specific date when the events took place. On the other hand, they were sure they had heard the news of Frederick Dalston's death within a very few days of their brothers coming home with the story. They also told me no one had seen Frederick Dalston in Norwich between the night on which Leonard Hamilton claimed he'd been robbed and the day the murder must've taken place.'

As they sat together after dinner that evening, Lady Alice was sharply aware of her husband's frustration. Once again, he had said little during their meal and had been nursing a glass of brandy and staring into the fire for almost half an hour. She decided, therefore, it was high time she asked him to tell her what was upsetting him.

'It's this cursed investigation!' he told her. 'Before we came to Norwich today, I'd dismissed the notion of seeking a suspect for Dalston's murder amongst the circles of wild young men who were his companions and acquaintances. That allowed me to narrow my search, and I was beginning to feel I was finally moving forward in the right direction. Now, thanks to Ruth and my mother, I have been presented with two strong suspects from amongst those same young men; both possessing compelling reasons for hating Frederick Dalston and both having sworn to encompass his death. I'd like to believe their threats were merely products of their overwrought emotions at a specific time but, if I'm honest, that's merely wishful thinking on my part. I feel as if I'm back at the very beginning!'

'That's clearly not true,' Lady Alice said, relieved that it was nothing worse. 'You may feel confused and muddled at present, but I'm sure you'll be able to sort it all out. What you need is a good night's sleep and a chance to reflect on what you've been told. Let us retire to bed early so that you may have the first right away. If sleep eludes you and you need your mind freed from going over and over the possibilities, come to my room where I can show you a very suitable way to bring this about. Forget this investigation for a while, my dear. Tomorrow there will be a lengthy drive back to Aylsham, during which you will have ample time to think. Now, finish your drink and I will ring for the maid to bring us candles so that we can go upstairs.'

❧ 13 ❧

The next morning, refreshed and revived, Adam took his time over his breakfast, enjoying the sight of the fresh growth on the trees of his garden and musing on the chances of the current sunshine lasting all day. The bitter, easterly wind had finally given way to a warm southerly one, bringing a hint of the hotter lands to the south whence it had originated. As his wife had predicted, his frustration had now abated. He could take a more balanced and measured view of his progress towards finding a satisfactory answer to who had murdered Frederick Dalston.

Once back in Aylsham next day, Adam set out in in pursuit of answers to more questions that lurked at the back of his mind. In the middle of the afternoon he walked the short distance to his friend Peter Lassimer's apothecary shop. Many times before, he had spent hours sitting in Lassimer's compounding room, describing his ideas to his friend and listening to his response. It had usually proved to be an excellent way of reducing a collection of seemingly unrelated facts to a clear and coherent plan for future action. Unfortunately, this time it was not to be. When Adam strode into the shop, expecting to find his friend, he found it half full of customers being served by a rather harassed young man behind the counter; one of

Peter's two apprentices and the one whom Adam had not so far encountered.

The customers responded to Adam's entrance as they might have done had the king himself arrived in the shop. All conversation ceased abruptly, including that between the apprentice and the customer he was in the middle of serving. People began to edge towards the door, trying to slip away unnoticed. Meanwhile, Peter's apprentice stood and stared at Adam, his mouth wide open and a look of out-and-out horror on his face.

It took a moment for Adam to realise the dreadful mistake he had made. These people were deeply embarrassed by his presence and rendered unbearably uncomfortable by being in the same shop with someone so far above them socially. They probably feared being rebuked or suspected of hoping to eavesdrop on whatever Adam said. The poor apprentice, nearly undone by the necessity of dealing with someone titled and wealthy like Sir Adam Bascom, stuttered and stumbled through explaining to Adam that his master was absent visiting patients and was unlikely to return for several hours. When Adam told him that he would send a servant later in the day to discover whether the apothecary had returned and when he might be available for a private word, the poor lad's look of relief was almost laughable. He could hardly wait to show this unwanted visitor from the shop so that the others might be persuaded to return.

Adam reproached himself all the way home. Why had he not considered the effect his presence would have on a group of ordinary people of the town? Members of the upper gentry did not go to speak with tradespeople in person. Nor did they arrive on foot, even if they lived barely a hundred yards away. They either sent a servant to conduct their business for them or summoned the person they wished to see to come to their house. In terms of strict social standing, an apothecary was a tradesman and should present himself only at the back door.

In recent times though, such rigid class distinctions had started to be relaxed, though the distinction between physicians and apothecaries remained in there in various subtle ways. For example, physicians charged fees for their services and their time. Apothecaries were only allowed to seek payment for the medicines they prescribed or sold over the counter and followed an apprenticeship like other trades-men. Many physicians, like Adam himself, now studied at a university and were increasingly treated as gentlemen as a result; though he had still found it prudent to go to the tradesmen's entrance unless told otherwise.

Adam, undoubtedly a member of the gentry, had thus broken the social conventions by appearing in Peter's shop in person. What made it worse was that he was now a baronet, which in most ordinary people's eyes meant he was close to counting as a nobleman. The people in the shop had been rightly embarrassed by the impropriety of Adam's behaviour. The fact that he would never dream of submitting his old friend, Peter Lassimer, to the indignity of being summoned to present himself as and when required had nothing to do with the matter. He would need to remember that for the future. The last time he had been to see Peter, which was only a few days ago, it so happened that the shop was empty at the time and he could be taken through into the compounding room and out of sight, before the next customer arrived. He had wondered a little at the time when Lassimer had let him out after their talk through the door that linked his busi-ness premises to his house next door, instructing the maidservant to make sure that Sir Adam was able to leave through the front door. Now he knew the answer.

Very well. He would need to agree on some kind of signal by which their old, easy intimacy, sitting in the compounding room behind the shop, could be reinstated. A way by which Adam could enter the premises without encountering Peter's customers and interrupting his trade. When the butler let him in at his own front door, he quietly instructed the man to send a servant later to see whether Mr Lassimer had returned from his rounds. She could also enquire what would be the best way for her master to arrive without causing any upset.

After that, Adam retired to his library to think through the ques-tions still facing him on his own. Two in particular still occupied his mind. Together they prevented any of the theories which he or others had formed to date being fully acceptable.

Despite all that he had heard from his mother and Ruth Scudamore, including the specific threats made by at least two young men, Adam remained unconvinced Dalston's behaviour and threats of extortion were the reasons for his murder. The families he had preyed upon were too respectable to resort to such a crude form of revenge. Several had even paid what he had demanded, despite suspecting he would be bound to return for more at some time. The threats of the Helston brothers sounded ominous yet would they truly be willing to face the gallows? It seemed more likely that, even if they managed to catch up with the man who brought disgrace to their sister, they would have been content to make some kind of public spectacle of him. They would make him a warning to others and ensure that his humiliation would be significant and long lasting. It all sounded dramatic enough, but none of it was plausible.

As an aside, Adam wasn't convinced Frederick Dalston was in hiding in the days before he was killed. It could have simply been that the members of the family Ruth had spoken with had failed to notice him. He might even have been travelling elsewhere at the time.

If threats of violent revenge and supposed indications that Frederick had been hiding in fear for his life didn't ring true, what was the other oddity that remained?

Adam was still grappling with that intractable question which had bothered him almost from the start. Why was Frederick Dalston killed where he was? All the suspects he had so far lived in Norwich, even Obadiah Webley. There were plenty of places in the city where you could wait in ambush, especially by night, then escape unnoticed after the deed was done. Why trail seven or eight miles after your victim to a lonely country area not far from the coast?

Adam sought out his wife and put these two questions to her. She agreed with him on both matters. She too found it impossible to believe that any decent person would resort to murder on a country road to punish a wrong done to them or theirs. That sounded more like the actions of a hardened criminal like Webley. Why should he do it either? From all that Adam had told her, he was likely to make a great deal more money from a living Frederick Dalston as dead he would be worth nothing at all. On the question of the spot where the murder had taken place, she could only shake her head and say it was either a matter of blind chance or the reason had so far escaped them entirely.

Disheartened, Adam returned to his library. If the respectable families of Norwich whose daughters had been wronged were not believable suspects, the same was also true of Mr. Hamilton — the lucky gambler whose luck had run out when he encountered Frederick Dalston. Nor was it likely the threat from Mr Hamilton would be turned into action. To kill the thief wouldn't help him to recover his money and would leave him too facing the possibility of execution. That only left whatever criminal activities Dalston and Webley were engaged upon between them.

At this point, Adam felt such frustration he would have abandoned the whole matter if his conscience had allowed it. Instead, he called for a servant to bring him his outdoor coat and hat and went out into the garden. There he stood for a time, gazing at the clouds moving serenely overhead and letting the sun's gentle warmth fall on his upturned face. How petty the sordid quarrels of mankind seemed compared with the majestic procession of the seasons and the unchanging splendour of the hills and rivers of his home county. How silly it was to fret and fume when you could walk out into the sunshine and listen to the birds in the trees and admire the fresh greens of spring.

Walking had always been Adam's answer to frustration with any problem. Somehow, the regular movement of his legs and the sense of progress it induced freed his thinking from whatever tangle it had got itself into. All he needed to do was allow his mind to drift while he looked about him and focused on the reality of the world in place of the phantoms his mind had been struggling with. He set off along the pathway towards the lower part of his garden in a state of mind that was almost calm again.

It worked. From somewhere inside himself — he had no idea of its source — a fresh possibility popped unbidden into his mind. What if the criminal enterprise between Frederick Dalston and Obadiah Webley was linked to the increased activity of the privateers in the German Ocean?

In an instant, Adam could see how such a business must work — at least in part. They would need to know which ships were sailing from the most significant ports along the coast, from King's Lynn to Lowestoft at least, what their cargoes were and when they were departing. That implied a network of informants collecting this information. Dalston's recent absence from Norwich could now be explained by assuming that he was away contacting these informants, learning what he and Webley needed to know. That done, he would return to the city where he and Webley would choose which ships the privateers should target in order to make the most valuable captures.

So far so good. Then came a blank he needed to be able to fill. What was the means that Webley used to convey their messages to the privateers? The most likely route would be via the smugglers, since the privateers would be somewhere twenty miles or more offshore. That still left the question of how to contact the smugglers without leaving Norwich to do so. Was Dalston doing this as well? Did that explain why he had been on that lonely road on the night of his death? It sounded plausible enough, until you considered the sheer number of attacks that Captain Mimms had told him were taking place. The assumption that Webley remained in Norwich, like the spider at the centre of the web, while Dalston dashed about all over the county bearing messages hither and thither, was almost enough to pour cold water on that whole explanation. It was high time he talked to Peter in search of some better ideas on that at least.

Adam's long-serving maid, Hannah, returned from Peter Lassimer's shop at around five in the afternoon. She brought the message that Mr Lassimer would be occupied until the shop closed. After that, to avoid interrupting Sir Adam and Lady Alice's dinner, he would present himself at their door at eight o'clock. He was confident that the excellent brandy his host was doubtless preparing to offer him would more than compensate for the slight inconvenience caused by walking the hundred yards from his house.

They met in Adam's library, where they could smoke if they wished without upsetting Lady Alice or leaving the smell of tobacco on her fine clothes. A decanter of Adam's best brandy, together with suitable glasses, had been placed in a prominent position and both men helped themselves generously before proceeding any further. After that, Adam explained his notion of a criminal enterprise involving Frederick Dalston, Obadiah Webley and the French privateers. To his delight, Peter thought it a splendid solution to understanding what had tied the two men together.

'If the shipowners found out who was tipping off the privateers,' he said, 'I wouldn't give much for the survival chances of the culprits. Would they resort to murder though? Wouldn't it be simpler to haul them before a magistrate and see them taken to the assize instead? What they were doing would amount to treason in time of war and the penalty for that is execution.'

He paused; his gaze fixed on the portrait of Adam's grandfather which hung over the fireplace.

'There's another reason why the idea that Frederick Dalston met his end at the hands of some furious shipowner won't work,' he said after a few moments. 'Didn't you tell me this Webley is alive and well and going about his business as usual?'

'That's what Ross said,' Adam replied.

'I thought so. So, why murder Dalston and leave Webley untouched? Ross knew the two were in this together. Why would the shipowners and captains not have discovered the same thing?'

'True enough,' Adam said sadly. 'Maybe it isn't such a good idea after all. I've been cudgelling my brains on another problem as well. How would Webley be able to send messages to the smugglers, for onward transmission to the privateers lurking offshore. Ross seems sure the man never left Norwich. Dalston could have gone, of course, but he was also in Norwich all the time until recently. That absence I had put down to the need to collect the information on ships and sailing from their informants in the ports.'

'Am I right to assume that Webley's plan would be for all to be carried out with the greatest secrecy?' Peter asked him.

'Very much so,' Adam replied. 'If either the shipowners, the captains, or the authorities discovered what Webley was doing his future prospects would be bleak indeed, as you yourself said.'

'There's a simple answer, you know,' Peter said. 'Use some of the travelling tinkers and packmen. They roam everywhere about the countryside, selling their goods in villages and farmhouses along the way. No one would take the slightest notice of their comings and goings. They do it all the time. All that would be needed would be to instruct one or more of them to pass Webley's message onto a specific fisherman. He would either tell the smugglers the next time there was a landing of contraband on his part of the beach or go out in his boat to fish and make sure to encounter a smugglers vessel once he was out of sight offshore.'

'Damn me!' Adam cried. 'I never thought of such people. I suppose I understood they existed, but I've never had any contact with them, so far as I know.'

'Of course, you haven't,' Peter said, between laughing at Adam's descent into profanity and replenishing his brandy glass. 'Fine gentlemen like you don't involve themselves in mundane matters like buying everyday household things. Your housekeeper orders what is needed, probably from tradesmen in Norwich. Even people of the middling sort, such as I am, usually send their servants to obtain whatever is needed from the local tradesmen in their locality. On the other hand, the poor families of labourers and fishermen, who populate the bulk of the county, rely on what they can grow or catch for themselves for food — supported by a little poaching along the way, I dare say. All the other things they need such as used clothes, which they can alter to use again, knives and other simple tools and perhaps a little salt, they buy from the packmen. They wander from village to village, their packs full of cheap goods and trinkets. They're the men who supply most of the common peoples' needs. Them and the tinkers who mend folk's pots and pans to avoid the need for them to buy more.'

'But wouldn't such people be far too slow for Webley's purpose? By the time they got to the coast to take the message to the smugglers, the chosen ships would be well on their way.'

'Don't you believe it. Suppose he wanted one to go somewhere like Bacton or Mundesley — or even Kessingfield. Somewhere small where he was unlikely to encounter customs men or other officials. If he started from Norwich, the furthest distance to Mundesley, I imagine, would be a little over ten or eleven miles. If he was paid well enough, he could easily walk that in the course of a long day, then call at the regular villages he visited afterwards. No one would know, or care, what precise route he had taken. Most packmen go to somewhere like Norwich market to fill up their packs, so anyone seeing them there would think nothing of that either. After our packman left the city, he wouldn't use the turnpikes or the main roads either. He'd be travelling by the drove roads, the local tracks and even the routes used by the pack horse trains. He would save many miles that way, as well as avoiding local villages and the prying eyes to be found there. If you ask me, what I've described is a perfect way to send messages without drawing attention. Don't you agree?'

Adam leapt to his feet, almost upsetting his brandy glass while doing so. 'That's it! Of course!' he said. 'That's how it's done. Thank you, Lassimer. Thank you. I would never have thought of it. Now, drink up your brandy and make your way home, there's a good fellow. I have an important letter to write and it's imperative that I send William to Norwich with it as early as possible tomorrow morning. Off you go. I'd love to spend more time talking with you, but I really have to get this letter written. I must ensure Ross comes to see me with all possible speed. Now I know what to tell him to do. If we don't proceed as fast as we can, the people we need to lay our hands upon will slip through our fingers.'

THAT EVENING, AS THE TWO OF THEM SAT IN THE DRAWING ROOM IN their usual fashion, Lady Alice congratulated her husband on his latest discovery. Afterwards, having thought about it a little more, she turned more pensive, confessing herself to be in two minds about the likelihood that Adam would track down the murderer.

'When you first told me of Frederick Dalston, I felt sorry for him,' she said. 'However wild he'd been, it sounded as if his behaviour was no more than a worse version of what scores of other young men from good families get up to. It's not unusual to find those fine fellows spending time sowing their wild oats, as the saying goes, before they settle down to conventional and respectable lives. Young Dalston's life had been cut short in the middle of such a period, as I thought then.

He would never now have the opportunity to calm down and become a useful member of society.'

'Now you feel differently?' Adam asked.

'The more you tell me about Frederick Dalston, the worse his character and behaviour turn out to be. I'm beginning to wonder whether the world is not better off without him. I am also curious about what changed his behaviour so drastically. Was it really no more than anger — pique might be a better word — at being ejected from the university? No one has suggested his father punished him in any way when he returned.'

'He almost certainly did not,' Adam replied. 'As I have mentioned several times, William Dalston is an easy-going man. All the evidence is that he displayed the greatest possible indulgence towards his elder son. The stern discipline meted out by Frederick's college may well have been the first he had encountered.'

'And it alone effected this disastrous change? Surely not.'

'It may have started the process, but I agree with you. On its own, it would have been unlikely to have such a profound effect. It occurs to me another person might well have proved more important in that regard.'

'Who?' Lady Alice asked him. 'Not his brother?'

'No. The one I have in mind is the Reverend Simon Geddy. I cannot imagine he would have stayed silent on the subject of Frederick's disgrace. He would probably have subjected the young man to a long series of angry tirades on the subject, heavily laced with biblical quotations and threats of hell fire. Even worse, he seems to have almost lived at Kessingfield Hall, having appointed himself as William Dalston's perpetual adviser. Maybe I should also add that, from what I have seen of the man, his bitter denunciations would not have died down for many weeks.

'Suppose the very sight of Frederick — the one on whom he had placed his highest hopes, the one who had now failed him so spectacularly — continually excited him to fresh reproofs and admonitions. That alone would be surely enough to make the young man long to escape. If, as a result, Frederick came to see Geddy as a representative both of the established order and the life of a country squire, it might have been enough to stir him to furious rejection of everything the rector stood for.'

'I see what you mean,' Lady Alice said. 'Geddy embodied the established church and its moral teachings, but also the deeply conservative country elite.'

'And epitomised both in their most disagreeable manifestations,' Adam added. 'Frederick must have been especially vulnerable to criticism. He had tasted a world of wider horizons and greater intellectual challenges, only to have it snatched away by those appointed to be its guardians. To be further assaulted with accusations and moral homilies might have been enough to turn adolescent rebellion into a fixed determination to escape, while taking revenge at the same time.'

'Now you make me sorry for him again,' Lady Alice said.

'I think he deserved some sorrow,' Adam replied, 'at least until he went so far that no one could feel anything beyond revulsion at the way he chose to live his life. To me, he was both pitiful and sickeningly cruel and selfish at the same time. We are, all of us, mixtures of goodness and wickedness. In most, the goodness prevails. In a few, it is pushed aside by evil thoughts and wicked deeds. In Frederick Dalston, my dear, the goodness had disappeared almost entirely by the time he died.'

❧ 14 ❧

A dam had given William, the groom, his instructions before he
and Lady Alice had retired for the night. He had stressed the
urgency and importance of his mission, telling him to leave
for Norwich as early as he could. Once he arrived, he was to see the
letter his master had entrusted to him was delivered only into the
hands of the person to whom it was directed. After that, he should go
to the livery stables used by the Norwich house. There he could feed
and water the horse and rub it down, then give it several hours to rest
before starting on the return journey. He should take rest and refreshment at the same time. Adam was always attentive to the needs of his
servants. He would not ask them to undertake tasks he would not be
willing to do himself.

When Adam finally surfaced from sleep, still wrapped most deli-
ciously in Lady Alice's arms, William had been on his way for almost an
hour. In fact, before Adam managed to drag himself out of bed —
entirely due to an urgent need to use the chamber pot — the letter had
been delivered and his groom was already on his way to the livery
stables.

Ross must have tossed aside all consideration for his mount when he covered the distance from Norwich to Aylsham in record time, urging the poor creature forward at full tilt nearly all the way. He arrived while Adam and his wife were still finishing their breakfast and so was forced to wait a short while in the library until Adam could join him. It then took some considerable persuasion on Adam's part to persuade him even to drink some coffee and eat one or two of the warm rolls sent up from the kitchen. He was more bewildered when Adam began their discussion by asking whether he was now any clearer about the precise nature of the business that Webley and Dalston were conducting between them.

His reply was brief and to the point. He was not.

In reply, Adam recounted the idea he had shared with Peter; that Webley and Dalston were acting as partners in sending messages to French and Dutch privateers offshore. The intent being to allow those raiders to pick out the richest, least protected vessels to fall upon. Captain Mimms had told him the rate of seizure of British merchant ships passing along the coast had increased steadily in recent weeks, rising from an average of one or two per week to four or even five. In the previous week, the old mariner had said, six fat merchant ships had been seized by French privateers and a further one by the Dutch. None had been ransomed. This represented a rate of loss that the merchants and shipowners could not possibly bear.

'Was it Frederick Dalston who had been collecting news about the ships' cargoes and times of departure?' Ross asked.

'I am sure that it was,' Adam told him. 'He'd been absent from Norwich for many days during the two or three weeks prior to his murder. I suspect he'd been to King's Lynn as well as Great Yarmouth. There he would spend his evenings in the better class of inns, buying drinks for the ships' captains and asking them about their work. They might have been suspicious at first, thinking that he was an agent of the Revenue. After a time, however, his ceaseless generosity, coupled with his amusing conversation, would have made them relax. He and Webley had almost certainly also recruited suitable informers in those ports. For a few shillings, such men would be willing to pass on all they knew about when certain ships would sail and whether they planned to join a convoy or not.'

'You put me to shame, Sir Adam,' Ross cried. 'You put me to shame. It is my job to nose out the plans of those intent on sedition — for that is surely what this amounts to. To seek to profit by aiding the country's sworn enemies in time of war is treason of the most heinous kind. Sir Percival will cast me aside when he learns of my failure.'

'Hush, sir!' Adam replied. 'It is not so bad as that, nor am I some genius in such matters. You told me before that Sir Percival had given you several tasks to complete for him in addition to helping me. Your attention has doubtless been divided, while I have had the time to concentrate my thoughts on a single set of circumstances. You may be sure I will inform Sir Percival that this has been a joint effort between us, not my supposed brilliance. It is the truth, you know. I could not have reached this conclusion without you.'

'You ease my mind, sir, though I swear I don't deserve it,' Ross said, looking like a man who has discovered the loss of a purse full of guineas. 'My master in London may forgive me, but I will not forgive myself in a hurry.'

'No more of that, Ross,' Adam said. 'Let us turn our minds instead to how we may prove or disprove my idea. It is only that, you know. I have not a shred of proof to back it up.'

'You may be sure I shall make finding that proof my first priority,' Ross said earnestly. 'I have good men in both the places you mentioned. I shall set them at once to looking for signs Frederick Dalston had been there and acted as you suggest. I shall also tell them to look for indications of who amongst the sailors and dockworkers might have been selling information on sailings and chosen routes. When I find them, I'm certain the Press Gang will be most willing to find them better ways to spend their time.'

'I wonder if Webley and Dalston realised the terrible risks they were taking by trying to carry out such a scheme in haste,' Adam said. 'If they had taken their time and limited themselves to providing the information necessary to allow the privateers to seize maybe one or at the most two more ships every two weeks or so, the conspirators might have escaped discovery for a long period. To encourage the privateers to increase their depredations four or fivefold was close to madness. In fact, I'm quite amazed that Webley is still in Norwich.'

'From what you've told me previously, Sir Adam,' Ross replied, 'I can only assume that young Mr Dalston was eager to accelerate his plans to leave the country for North America and was prepared to take quite extreme risks to add to his capital before he went. I can't believe that Webley wouldn't have told him how dangerous this might be, even if the young fellow hadn't realised it for himself.'

'Yet why is Webley still in Norwich?'

'My best guess is that he's waiting for the final payments from the privateers, sir. Either that or his greed has got the better of him and he thought he could continue his activities at a slower pace after Dalston had gone. Come to think of it, he could easily have denied more than a superficial involvement. After all, he didn't live in a port town, so how could he get any information about ships and cargoes? With Frederick Dalston dead, he could have suggested to any who sought him out that Dalston alone must have been the source of the tipoffs to the privateers. That was why he was now dead. Some group of shipowners or captains had taken their inevitable revenge.'

'But the rate of seizures doesn't seem to have gone down since Dalston's death, does it?'

'Maybe Webley is ready to make a run for it as well. He could be trying to get together as much money as possible beforehand in the same way that Dalston did. There might be another, less dramatic explanation too, I suppose. It would take some days for messages to reach the privateers. Still more time for them to sail to the spot where they now planned to intercept each ship. If he and Dalston had been sending them information right up to the point of Dalston's death, you wouldn't expect the number of seizures to fall back immediately to the level before.'

'I prefer your first explanation,' Adam said. 'I think you're right about Webley being on the point of making his escape. We must act in haste to prevent that happening or we will lose him. He's been trying to get together as much money as possible before making his escape overseas, just as Dalston was. Wait! Frederick Dalston's ill-gotten gains must be somewhere. He has no need of them now. Obadiah Webley is a greedy man, I suspect, as well as a dishonest one. He will have had his men out hunting for Dalston's money. Have you searched Dalston's lodgings?'

Ross's stricken expression gave the answer in an instant. 'My God!' he cried. 'I never thought of doing that. What a fool I have been! Oh, heaven forgive me! I didn't think I could be shown up so badly twice in a single morning. I should give up this job and take to serving beer in a tavern instead.'

Adam ignored the man's wails of anguish and pressed on. 'It's probably too late, but I think you should do so anyway. There's still an outside chance that Webley's men may have missed wherever it is the money is hidden. He probably used local ruffians without any skill or experience in searching correctly.'

'Nor the intelligence and experience to work out where the hiding places might be,' Ross added. He felt more cheerful facing a task he knew he could do and do well. 'But wouldn't it be an enormous risk to hide large amounts of cash? Especially in your own lodgings which is where people would search first? Wouldn't Dalston have put his money with one of the bankers?'

'He might have done so, but I doubt it. Everyone knew that he was always short of money. If he was seen to have an unusual amount available to entrust to the bankers, it would have attracted comment. He probably thought it was better to hide the money somewhere until he was ready to make his escape. Then he would travel to London and exchange the coins for paper at a series of banks there. None of them would know him. He would have had little difficulty in exchanging a whole series of modest amounts for bankers' drafts. Those he could take to a bank with international contacts, such as Rothschild's, and exchange for letters of credit drawn on their offices in Boston or New York. If they seemed suspicious, he could say he had sold his property in Britain, since he was intending to emigrate to the New World. A story like that would probably have satisfied them. With those letters of credit in his hand, he could next travel to Bristol or to Liverpool and take passage to America.'

'Simple, when you think about it, which is exactly what I didn't do.'

Ross was clearly still disgusted with himself. Here was an amateur and a gentleman explaining a second obvious action which he had missed altogether.

For Adam, this was no time for recriminations or self-abasement. He wanted to send Ross on his way with all speed to marshal the men necessary to track down Obadiah Webley and take him into custody.

'I have also been talking with a friend about Webley's need to make contact secretly with the smugglers,' he said. 'He reminded me of the many packmen and tinkers who travel about the county. They're such an obvious part of rural life no one would take the slightest notice of them. They're also likely to know about all kinds of shortcuts and hidden roads where they could travel unseen. Things like the pack-horse roads, or the drove roads, or even local footpaths through the fields. If we assume Webley paid one or two particular ones to go directly from Norwich to one of the small fishing villages along the coast where smuggling is endemic, the packman could deliver his message to a certain fisherman within a day of leaving Norwich — maybe even sooner. The fisherman would simply row out to sea and meet with the smugglers — or even the privateers themselves. Webley's message about an approaching ship could reach the captain of a privateer within eighteen hours of it leaving Norwich.'

Ross was stunned for the third time that morning. For several moments, he stared as if Adam was a creature from some other world.

'I'm a city boy,' he said after several more moments. 'I would never have thought of anything like that. What you say makes perfect sense. Now I can see why Sir Percival Wicken values you so highly. He told me you were clever and resourceful. In my arrogance, I thought I could be your match. What a fool I was! What a wretched fool! I am far below you as an investigator.'

'Never mind that,' Adam said. 'What we need now is action. You must leave and return to Norwich at once. There you should instruct your men to do two things. One is obvious: to keep a close eye on Webley and arrest him should he attempt to leave the city. The other is to keep a sharp watch out for any packman or tinker who tries to make contact with Webley. They should leave him alone until he has had the chance to receive the message or letter that Webley wants him to deliver. Then they should follow him until he is safely out of sight —

we don't want to alert Webley that we know what he's doing — then arrest the man and uncover the nature of the message. It's quite likely Webley will be trying to get in touch with someone to take him out to sea where he can be picked up by one of the privateers and carried to safety in France.'

'Of course! Of course! This is the route we've been looking for!' Ross almost shouted. 'The latest secret means of taking messages, as well as people like spies and escaped prisoners of war, across the sea to the French. We've all been looking for it for months, with not even a sniff of success. You found it in a week! Wait until Sir Percival Wicken hears about this!'

All his previous gloom had fled in an instant. This was his discovery; his revelation which linked Webley to more than a straightforward expedient to make money by earning rewards from the privateers.

'Yes, yes,' Adam said in exasperation. 'You may well be right, but that will hardly matter if Webley escapes. Now, on your way, man! Since you arrived here so quickly today, I imagine your poor horse is already exhausted. Take another one from my stable. It's my own riding horse, though I ride very little nowadays. She is fleet of foot when you allow her to be. Just don't ruin her wind for ever. Now hurry, Ross, hurry! Send your people at once to keep watch on Webley. Send one or two others to search Dalston's lodgings, as I suggested. If you find anything, let me know at once.'

After Ross had left, Adam realised he'd forgotten to tell Wicken's man he could cease from investigating Dalston's gambling companions. The solution to the murder would not be found there. For a few moments, he wondered whether to sit down and write a letter to that effect, then set it aside. Ross would be far too busy with Webley to worry about anything else. Obadiah Webley was about to try to make his escape, taking whatever cash he could get together with him. Adam felt it in his bones. The wretched man must realise that the captains and shipowners would be searching for the person who was tipping off the privateers, using every means available to them. They were bound to succeed before too long. If he didn't get out of the country quickly, he would certainly lose his life.

Adam should have been elated and excited by his success. In fact, his sense of frustration had returned in full measure. It looked as if he might very well have solved Wicken's problem of the new delivery method for espionage and escape route for spies, while leaving his own investigation no further forward.

He sat down again in his chair and closed his eyes. He couldn't accept that Dalston's death had anything to do with Webley and the conspiracy they had hatched between them. He didn't think the smugglers were involved either. How could they possibly have known Dalston would be travelling along that particular road at that time on that particular night?

Had Dalston been followed all the way from Norwich? Adam didn't think so. Anyone doing that would have been obliged to follow him on horseback. Dalston would surely have heard their approach, there in the wood. The night had not been windy, and the roadway was too firm to deaden the noise of a horse's hooves. Would Frederick have allowed them to get so close to him on a deserted road without making some kind of challenge or trying to escape? Surely not. Such an explanation failed at too many points to be worth considering further.

As for some injured father or enraged brother being the culprit, he had discounted that some time ago.

That appeared to leave him only the explanation the magistrate had favoured: either an attempt at robbery that went badly wrong or a random killing by a madman. Both were too convenient and ignored too many pieces of evidence. The lonely location on a little-used country road. What robbers would choose to lie in wait at such an isolated spot — and in the middle of the night? Only fools, he was sure of that. The same applied to a random killing by a madman, unless you believed he'd simply been wandering in the woods and found Dalston by chance. Then there was the odd nature of the wound and the way the body had been left so neatly laid out. Neither suggested a frightened robber or a wandering lunatic.

Adam tried again. What if he assumed his whole approach to the murder of Frederick Dalston was fundamentally flawed in some way? That he had been approaching this investigation in the wrong way from the start? Collecting the wrong facts, looking in the wrong places and setting himself the wrong puzzles to unravel? What if Frederick Dalston's death was really due to some cause as yet unknown and unsought?

It was time to begin again.

❧ 15 ❧

Late in the afternoon on the following day yet another letter arrived from Ross. In it, he told Adam that, as requested, he'd set his snares all around Webley's house. His men had concealed themselves where they could observe the house and take note of anyone approaching. Others walked slowly past along the street, turned the corner, organised themselves into different groups, changed tricorns for slouch hats or vice versa and swapped coats before walking back again. Others hid in the gardens behind the house, keeping a close eye on the back door. It had taken several hours before they had been rewarded with what they were seeking: a man carrying a pack who went boldly up to Webley's front door and was admitted at once. When he came out again, they waited for him to pass out of sight and then arrested him.

As he read through the letter, Adam pictured the scene in his mind. Ross's men loitering in doorways and at the mouths of foul-smelling alleys, trying to pretend they were doing anything except keeping watch on the house where Webley lived. Others walking past again and again in different guises. They might even have organised one of their number to pose as a beggar, squatting near Webley's door, holding up a hand and pleading for "just a few coppers, please" when anyone came close enough.

Then that moment of sudden excitement, when a man carrying a pack on his back was spotted walking steadily towards the house they were watching. What would he have been wearing? Adam envisaged a man dressed in the typical smock of the Norfolk countryman, his britches splashed with mud from the road and heavy hobnailed boots on his feet. As instructed, the watchers would let him enter without hindrance, though the fake beggar might have tried to wheedle a ha'penny out of him and been rewarded with a curse or two and an attempt to cuff him around the head, easily avoided.

After that, more waiting. How long would he remain inside? Would he leave by the same door as he had come or try to slip out via the back entrance? Could those watching the back door be trusted not to miss him?

Five minutes probably passed, then seven. Excitement turned to anxiety. Had they let him get away somehow? No, there he was again, leaving through the front door and striding away full of purpose, intent on what he had just been ordered to do. According to Ross's letter, three men had been detailed to follow him and arrest him once he was out of sight.

At first, the man had blustered, Ross said, trying to get his men to believe he was simply visiting a customer. They ignored him. Instead, they dragged him off to where Ross himself was waiting in the Bridewell. There they searched him, their rough hands seeking out the written message he must have been given. There was a moment of doubt at first when they found nothing; a concern that the message may have been oral, a phrase to be repeated verbatim, and the man they had seized might refuse to divulge what it was. Finally, success — only two messages not one.

By the time the packman was brought to him, Ross wrote he had been waiting impatiently for several hours, eager to question the prisoner. First, however, he opened the two messages and scanned the contents. The first was simple, "Two 200-ton schooners leaving for Baltic on tomorrow's high tide. Barley, wheat and malt". The other was written in some sort of cipher, addressed on the outside merely to "Le

Capitaine". That he had sent at once to a local man they had used before to decipher such messages.

There was no bluster from the packman after that. The messages found on his person had already condemned him. Confronted by this grim-faced, professional inquisitor, Adam thought, he would quickly answer every question put to him, stressing over and over again that he was merely a messenger. He had no idea of the meaning of what he was carrying. He wasn't even able to read.

Stripped of the whining, the pleading for mercy, the repeated excuses of ignorance, Ross continued, his story was simple. He had been told to head for the cluster of fishermen's huts at Kessingfield, travelling as fast as he could and keeping out of sight wherever possible. The moment he arrived he was to hand over the letters entrusted to him to a certain Jethro Clayton, one of the fishermen there. What happened after that the fellow didn't know. All he could add was that this was a regular assignment undertaken every time he returned to Norwich to refill his pack.

Was he the only one employed in this way? Certainly not. He knew of at least four or five others, packmen like himself, who were involved. Were messages the only things they carried? He shook his head. Sometimes it was bundles of papers, he told Ross, thick ones. Once or twice he had guided foreign-looking men and left them hiding in Clayton's hut.

At this point, Ross added, he broke off briefly to dispatch two men to ride as fast as they could to Kessingfield and arrest Jethro Clayton. Then it was back to the questioning. Was the packman always sent to Kessingfield? Not always. Sometimes he was told to go to Bacton or Mundesley, but always somewhere along the coast, somewhere quiet. Was he ever given anything to bring back with him to Norwich? Never. Once he had delivered what had been entrusted to him, he resumed his normal route through the villages, selling the goods that he was carrying.

There it ended. Despite fifteen or twenty minutes more of hard questioning, there was nothing else to be learned. The packman was now safely lodged in the gaol at Norwich Castle and the watch on Webley had been resumed.

There was a scribbled postscript.

News has just reached me that Webley has left his home and is heading out of the city northwards, along the road towards Cromer. Three of my men are directly behind him. As soon as they can find a suitable spot, they will arrest him and bring him back here to me. I will visit you very soon to tell you what I learn from him.

P.S. Almost forgot to tell you that my men searched Dalston's lodgings thoroughly and found the coins that Webley's men had missed.

What had caused Webley to try to escape, assuming that was what he was doing? Had Ross's men been spotted? Would Webley confess? All unanswerable questions at this stage. Once again, there was nothing that Adam could do other than wait.

※

Ross must have questioned Webley through the evening and into the night, because he presented himself early the next morning at Adam's house, looking tired but undeniably triumphant. Adam sat him down, called for more coffee and tried to contain his impatience until Ross had refreshed himself and was ready to begin.

'What happened when you seized Webley? Did he try to deny everything?' Adam realised he'd already caught something of Ross's excitement, though, in truth, the pursuit of Webley and his links to the privateers had always been something of a diversion for him from his main investigation.

'It was easy,' Ross said. 'Webley has been a criminal for many years. He knew there was no escape. Why try to struggle against what was inevitable. He made the usual, useless protest about being an honest businessman going about his lawful activities. He even denied having any knowledge of a person called Frederick Dalston, nor any dealings with privateers or ships of any kind. I think he felt doing that was a sort of ritual that had to be carried out at the start.

We had all the evidence we needed to send him on his way to the scaffold.'

'What evidence was that?'

'For a start, as I said in my note to you, we had his letter in plain English containing information about the ships which had sailed and what they were carrying. That would have been sufficient by itself. Then my men searched both Webley's person and the saddlebags on the horse he was riding when they arrested him. Altogether, they found a packet of papers in code, together with bankers' drafts from most of the major banks in the city of Norwich. They amounted to five thousand, eight hundred and seventy-five pounds.'

'Those would mostly be the plunder from Dalston's lodgings,' Adam said. 'In your note to me, you mentioned your men had also found more cash when they searched his rooms.'

'As you had worked out,' Ross replied, smiling, 'the men Webley had sent to search had little idea what they were doing. They left it entirely ransacked and found the bankers' drafts, but nothing else. I'd take a fairly large wager they never looked outside at all. My men found one bag of coins tied to a rope and dropped down the hole in the privy. Rather smelly and dirty to retrieve but providing a good haul of guineas and half guineas when they washed everything off and counted the contents. Then one of them noticed that the earth at the edge of a flagstone near the privy doorway had been disturbed recently. They lifted the stone, dug a little way underneath it and found another leather bag with more coins — mostly half crowns, shillings and sixpences this time. That made another three hundred and forty-five pounds, fourteen shillings and sixpence.'

'You said there were bags of coins in Webley's saddlebags.'

'Yes, three of them. They all contained a few guineas and half guineas, mixed in with Spanish dollars, guilders from the Low Country and some coins we haven't yet identified. With the coded papers were a number of French banknotes and drafts on Paris banks.'

'How much did that amount to?'

'Counting just the coins whose values we can guess at, I reckon there must be somewhere around four hundred to four hundred and fifty pounds worth. On top of that, the banknotes and bank drafts amounted to almost ten thousand francs. What that comes to in English money I have no idea.'

'Altogether a significant amount of money,' Adam said. 'Webley must have been planning to live in France, or wherever he was going, in some comfort. Do you think that was his complete hoard of ill-gotten gains?'

'It must have been. My men virtually tore Webley's lodgings apart and found nothing more. The wretched little runt knew the game was up and was trying to make a run for it to save his neck.'

'The other message that Webley gave to the packman — the one that was in code or cipher — was your man able to decipher it?' Adam thought he could roughly guess the content, but it would do no harm to be certain.

'I should have mentioned that earlier, if only because it was that message which made us realise that we had to act as quickly as we could and arrest Webley before he could slip away. Our man said it was written in quite a simple cipher. Obviously, Webley had neither the education nor the intelligence to use a more complex one or write in French. What it said was, "Your friend in the city has to leave urgently. He will be on his way by the time you receive this and needs safe passage. Tell the one who brings this where you will wait for your friend to join you". As soon as this man Clayton had returned from delivering the earlier messages to the smugglers, he would doubtless have found Webley hiding in his cottage, demanding to be rowed out to the selected spot where he could be picked up.'

'You confronted Webley with all that you had found?'

'We did. Against such damning evidence there was no possibility he could maintain his innocence. He tried a little bluster, gave up and then confessed all the details of his enterprise. It took a little more time to squeeze out of him the name of the person who brought him the coded papers. A man called Septimus O'Neill, as it turned out. Sir Percival had been keeping an eye on him for some time but had never caught him doing anything untoward. It was O'Neill who contacted Webley each time to tell him when to expect men to arrive who needed to be given safe passage out to sea.'

'Webley tried to protect O'Neill, did he? That was loyal of him.'

'I think that was due to pride more than anything else,' Ross said with a grin. 'He couldn't bear to think of himself being so craven as to send another man to the gallows along with him. Between us, we soon disabused him of that notion. You may be certain Sir Percival's men will have arrested O'Neill too by now. He's doubtless being questioned with some severity to make him disclose the names of anyone else involved. Within a day or two, we'll have all the conspirators. Traitors every one of them. Passing secret messages to the enemy and helping prisoners of war and spies to escape are worse crimes than making it easy for foreign privateers to seize English ships and English cargoes. The whole lot will be tried in London — probably *in camera*. The government won't want the details of how the escape route was arranged and managed to become public, in case somebody tries to do it again somewhere else.'

'Does that mean that Frederick Dalston's part in this enterprise will also remain hidden?' Adam asked.

'I imagine it does. As it turned out, he was really no more than Webley's messenger boy; the one who rode to and fro collecting the details on ship sailings and passing them to Webley. He'll be mentioned during the trial but his name, along with the rest of the evidence, will not be released. It's possible nothing will be said about this matter at all outside the courtroom. Even the executions may be carried out secretly in the grounds of some prison. If any mention of this business appears in the newspapers, it will be no more than to say that members of a dangerous group of French spies have been rounded up and executed.'

'One last point,' Adam said quietly. 'What did Webley say when you asked him about the murder of Frederick Dalston?' He knew Ross was eager to get away, back to Norwich and his prisoner. Still, it was this part, left to the end as he knew it would be, which was of real interest to Adam.

'He swore he had nothing to do with it,' Ross replied. 'Wouldn't be shaken from that refusal whatever I said. He was happy to admit he intended from the start to defraud the young fool. Even if Dalston hadn't been killed, Webley planned to wait until he knew Dalston was getting ready to leave Norwich and then he would send his men to break into Dalston's rooms and steal everything of value they could find there. The murder simply made it easier to take what he wanted. Since he would have taken the money anyway, he kept repeating that he had no reason whatsoever to add murder to theft.'

'You believed him?'

'I did. Webley knows he is going to be hanged. Confessing to murder would not make any difference to that. To my mind, both his words and his manner had the ring of truth. During my career, I've seen many men who proved to be skilful liars under pressure. I've learned through long experience how to see through their protestations and ignore their deceptions. Webley was telling the truth, you can take that from me. Nothing will make me change my mind on that point. Whoever killed Frederick Dalston, it was not Obadiah Webley.'

'So, what comes next?' Adam asked. 'You have Webley together with all the evidence you need to see him pay for his crimes. I imagine he'll be taken to London and you'll hurry to report to Sir Percival Wicken yourself.'

'Unless you tell me you still need me here, Sir Adam. We've organised a party of dragoons to escort our prisoners to the capital tomorrow. I plan to go with them, unless that causes you any problems. I'll then return to Norwich in a few days, I imagine, to get on with my normal work. Of course, I'll continue to be at your disposal if you need me. You know how to make contact.'

'For you to go to London will cause me no inconvenience at all, Mr Ross,' Adam said. 'Nor do I believe that you can be of further assistance to me in discovering the murderer of Frederick Dalston. I was certain in my own mind that Webley wasn't the assassin before this and would have been amazed had I found I was wrong. I must look for my killer elsewhere.'

'Where will that be?' Ross asked.

'I wish I knew. Every avenue I have explored so far has proved unfruitful. I'm certain I'm missing something — something vital to the discovery of the truth. Sometimes I think I feel it hovering somewhere at the back of my mind, always slipping away when I try to look at it closely. I fear I may eventually be forced to admit I'm going to fail this time.'

'You won't fail, Sir Adam,' Ross said earnestly. 'Of that I have no doubt. I only have to look at the way you took the investigations I had been pursuing for months, without even a sniff of success, and brought them to a conclusion in a little over two-and-a-half weeks. You'll find the person you're looking for. All you need to do is to be patient with yourself.'

'I do hope you're right,' Adam said. 'Now, Mr Ross, give me your hand and let me express my deep gratitude to you for all you have done. Please give my best regards to Sir Percival when you see him.'

'I have already heard that Sir Percival is elated with the success here,' Ross said, 'and I have no doubt that he will be writing to you in due course to convey the thanks of the government as a whole, for your part in bringing it about. Goodbye, Sir Adam. Don't forget what I have told you. Just be patient.'

AFTER ROSS HAD LEFT, ADAM STAYED IN HIS LIBRARY. THERE HE could be heard, walking up and down, talking to himself, sometimes loudly enough for anyone outside to pick up most of the words, often so softly it sounded like a whisper or faded out altogether. The servants had been given no instructions on the matter, but none of them ventured to disturb him. Lady Alice had gone out to make calls on various friends. She could be neither consulted on the proper course of action nor persuaded to intervene in whatever was going on behind the library door.

'Master hasn't taken a drop o'drink or a bite o'vittles all day,' Hannah said to the cook as the hours passed and the door stayed shut. 'He must be powerful hungry and thirsty by now. Should I take him something d'you think?'

'I reckon he'd be best left on his own when such a mood comes upon him,' the cook replied, turning aside the maid's anxious enquiries with a smile. 'If he do need anything, I'm sure he'll call. Doesn't do to interfere with the ways of the gentry, in my opinion. There's times when no sensible body can make head nor tail of what they does. But you can be sure that if you try to help 'em out — return 'em to the real world, as you might say — all you do get for your troubles is a mouthful of abuse. Wait till her ladyship comes home. She knows how to handle him. You leave things be.'

Adam finally emerged in time to join his wife at the dining table, though he scarcely spoke during the meal. He ate mechanically, his mind still far away. If anyone had asked him, when the meal was over, what had been set before him and what he had actually consumed, he would have been at a loss to give an answer. Only when he sat with his wife in the drawing room, nursing his usual glass of brandy in one hand, did he emerge sufficiently from his cogitation to give her a summary of all that Ross had reported to him.

'Mr Ross must be pleased and proud with what the two of you have achieved,' Lady Alice said when her husband's narrative came to an end. 'It's quite a feather in his cap as well as yours.'

'Oh yes,' Adam responded, 'Ross was like a dog with two tails, unsure which to wag the most. It's all right for him. His task has been completed more than successfully. He can hurry back to London to bask in the applause. None of it helps me find Frederick Dalston's killer though, does it?'

'It doesn't hinder you either, my dear, so there's really no cause for being so gloomy. Just think through what you know and look for something you've missed along the way.'

'What do you think I've been doing ever since Ross left?' Adam cried. 'I know that somewhere I've taken a wrong turn, but I'm damned if I can see where.' Noting his wife's frown, he hastened to apologise. 'Sorry for the language, my dearest, but I couldn't help it. This business is driving me nearly mad with frustration.'

'May I make a suggestion?'

'Anything! I have no new ideas left.'

'All along, you've been looking for someone who hated Dalston enough to want to kill him. Someone driven by the need for vengeance or the desire to make the man suffer as he had made them suffer. Naturally, that had to mean someone Dalston had hurt fairly recently; probably someone in Norwich, since that was where he had been living.'

'That's right and I found no one.'

'You've also told me more than once that you couldn't understand why any of them would have chosen to kill the man seven or eight miles away in a remote area amongst woods and fields.'

'Right again. It still makes no sense. But if you recall, I went to see the only more local family which he had damaged — at least as far as I could discover — and came away convinced of their innocence.'

'Yet you have ignored people living barely a mile from the spot.'

Adam jerked upright. 'Whom have I ignored?'

'His own family.'

For perhaps thirty seconds, Adam sat rigid. It was as if all his blood had turned to ice and his muscles to iron bands. His brain was working so fast it had abandoned all ability to change his expression or the movement of his limbs. At length, he made an inarticulate noise, sprang from his chair, strode across to where Lady Alice was sitting, and pulled her to her feet. Towering over her — she was barely five feet tall and slightly built — Adam enveloped her in a hug worthy of a performing bear. Then, without releasing his hold, he kissed her so hard and for so long she had to flail her arms to let him know she still needed to breathe.

'How did I ever manage before you were insane enough to consent to be my wife?' he exclaimed after a moment, dropping his wife back into her chair, where she half sat, half lay, gasping for air. 'All day I've been looking for my mistake. You put your finger on it in five minutes. What a fool I've been! What a blind, thick-headed numbskull! I've done what Ross did several times: become obsessed with one route through this maze and ignored the possibility there might be others. Now you've given me the answer I've been searching for.'

'I have?'

'Of course! It wasn't hatred that caused Frederick Dalston's death. It was love. Whether love for him or love for some other family member, I'm not yet certain, but it has to be one or the other.'

Lady Alice had, by now, recovered her breath sufficiently to try to speak in a complete sentence. 'But Mr William Dalston said—'

Adam was far too excited to let her finish. 'Mr William Dalston has lied to me from the start. So has his younger son, with his neat assurances he was far away at the time. Liars, both of them!'

'But it was Mr William Dalston who asked you to find the killer,'

Lady Alice objected. 'Why set you on the trail, then tell you lies to stop you finding the answer?'

'He may have asked me to find the killer, but that wasn't his real reason for starting an investigation, was it?'

'It wasn't?' Lady Alice said. 'Now I'm completely confused. What did he want?'

'He already knew who the killer was — or thought he did. That's why he's been steadfastly urging me along the wrong path from the start.'

'So, he didn't want you to find the killer, even though he asked you to do so?'

'Only if I came up with someone other than the person he had in mind,' Adam said. 'He's been trying to protect that person all the way through this wretched business.'

Lady Alice didn't even try to work that out. 'But why should the younger son — George, isn't it? — have lied to you as well?'

'For the same reason — or near enough. He also thinks he knows who killed his brother. I would also take a large wager that his so-called alibi is actually worthless. The last thing he wanted was for me to look at it more closely. Instead, like the fool I am, I took it all at face value and went on chasing Will o' the Wisps.'

'So, what will you do now?'

'First thing in the morning, I'm going to Kessingfield Hall to have it out with both of them. But first ... first, I need to relax and you need to know how much I love you. The best place to achieve both of those, your ladyship, is not here but in your bedroom, I think. Call your maid, get her to do whatever she does to prepare you for bed, and I will join you in, say, twenty minutes — if I can wait that long.'

ᘏ 16 ᘏ

When he set out the next morning to go to Kessingfield Hall, Adam was still boiling over with rage. How dare William Dalston treat him like this! How dare he misdirect him and lie to him so that he spent days and days running around to no purpose. He had had more than enough of dancing to William Dalston's tune. He was on the right track at last. All he needed now was to somehow shake the truth out of the father and son. He was no longer seeking a killer at the request of William Dalston. This was a personal matter. His self-respect was at stake.

As a result, Adam ignored everything outside the carriage. Even when they turned once again onto the country lane to Kessingfield, he remained wrapped in angry gloom while they lurched and rumbled over the ruts left over from the frost and rain of winter. The birds spurting from the hedgerows in alarm as they heard the clatter of wheels and hooves failed to attract his attention and he paid no heed to the massive clouds, like men o'war, sailing ponderously through the immense Norfolk sky overhead. The scores of rabbits darting about on the heathland failed to draw his eye. Even when a bittern burst from the reeds nearby, only to fly straight into the path of a passing peregrine falcon seeking a meal, Adam noticed nothing.

William, the coachman, saw them and rejoiced when the bittern managed to make its escape, losing only a few feathers and a great deal of its dignity in the process. Had one of the great seagulls from the coast — one of those as big as a goose, with black wings and a wicked, yellow beak like a pirate's sword — been perched in the birch tree they were passing, singing a tune from the latest Italian opera, Adam would have been blind and deaf to it all. His thoughts were fixed on one matter only: why did William and George Dalston lie to him?

Only when he finally realised what the answer must be did Adam's fury subside. That's the trouble with upright people, he told himself. Confronted with a desperate situation, they behave like idiots. All those complicated attempts at deception were unnecessary. They'd been muddying the water and obscuring what each imagined was an unpalatable truth to no purpose.

Adam was certain neither Frederick's father nor his brother had any hand in the murder despite their lies and evasions. He was just as sure one of them, at least, knew why Frederick had been where he was that night and what the reason had been for his journey. Adam could make a good guess at the answers to both of those questions too. What he was as far as ever from discovering was what the young man had done, or what he had been about to do, that made putting an end to him so imperative.

When the carriage finally came to a stop outside Kessingfield Hall, Adam had decided he would play-act the angry victim of deception. If nothing else, it would relieve what was left of his annoyance at the way he'd been treated. Besides, there was no reason to let either of them avoid the consequences of their stupidity. If he gave them a good fright, it would shake the truth out of them. It might also prove a salutary lesson for the future.

The most pressing question now was whether he would find William Dalston and his son at home. He'd deliberately given no warning of his coming. He didn't want them putting their heads together and planning yet another set of lies to send him on his way empty-handed. He wanted to take them by surprise while both were still convinced he was away chasing shadows. He would soon put an end to that! This was no time to observe polite conventions. The more they were thrown off balance by his manner and his entry, the better.

The moment the butler answered the door, therefore, Adam pushed through it, demanding to speak with Mr William Dalston on the instant.

Some butlers would have managed to withstand the typhoon that Adam's presence had just set loose in the house. The Dalston butler was not one of them. Pale and shaking, he led the way without a word to the morning room, tapped on the door and opened it wide in response to a grunt from inside, then closed it with a sigh of relief as this terrifying visitor swept past him, still wearing an outdoor coat and hat.

William Dalston stared at Adam in horror. Then, after a moment, he began to shake and his skin turned deathly pale.

'I can see you realise why I'm here,' Adam snapped. 'I'm going to have the truth this time. The truth, the whole truth and nothing but the truth. Understand that! No more lies!'

'Sir Adam, please,' Dalston stuttered. 'Your coat ... your hat ...'

'Damn my coat and hat! There, I'll throw them on that chair if they offend you. Where is that other liar, your son, George? For heaven's sake, sit down, man, before you fall down. If the prospect of telling me the truth upsets you so much, you only have yourself to blame. Now, for the last time, where's George?'

'He's ... he went out early to shoot a few rabbits for the kitchen,' Dawson replied, his voice quivering and his eyes as round and staring as an owl's; though, in truth, he was the cowering mouse and Adam the predator, diving down to make his kill. 'He'll be back very soon ... I imagine it'll be in less than half an hour at the outside.'

'He'd better be. Next question. Where is that self-righteous friend of yours, the rector? I don't want him bursting in on us halfway through, is that clear? Tell the servants to keep him out of this room or I'll throw him out myself. This is between the three of us — me, you and your son — and I won't have him interfering, man of the cloth or not. To be honest, I find it impossible to understand how you tolerate such a fellow at all. All that pious religious cant and those biblical quotations all the time make me feel sick.'

'Mr Geddy is a good man, when you get to know him. It's just that he has an unfortunate manner at times. He was a friend of my father's and my tutor when I was a boy. He was Frederick's tutor too and George's. He's been devoted to this family for almost fifty years.'

'I didn't ask for a reference for the man, I wanted to know where he is.'

'He has a prior commitment, I believe,' Dalston said. 'Mr Geddy is something of an expert at the butts. A number of young persons from better class families round about, people of both sexes, have formed a group to practice archery. Many think it an ideal exercise for young ladies especially. It is done in the open air and demands technique and skill, rather than strength. I daresay the young men relish going along for the opportunity to flirt a little and look for potential marriage partners. Mr Geddy is their instructor.'

'How long will this archery lesson last?'

'The best part of the morning,' Dalston replied.

'Good!' Adam said. 'Before we go any further, let me make certain things clear. I know that, from the very start, you have tried your best to keep me looking in the wrong direction, telling lies whenever necessary. I am also certain you know exactly why your son, Frederick, was on that road the night he was murdered. He was coming here, wasn't he? You knew that. You'd probably arranged it between you in advance. You'd also made certain your other son, George, was safely out of the way, or rather you thought you had, but we'll come to that. I'm right, aren't I?'

William Dalston knew he was a beaten man. He had nothing left with which to respond to the furious onslaught Adam had unleashed on him. It was time to make his confession and hope to receive mercy. The only way out now was to tell the truth.

THE STORY WHICH EMERGED IN FITS AND STARTS, INTERRUPTED BY cries of distress and once by tears, revealed William Dalston in his true colours: a weak man and a mild and caring father. A man raised in an atmosphere of respectability who had been driven to desperation by a situation he was unable to understand or control. Many times, Adam was moved and saddened by it all. Even so, he kept his face stern and unyielding. Any sign of sympathy would probably have provided the man before him with an excuse to step back and avoid the most painful elements of what he had to relate.

He had been unable to curb Frederick's wildness, he told Adam. He'd tried — how he'd tried! — but always to no avail. To make his life still more wretched, George had been understandably furious at his brother's actions. As well as cursing Frederick in the most colourful terms, he turned on his father for allowing Frederick to plunder the estate to support his wild and indulgent style of life. Having a brother who was fast becoming notorious as the most abandoned of rakes had reflected on him, George said, despite his disapproval of everything Frederick had done. He'd had to suffer sideways looks and half-concealed mutterings whenever he went into Norwich. He could no longer move about in society freely, as was his due, without encountering problems caused by his scape-grace elder brother. Frederick's constant antics were ruining George's life and his sister's as well. One day, in a towering rage, the normally calm and peaceful George said he'd see Frederick dead before he let him get what he wanted. William did his best to calm matters down but could see he was not placated.

'You sent George away after that,' Adam said, 'in the hope you could persuade Frederick to lower his demands, didn't you? George was so angry you feared he would do something rash if Frederick came to press his demands and the two brothers met.'

'That's correct,' William said. 'I told you that earlier.'

'Based on your past dealings with him, it's obvious Frederick assumed you would give in again. All he needed to do was keep up the pressure. You would have done as he asked, wouldn't you?'

'I expect so. I could see no other way out. If he kept his word and went abroad, we would be free of him.'

'Had he ever kept his word before?'

The answer came in a whisper. 'No. George knew I would eventually give in to Frederick's demands, whatever I said to the contrary. He told me as much.'

Adam was still playing the implacable investigator.

'What you haven't told me up to now is that there was a period, coinciding with the time Frederick met his death, when George went missing. I expect he'd only just come back to where he should have been when your message reached him that his brother had been killed and he should return home at once. That's right too, isn't it?'

For several moments, William simply stared at Adam, his expression stricken and his eyes empty of all hope. 'It is so,' he murmured. 'How did you discover it? Why did I ever think I could deceive you?'

'Because you're a fool,' Adam said coldly. 'I didn't discover it for a long time. You and George saw to that. I wasted my time pursuing other explanations of events. Only when all of those had been exhausted, did I finally realise the truth. You're afraid that your son, George, murdered his brother. That's why you've been trying so hard to protect him. Once I realised that, the rest was obvious. You would not have imagined George was the murderer, unless you knew that he'd slipped away in secret at the critical time. Have you asked him where he was? No, I don't suppose you have. Too afraid you would recognise the lie and be forced to face an unacceptable reality.'

'I didn't dare ask him and I can only beg that you don't ask him either.'

'Oh no,' Adam replied. 'I shall ask him. Indeed, I shall demand that he tells me the truth. The only way to lance this boil that is destroying your family is to face the pain and let all the poison out.'

'I beg you, Sir Adam. Please! Have mercy! I do not think I can bear it anymore.'

'Bear it you must, Mr Dalston,' Adam replied. 'The road to healing can be very bitter. I tell you that as a physician who has had to bring immense pain to many patients in order to effect a cure. If I take pity on you now, I will be condemning you and your children to lifetimes of growing bitterness and suspicion. I will not do it! I cannot do it, on my oath as a doctor. Now, go on with your tale. We will call George in here when you have finished.'

Exactly as Adam had reasoned, the moment William Dalston had sent his son George away, he began to wonder whether it would prove to be in vain. If, as he feared, George had been angry enough to repeat his threats to other people, the news must soon get back to Frederick.

Then he would lose his temper, with the result that it would be impossible to persuade him to moderate his demands.

When Frederick came to the house unexpectedly, only a day or so after George had left, and made his demand to be paid the immediate cash value of the estate in return for abandoning all claims in the future, William felt his whole world had fallen into ruin. He'd tried his best to reason with his son, but Frederick was in no mood to compromise. Not even when his father swore to him that it would be impossible to meet his demands without bringing ruin on the rest of the family. Soon, Frederick turned to open threats, saying that if he didn't get his money within a week, he would make sure everyone in Norwich society knew the full extent of the ways he had brought disgrace on his family and on the name of Dalston.

That was the last time his father had seen him alive, storming out of the house and shouting that he would ruin them all, and that it was they, not he, who were the degenerates and the parasites. When, that same afternoon, a message reached him that George had disappeared from the house where he had been staying, William decided his very worst fears must soon come to pass. If the brothers met, they would surely come to blows. It was the following morning when the groom came to the house and told him Frederick's dead body was lying by the side of the road less than a mile away. He instantly jumped to the conclusion that George had murdered his brother to secure his own future and that of his sister. What else could he think?

At first, the coroner's inquest seemed likely to allow him to grieve without the anxiety occasioned by his fears about George. A verdict of "murder by person or persons unknown", with a heavy suggestion that it had been a botched robbery which would never be traced back to any particular criminal, should have put an end to the matter then and there. Sadly, the coroner's heavy-handed approach during the inquest started rumours that he knew very well who the murderer was and was trying to move on quickly to avoid a certain family's embarrassment.

'It looked as if your fears for George were proving correct,' Adam said. 'People knew how angry George had been about his brother's activities and were jumping to the obvious conclusion.'

'It was a nightmare and getting worse,' William Dalston said. 'The magistrate's lack-lustre attitude to any investigation was bound to convince people the rumours about George being involved were correct. I had to stop those rumours, if I could. To stay silent would give them substance. I felt I was facing the ruin of my family just as surely as I would have been if I'd given in to Frederick's demands. That's when I began to agitate for a proper investigation to be made. I told everyone that I wanted someone thorough and impartial, someone whose findings would command respect, someone who could finally discover who had killed my son.'

'What if this impartial investigator found that George was the murderer?'

'That was a risk I had to take. I had heard of you and knew you had investigated suspicious deaths before. I also knew you had a fine reputation for discovering the truth. That was why I approached you. My plan, such as it was, was simple enough. I would do everything I could to direct your suspicions onto people in Norwich or anywhere else, save only the inhabitants of Kessingfield Hall. If you then discovered someone who could be prosecuted, my nightmare would be over. Even if you didn't, I'd be able to say, truthfully, that there had been a full investigation. No explanation for the death could be found that was better than the one the coroner had given. Either way, George would be freed from suspicion and we could get on with our lives. You must understand this seemed to me the only legitimate path I could take. As soon as Frederick had returned from Oxford, I knew I had lost him. I couldn't bear to lose George as well, nor see my daughter's marriage prospects reduced to nothing.'

'Tell me exactly what happened in the two weeks or so before your son was killed,' Adam said. 'The truth, I mean, not some edited version.'

Dalston looked at him reproachfully, took a deep breath and began.

'Frederick came to see me, quite unexpectedly, about ten days before his death. He came late in the afternoon, when he knew that he was certain to find me at home. George had gone visiting friends and I was on my own. It was the old, old story. He wanted money, lots of money. It wasn't to pay his bills and debts this time, he told me, but to allow him to make a new life in America. He seemed proud of this idea. He spoke as if it made his demands reasonable, even laudable. When I said there was no more money available, his mood changed, and he became angry. I tell you, Sir Adam, I was in no doubt at that moment that something very bad was hanging over Frederick's head. He wasn't his usual, blustering self. This time he was deadly serious. If I'd had to guess, I would have said he was mortally afraid.'

'Still you refused him?'

'I had no choice. I had already mortgaged the estate more than was prudent. I tried to explain this to Frederick. It was no use. It only increased his fury.'

'That was when he threatened you?' Adam said.

'He told me he was prepared to accept nothing less than what he judged to be the immediate value of the estate. It was a ridiculous sum of money, but I could see he was entirely serious. When I still refused, pointing out that, even if I could meet his demand, it would reduce the whole family to penury, he said the rest should simply get used to poverty and disgrace. He would return on an appointed day, probably late at night, when he would expect me to have the money available. The night he set for his visit was the one on which he was murdered. If I didn't meet his demand, he declared, he would tell the whole world what he had been doing since the time he moved into Norwich. He then gave me a long list of frauds, lies and extortions, each more hideous than the last, until he ended by saying that his final acts in this country were going to bring him a fortune.'

'Did he give you any reason for wanting to throw his family's future away and leave for another country?' Adam asked.

'Oh yes,' Dalston said. 'Several. He said he had never wanted to inherit what he called "a crumbling pile of bricks, with a few fields unable to earn its owners more than a pittance". He denounced me for being weak and stuck in old fashioned ways. He called George "another tedious weakling who would never make anything of his life". He even attacked the rector, labelling him "an aging, narrow-minded, puritanical and domineering cleric, with no more idea of the world than a mole has". He, Frederick, alone knew how life should be lived. He was going to shake the dust of the land of his birth from his feet and go where people were full of enterprise and the desire for freedom. There he would start a new life.'

'And he needed to do this in a great hurry?'

'He told me that his last scheme would probably prove to be the most dangerous of them all. If he didn't leave England as soon as he could, he would most likely lose his life, either by murder or on the gallows. That was when he stormed out of the door. I never saw him again.'

Adam knew they were coming to the end of what William Dalston would be able to tell him, but there were still a few points which had to be raised.

'What did you do after that? Did you talk to anybody? Did you send a message to George asking him to come home?'

'George was better off where he was — or so I believed. What did I do? Lost a good deal of sleep. Probably reduced my lifespan by a good few years through worrying. There was nothing I could do.'

'Did you discuss the problem with the rector?'

'I did, fool that I was. I thought he might offer me some support and comfort. Instead, what I told him seemed to bring him to a state of blind fury. Of course, he knew exactly what the effect on the family would be if I gave in to Frederick's demands. His first response was to call down the wrath of God on my errant son, declaring that he wasn't going to sit back and see the Dalstons disgraced in such a way, even if I was. It took some time to calm him down so that he could give me a more rational response. I won't bother you with how earnestly he urged me to pray for deliverance — I know you have little truck with such things — so I'll tell you the practical suggestions only. The most sensible one, to my mind, was that I should speak to my bankers and obtain the very smallest loan that could appear to be an attempt, on my part, to satisfy Frederick's demands. If Frederick was truly desperate to escape revenge for his misdeeds, the rector thought he would most likely take whatever he was offered and leave. If that didn't work, I should try saying that the amount I had was all I could obtain at short notice. To raise any more money would take several months.'

'Did the rector really believe that either of these excuses would be sufficient to prevent Frederick from carrying out the threats he had made to you? To me, it sounds more like standing in front of a raging tiger and hoping to distract it by offering it a small leg of lamb.'

'I agree with you,' Dalston said wearily. 'Even praying would have been more effective.'

'Let me be certain I am understanding this correctly,' Adam said. 'You knew that Frederick was coming to Kessingfield Hall, late at night, on the day on which he met his death.'

'Yes.'

'What did you do when he didn't arrive?'

'In essence, nothing. What could I do? I wasn't sure where he was coming from nor how he would be travelling. If I am to be totally honest, I rather hoped he had been forced to flee the country sooner than he had expected. That way I would be free of his demands and his shameful deeds for good. I would go to my lawyers, explain the situation as I understood it and seek a legal way to break the entail my grandfather had included in his Will, on the grounds that the heir had gone abroad leaving no means by which he could be contacted and declaring he had no intention ever to return. If that failed, I would wait for the statutory period then try to have Frederick declared dead.'

'But none of that proved necessary, did it?'

'Surely you aren't suggesting that I murdered my son?' William Dalston said in horror.

'I'm not,' Adam replied, 'but it's quite possible that's what your son George thought had happened. While you've been trying to protect him, he'd been doing the same in reverse. That's why he tried to avoid my questions, all the while going about looking as if his brother's death was of no more importance to him than the likelihood of rain tomorrow. Well, let's have him in and get the truth out of him as well. It's time both of you started supporting one another, instead of giving in to unsubstantiated suspicions.'

GEORGE DALSTON WAS SUMMONED AND ARRIVED LOOKING determined and mulish. As Adam had noted previously, he bore a close resemblance to his father, though he was somewhat taller and less weather-beaten. He sat down without greeting Adam or even acknowledging his presence.

'I've told Sir Adam everything, George,' his father said. 'It's best that way.'

'You should never have asked him to poke his nose into our affairs,' his son replied. 'We should have let sleeping dogs lie. Frederick caused us far too much trouble during his life. Now it seems he's going to cause even more because of his death.'

Adam decided it was time to break up this cosy conversation. Dealing with people harshly was not something which came naturally to him and he didn't like doing it. However, in George Dalston's case, as it had been in his father's, he would get nowhere until he broke through the shell he had built around himself.

'You're a liar!' Adam began, trying to sound as formidable as he could. 'When I spoke with you before, all you gave me was a series of falsehoods. That stops now! Do you understand that? No more fabrications! You knew your supposed alibi was worthless, didn't you? That's why you tried to deceive me. You're a liar — and quite possibly a murderer.'

In one series of short sentences, Adam could see he had shattered the young man's initial composure. George turned deathly pale, his hands started to shake and he stumbled over his words.

'But ... but ... you've got to listen to me! I couldn't have killed my brother. I wasn't even here. My father can verify that fact.'

'He can't and he won't,' Adam said coldly. 'He's already admitted as much. On the morning after the day your brother's body was found, he received a message to say that you had disappeared from where you ought to have been. No one knew where you were.'

'But my father's message telling me my brother had been killed reached me there,' George objected.

'It may very well have done, but that won't help you. Your father's message and the one telling him you'd gone missing crossed in transit. As it stands, you have a perfect set of reasons for wanting to see your brother dead — he was about to plunge the whole family into penury and disgrace. You also had ample time to sneak back, hide in the wood, kill your brother and return the next morning in time to receive the message from your father. If you want to convince me, and very possibly a jury, that you were not Frederick Dalston's murderer, you have to tell me where you were.'

'I already told you. I was miles away.' It was a feeble attempt to defend himself and Adam brushed it aside.

'Prove it! Tell me where you were. Even your father thought you might be the murderer. That's why he's been trying to shield you by sending me off in the wrong direction. I say again, where were you?'

'For the love of God, George,' William Dalston said, 'tell him and be done with it. He'll keep on and on at you until you do.'

George's complexion had now turned from white to a sickly green and he appeared to be struggling to keep himself upright in the chair.

'I ... I ... I can't!' he moaned.

'Can't or won't? You have to tell me where you were and why you went there. So long as you stay silent, rumours will spread that you came back in secret to put an end to your older brother's demands once and for all. Is that what you want? Is that what you want your father to have to deal with? Get this clear in your mind. It's not just me you have to convince, it's the whole of Norfolk society. That's why your father decided to involve me in this mess. He knew that if I found the murderer and declared you and him to be innocent, those nasty rumours would be silenced forever.'

'I didn't kill Frederick! I didn't come back here, I swear it. The place I went to was not even in this direction. You do believe me, father, don't you? Please, say you believe me.'

'Sir Adam, I beg of you, stop this!' William Dalston cried, his voice throbbing with emotion. 'I can stand no more of it. Yes, I lied to you and so did George, but this punishment is more than any person could stand. Bring an end to your cruelty, I implore you. Please!'

Adam sat back in his chair. He hated himself for what he had been doing, but he knew it was inevitable if he was to clear the family from the clouds of suspicion which surrounded them. In trying to protect each other from rumour and innuendo, they had been steadily making matters worse. He suspected he could break down all George Dalston's defences if he kept going, but that really would be cruel. He knew he didn't have the stomach for it. Instead he decided to try a stab in the dark, a guess, if you like, but one he felt had a good chance of being correct.

'Very well. It doesn't matter so much anyway,' he said to them. 'I know where George was and what he was doing so secretly. He was with a woman.'

Those five words proved enough to make George Dalston explode in fury. He sprang from his chair, clapped his hands around Adam's throat and tried to squeeze the life out of him. It seemed possible he would commit murder there and then, if his father had not pulled him away.

For a few moments, Adam massaged his throat. It was as much to give William Dalston time to calm his son as for his own benefit. George's attack had appeared dramatic, but in truth had done him little harm. He blamed himself for forgetting how extreme young men's emotions could become, especially when a member of the opposite sex was involved.

By now, William Dalston was pouring out incoherent apologies on his son's behalf, begging Adam to forgive him. George, thrust back into his chair, continued to glare murderously at his supposed oppressor. Adam waved William Dalston's apologies aside and told them both, in as stern a voice as he could manage considering he'd just been half strangled, to put an end to the histrionics and listen to him carefully.

'Despite what you may feel, I'm not trying to do anything other than save you from the lifetime of misery the two of you seem determined to bring down upon your own heads. You know the rumours that are going about. I'm sure you've seen the look of suspicion in people's eyes, their attempts to avoid you whenever possible, your growing exclusion from polite society. That's due to two simple things: your own mistaken suspicions of each other and the fact that neither of you had the plain common sense to share your fears and concerns about Frederick and his death with the other.

'While I ran around, peering down blind alleys and inevitably reminding people of the wrongs Frederick had done in the past few years, the two of you probably congratulated yourselves on the way you were deceiving me. Fools you were and fools you are still; fighting me at every step of the way when I'm the best hope you have for returning to something like your previous existence.'

Father and son sat in front of Adam. They looked like two naughty boys being lectured by an enraged father. Maybe they recalled past occasions when they were told to bend over and receive a good hiding to remind them not to do something again.

Adam sighed. All he wanted to do now was get away from here. His mind was whirring with fresh possibilities and he needed time to sort them out.

'Let's begin again,' he said. 'George. If it helps you to keep your temper, let me tell you that I don't think you are involved in your brother's death in any way, however much you keep trying to put a noose about your own neck. Nor do I think your father was involved. Just tell me, plainly, everything you did between leaving here and when you received the message from your father telling you to return. If you do that, I shall leave immediately and this wretched business will be almost at an end.'

George looked at his father for a long moment, then nodded slightly and started to speak. He passed quickly through the first part of his narrative, merely confirming what his father had said many days before. Even now, it appeared, he didn't know precisely why he had been sent away. All that mattered was that he had, and at a time which was most inconvenient for what he had in mind. He confessed he had fallen deeply in love with a young woman and, so he believed, she loved him with equal fervour. They wanted to get married only to find what appeared to be insuperable barriers to bringing that about.

'Your father would not have approved of her?' Adam said.

'I have reason to believe that my father would have been delighted,' George replied. 'Her family were the problem. Thanks to my brother's antics, they felt I was an entirely unsuitable person to be considered as a husband for their daughter. Indeed, when they discovered we were in communication with one another, they forbade her to have any further contact with me on pain of being sent away.'

'But the two of you ignored this prohibition. Am I correct?'

'You are. There is a mutual friend who is aware of the love we bear one another and was willing to help us. She—' He stumbled. He'd been going to use the young woman's name and realised it only at the very last moment. 'My love would write to our friend, folding a short note to me in with the letter before she sealed it. Our friend would then pass it on to me and I would reply in the same way.'

'Yet you were still desperate to meet, weren't you? That's where you disappeared to.'

'It was,' George said, 'and I was telling you the truth when I said it was not even in the direction of the road to Kessingfield Hall. Happily, for us both, the woman I love and her family live not too far away from the place where I was staying. Dearest——' Again the slight stumble. 'My fiancée is an excellent horsewoman and goes riding nearly every day. We had arranged that she would take her ride that afternoon. I would be waiting for her in a suitable spot out of sight of prying eyes.'

'And you stayed away all night,' Adam said in a level voice. 'Many people would find that suggestive.'

'Then they would be wrong!' George replied. 'I stayed away because she was unable to come. Instead, she sent a young groom, something of a favourite of hers, with a message explaining that her mother had suddenly decided to require her presence on a visit to an elderly relative who lived several miles away. Now the only time my friend could get away would be very early the next morning. I decided it was too risky to try to slip away a second time, so I took a bed at a local inn for the night. Alone, in case you still wondered.'

'And the next morning? You met as arranged? What was the purpose of your meeting, beyond, I don't doubt, a chaste kiss or two?'

'We were making the final arrangements to elope,' George said. Something of his previous defiance had returned. 'I can see you laughing at me, but I can assure you it's true. It was the only way we could ever be together, even if it meant her family disowning her and the consequent loss of her dowry.'

'How heedless those in love can be of practical matters,' Adam said, and then suddenly realised how much he sounded like his mother. 'You may find that much has changed, now that you are the heir to the estate. A younger son has few prospects, unless his family can afford to give him enough money to get started on his own. Perhaps by buying him a commission in a favoured regiment or funding the education that would allow him to enter the church. That will all have altered, especially if you and your father start to work to improve the estate and, thus, increase its overall value. I suppose you still won't tell me the young lady's name.'

'Not if you threaten me with death,' George said fiercely. 'I cannot risk her being sent away somewhere where I can no longer communicate with her at all.'

'No matter,' Adam said, his voice mild. 'It has taken me a good deal of unnecessary effort, but I can see that you have now told me the truth. I suggest you and your father put some of the energy you have previously put into trying to deceive me into thinking of ways to convince this young woman's family that you are acceptable after all.'

'So, you believe me?'

'I would have believed you at the very beginning,' Adam said, 'had you told me the truth.'

❧ 17 ❧

Once Adam was safely back in his carriage and heading home again, his mind began working furiously. Several times during his conversation with the two Dalstons, father and son, he had registered a tingle as something they said alerted him to an aspect of his investigation or a connection he had somehow missed. At the time, he could do no more than hope to be able to recall whatever it was later. Now he sought desperately to make sure none of these revelations had been lost.

The essential point, he realised, brilliantly clear at last, was that he had not only been misled into looking outside the Dalston family, he had also allowed himself to ignore things which should have been plain to him almost from the start. In particular, he had ignored the role of the rector. Even worse, his image of the rector and his likely actions had been too simplistic and coarse-grained to reveal the truth. He'd viewed the Reverend Simon Geddy only as the very worst kind of clergyman: pompous, self-righteous, puritanical and narrow-minded. The kind of man who would respond to every situation — whether it was a cry for help or a request for advice — with an empty series of biblical quotations, or some hackneyed piece of conventional moral injunction.

All that was correct, but it was only part of the truth. Simon

Geddy had played a much more sinister role in events surrounding the death of Frederick Dalston. Like some evil puppet-master, he had lurked in the background, manipulating William Dalston into being his means to carry out what he intended and escape afterwards unscathed. Adam should have recognised him at once as a bully; the kind of man who would be brave only until the object of his anger stood before him. Then he would hide and avoid any open confrontation. If retreating into his role as a stern minister of the Established Church was not sufficient, he would throw out a fog of biblical quotations and pious cant; or hide behind William or George, while they played out the roles he had assigned to them.

Everything William Dalston knew, Geddy knew soon after. Dalston consulted him about nearly everything including his finances, his family situation and especially his wayward son, even on minor matters. Throughout his dealings with William Dalston, Adam had heard many times that he discussed this or that with the rector. Every worry, every decision, every piece of news, good or bad, all were raised with Geddy, probably within hours or even minutes of them reaching Dalston himself.

All of this Adam had heard or seen and set aside as irrelevant. The one time he had met Geddy, the man had set up such a barrage of ecclesiastical verbiage and pious twaddle that Adam had tried only to dismiss him from his mind. He had even sent him out of the room, believing by doing so he could remove his influence on his discussion with William Dalston. Geddy must have been delighted! Dalston would tell him everything afterwards and Geddy would ply him with "suggestions" about what his next course of action should be.

Adam now knew Frederick's father was aware of almost everything about his son's rapidly deteriorating behaviour. He'd had it from the best source, Frederick himself. All had been passed on to Geddy as well. William had described the rector's fury at Frederick's final demand. Once again, Adam had listened, but he had not heard.

The more he thought about it, the more Adam was convinced that, behind that old-fashioned, clerical exterior, Simon Geddy was a clever and unscrupulous man. One whose emotions were powerfully focused on the well-being of the Dalston family. To say he loved William

Dalston, and all he stood for, would be to express it in terms that were far too mild. The Reverend Simon Geddy, single, childless and with the kind of forbidding personality that prevented him making friends, must have invested himself, heart and soul, in the Dalstons as a surrogate family. He had been doing this for more than thirty years.

By the time he reached this conclusion, Adam's carriage had come to the edge of Aylsham itself. He had been so engrossed in his thoughts that he'd paid no attention to the journey. Realising that he would reach home in a matter of minutes took him by surprise. He was about to sit back and relax when the final piece of the puzzle he had laboured at for so long dropped neatly into place. That was it. He knew all that had taken place on the night Frederick Dalston met his death.

At once he took his cane and banged on the roof of the carriage to attract the groom's attention. They came to a halt and a surprised young William stepped up to the carriage door to ask what his master wanted. Adam told him that they must go at once to Dr Henshaw's house rather than his own. William climbed back up to the driving seat, coaxed the horse around in a sharp left turn and set off as he had been directed. Meanwhile, Adam was left to hope that his former junior partner would not be away making house calls or otherwise engaged. His confirmation of Adam's last insight was essential. Henshaw had examined Frederick's corpse in detail. By the time Adam himself had become involved, the man had been in his grave in the family plot for several weeks.

Adam was in luck. Dr Harrison Henshaw was at home and free to answer his questions.

'By all that is holy!' Henshaw said, when Adam had finished his explanation and posed all his questions. 'That's the answer! It has to be. What a fool I was not to have thought of it myself.'

'I didn't think of it either,' Adam said. 'Not until a few minutes ago and then only because I remembered what I'd been told earlier today and put two and two together.'

'It's incredible isn't it? So plain when someone suggests it, as you have done, yet unlikely enough not to have entered your mind in years of wondering. I must have run through scores of possible explanations yet missed that one entirely. It seems ... so old-fashioned. Something from three hundred years ago, not a serious option when committing a murder in these modern times, with King George III on the throne.'

'But are you sure?' Adam asked. 'It sounds right to me and it fits the story I have been putting together all the way home from Kessingfield Hall, but you're the one who did the autopsy. I wasn't even in the county at the time.'

'Of course, I'm sure,' Henshaw said. 'Short of having the thing in my hand and being able to make the comparison, I could not be more certain. This time you have surpassed even my previous lofty opinion of your abilities, Sir Adam. It's a stroke of genius!'

'Stuff and nonsense!' Adam said. 'At best it's no more than a belated realisation of something which should have occurred to me many days ago.'

'What next?'

'There's only one thing I can do. All that I have so far is merely supposition, backed up, I'm glad to say, by your expert opinion. Would it make a sufficient case to bring the man to trial? I doubt it. Would a jury convict him, especially given the status and background of the accused? I think they would be most reluctant to do so, especially if the defendant put up a spirited argument. It would be easy to point out there was not a single material fact — not one piece of independent evidence — to back up the prosecution's case.'

'He'll get away with it then,' Henshaw said. 'There's nothing you can do to stop that happening.'

'So far as I can see at present,' Adam replied, 'I have only one option. That is to go to his home tomorrow and confront him, hoping for a confession.'

'Take him by surprise, you mean.'

'There will be no surprise involved,' Adam said sadly. 'Of that I'm certain. He will have had his defences ready long before I can reach him.'

BACK AT HOME, ADAM FOUND A LETTER FROM ROSS WAITING FOR

him, sent from London. The principal matter it contained was to tell Adam that Obadiah Webley, the packman, and the fisherman from Kessingfield, Jethro Clayton, were now safely lodged in the Tower of London undergoing additional questioning and awaiting trial.

As Ross had expected, all trials connected with the matter were to be held in secret before a special panel of judges, headed by the Lord Chief Justice himself. In Webley's case, the verdict was as obvious as the sentence. He would hang. The other two might escape with lighter sentences on the grounds that they had been minor, if essential, elements in the conspiracy. However, since the crimes had been most serious, the least they could expect would be lengthy prison sentences.

Under questioning, and in an attempt to obtain mercy from the court, all three had hurried to name many others who were involved. As a result, Wicken's men in Norfolk had arrested three other packmen and a tinker. The constable from North Walsham was in the process of seizing five additional fishermen from various coastal villages. One other man was at sea but would be taken as soon he returned with his catch. After that, all ten of them would join their fellows in the Tower.

The names obtained from Webley were of the greatest value. These were people intimately involved in the affair, not mere messengers. Two conspirators had been taken in London and three more in Portsmouth and Chatham. So far, none had named all the spies whose messages were being conveyed via Webley. Still, these were early days. There was ample time to apply yet greater pressure. Perhaps as a foretaste of things to come, premises had been raided in several small towns in Sussex and Kent. A total of two undoubted spies, twenty-two escaped French prisoners-of-war and seven Irish rebels had been taken into custody. The spies would be interrogated, then executed. The prisoners would be returned to their cells in accordance with their status as prisoners of war. The Irishmen would be subjected to close questioning before being sent back to prison and trial in Dublin. If any proved to be convicted rebels who had taken up arms, they too would be executed. The Norfolk conspirators had been planning to help all of these men escape to France via the beaches of Norfolk and the privateers waiting offshore. Wicken was delighted that such an important route out of the country had now been blocked.

All in all, Ross wrote, an exceptionally satisfactory haul with the prospect of more to follow. Not surprisingly, Sir Percival had been loud in Sir Adam's praises; so much so that word of his contribution had already reached the King himself.

That evening, Adam showed Ross's letter to his wife and allowed himself a little time to bask in the warm sunlight of her pride and pleasure in what he had achieved. Then, as had now become his habit, he told Lady Alice all that had happened to him during the day.

When he had finished, she sighed and shook her head. 'A sad affair all told,' she said. 'I am appalled at the misery apparently rational people inflict on one another, merely by concealing what they should have brought out into the open and discussed with proper frankness.'

'They were afraid,' Adam replied. 'It was as simple as that.'

'I hope you weren't too hard on young George, or on his father, come to that. I know both had lied to you, but even so ...'

'William Dalston has been reaping the results of failing to take a firm stand with his eldest son after he returned from Oxford, so full of bitterness and resentment.'

Adam was in no mood to view the behaviour of either of the Dalstons indulgently.

'I suspect he hoped it was something Frederick would grow out of,' Adam continued, 'if he looked the other way and gave him his head for a while. It's impossible now to know how Frederick viewed his reception, but I wouldn't be surprised if he mistook indulgence for indifference and bewilderment for disdain. At that time, he was full of resentment at what he must've seen as the unfairness of the world. He and his father probably never had an honest conversation in their lives. If they had, maybe the son would have realised that taking out his anger on those around him would leave him isolated at the very time he most needed support and understanding. As for George ...'

'First love can be a terrible trial,' his wife said. 'Perhaps the ancients were right to see passion as a form of madness; something to be avoided, not sought out.'

'It's certainly been doing terrible things to George Dalston,' Adam replied. 'You're quite wrong, if you think I have no sympathy for the young fool. From what he told me, he became romantically attached to what first seemed to be an entirely suitable young lady. She reciprocated his affection and was quite willing, perhaps eager, to become his wife, despite the fact that George is too young to be considering matrimony, in my opinion.'

'I was just seventeen years old when I married my first husband, Sir Daniel,' Lady Alice said quietly.

'Young, innocent and in the first bloom of beauty,' Adam replied, grinning.

'Don't mock me, husband! I was all of those things, I assure you. Dear Sir Daniel died scarcely five years into our marriage, remember. Now, here I am, married to you just over a year later and not nearly as aged as you seem to believe.'

'I didn't know you then, but I can't believe that you were any more beautiful than you are today. Not quite so innocent, perhaps.'

'Pish!' his wife replied. 'A clumsy attempt at a compliment, my dear, though the sentiments are appreciated. As for losing my innocence, that is something you ought to see as a benefit.'

'Indeed, that is something for which I thank Providence daily. You know, I still can't quite believe you were willing to marry me. Surely a young, wealthy and incredibly beautiful widow could have found someone far better than a country physician.'

'Enough of this nonsense,' Lady Alice said, smiling at her husband in her turn. 'You can fish for compliments and lavish all the praise on me that you want at another time. Let us return to the sad business of Frederick Dalston.'

'If you recall, we were actually talking about brother George and his troubles. He doubtless saw his brother's increasingly deplorable behaviour was not only going to destroy the whole family, it was threatening to snatch away the woman he had set his heart on. Quite a powerful reason for murder, don't you think?'

'Unquestionably. Yet you tell me you don't believe the one brother murdered the other.'

'I am certain they did not. By the end of tomorrow, I very much hope that I will have proved it. George can return to pursuing his lady love and everyone can forget about Frederick Dalston for good. No, the local people will probably turn him into a bogeyman to be celebrated in folktales. Wicked, but harmless once the tale is over.'

'I just wish you hadn't caused father and son so much pain in the process of tracking down the killer,' Lady Alice said.

Her husband smiled at her. 'You forget that I am, first and foremost, a physician, my dear. Faced with a suppurating wound spreading its poison further into a patient's body, no physician can afford to be squeamish about causing pain. All that poison has to be drained away and the wound cauterised before healing can begin. If that isn't done, and done quickly, the patient will die. It's an intensely painful process, I'm sure, but utterly necessary. In his family, Frederick Dalston had become just such a wound. The poison of his behaviour had to be drained away and the lesion purged of further contamination. Had I held back through a mistaken sense of pity, the Dalston family would be facing poverty and disgrace.'

'Yes, I can see that,' his wife said sadly. 'It's like cupping and bleeding I suppose. Both inflict pain, yet may prove the best way to bring about a cure.'

'Exactly so. I'm grateful I'm not a surgeon. Imagine cutting off someone's limb, while they squirm in agony with only a draft of rum or brandy to dull the pain. Sawing away with your ears full of their screams of anguish. Only apothecaries are able to dispense their powders and potions without fear of inflicting pain.'

'Perhaps that would have been a better path for you to follow, like your friend, Mr Lassimer.'

'Handing out patent medicines and making up pills and potions all day?' Adam screwed up his face in horror. 'It would drive me insane within a week. It suits Lassimer well enough, but he and I are different in many ways.'

'You both pursue defenceless widows,' Lady Alice said archly.

'Lassimer undoubtedly hunts comely widows. He's more than happy to admit it,' Adam replied. 'Not me though. I only sought one widow and she was — and is — very far from defenceless. Once I had caught her — or was it the other way around? — it ended my hunting days for good. I doubt that the widows with whom Lassimer dallies are so defenceless either. They certainly don't seem to run away. If the man himself is to be believed, all have been more than willing to accept his advances. If he's escaped matrimony for as long as he has, it isn't for any lack of snares laid in his path.'

'Why do men always view matrimony as a trap?'

'Oh no, my dear,' Adam said, waving a finger at her in mock rebuke. 'I'm not going to join in that kind of dispute with you. Even I can see it's a trick designed to lead unwary husbands into condemning them-selves out of their own mouths.'

'What a shame,' Lady Alice replied. 'Then let us be serious again. You know who killed Frederick Dalston, don't you?'

'Yes,' Adam said simply. 'At long last I can see who it was. I also know why it was done and how. All that is left is to try to prove it. And that, I fear, may well be beyond my ability to bring about.'

✵ 18 ✵

dam was quiet and abstracted over breakfast the next morning. He wasn't looking forward to the prospect of confronting the rector of Kessingfield, in part because his own hand in this game of cat and mouse was so weak. He was sure in his own mind that the accusation he must put to the Reverend Mr Geddy was true. Geddy was the one who had sent an arrow into Frederick Dalston's back, then laid him out neatly by the side of the road. He was equally certain that he could prove none of it. If an appeal to the man's conscience failed — as he suspected it would — any attempt to make him admit to what he had done would prove hopeless. Some denials, accompanied by loud blustering and a torrent of biblical quotations, and Adam would be forced to return empty-handed. Adam's deep dislike of the rector and the particular variety of religiosity he espoused meant that what lay ahead amounted to a morning likely to leave a bad taste in the mouth for many days to come.

He couldn't back out now, of course, though that was what he would most like to do. He never relished being involved in angry confrontations. Escape was a nice thought, but impossible. If he shirked what was now plainly his duty to justice and his own integrity, he would never forgive himself.

If Lady Alice had been surprised when her husband told her where he was going, she wisely stayed silent. Only when he was about to leave the house to travel to Kessingfield did she place a hand on his arm and softly reaffirm her complete faith in him, whatever the outcome.

The route from Aylsham to Kessingfield Hall was becoming all too familiar by now. It began with descending the hill out of the town, followed by a route through well-cultivated fields, before crossing the River Bure and heading for the village of Itteringham. After that, there were several miles of mixed common grazing and heathland to be traversed until you reached the turnpike road. A short distance along it, in the direction of Cromer, there followed a left turn onto a rough, rarely used lane towards Kessingfield village. There you would find the Hall, the small parish church with its round, flint tower and the rectory sited conveniently alongside.

Adam tried to look out at the countryside as they passed and focus on noting signs of spring. It was no use. His thoughts kept returning to what must have happened to cause the rector to forget his Christian principles and opt for murder as the only way to end the Dalston family's descent into ruin.

It must have begun when Frederick returned from Oxford, full of rebellion and anger. Like the young man's father, Geddy would probably have been taken by surprise by the change. But where William Dalston was a weak man, the rector had enough strength of mind and moral certitude for ten. Maybe he calculated that, provided Frederick's father followed his advice, all could be set straight in time. With that in mind, he would have determined to do all he could to strengthen William Dalston's resolve to bring his son to heel.

Attempts to curb Frederick's behaviour in that way only made it worse. The weak, indulgent father was no match for a child bent on a mixture of naïve fantasy and personal destruction. The more Frederick rebelled against all his father and his family stood for, the more William tried to tame him with kindness. All Geddy's frantic efforts to persuade him to exercise stern authority were set aside. Frederick's debts were settled over and over again. He was allowed to set himself up in Norwich, where his father could no longer see what he was doing, nor make any effective attempts to curb his worst excesses.

What must have made it worse for the rector was that he had been Frederick's tutor. He would have seen the young man's scornful radicalism as a personal rejection, as well as a hopeless attempt to change English society single-handedly.

The carriage was now turning into the driveway to the rectory itself, passing between a pair of once imposing gateposts. Now the wrought-iron gates designed to close the entryway were sorely in need of repair. In several places, the metal had rusted through leaving gaps in the pattern. They had also stood open so long that brambles from the hedgerow on either side had grown around them, wrapping them tightly in their stems. The driveway itself still seemed solid enough, despite the large patches of weeds and grass which had spread in from the sides and left only a narrow strip of hardened earth and gravel in the middle. Either the rector travelled everywhere on horseback, or he did not possess any vehicle larger than a dog cart. Such driveways were usually edged by lines of mature trees. This narrow track wound its way instead between overgrown shrubs, before ending in a wide circle before the house with a cracked and moss-covered fountain in the middle.

Kessingfield Rectory must have been a handsome building once. By the look of it, it was erected perhaps some hundred years previously. It still stood, solid and imposing, with two bays either side of a neat front door with pilasters either side and a curved fanlight above it. Yet clear signs of neglect were everywhere; in the crumbling mortar between the red bricks with which it had been built and the windows too. Once edged with pale stone they were now soiled with the stonework flaking away in places. In the window frames, the paint had been long dimmed by the weather and the wood was cracking and rotting away. Like many other house in Norfolk of that period, the gable-ends of the house were curved in the Dutch style and the roof covered with baked clay pantiles. Ivy had been allowed to grow up one side of the building and spread itself across the front and up over some of the tiles. What once must have been low shrubs had been neglected so that they had grown tall enough to obscure several of the windows on the ground floor. Even the remains of the garden to either side looked as if they had long been neglected and unloved. The only striking element in all this dreary prospect was a magnificent cedar tree that a former rector must have planted to provide shade and a pleasant outlook. For the rest, the whole place looked to Adam like an elderly dowager, now living in greatly reduced circumstances, yet still showing unmistakable signs of the elegance which had adorned her younger days.

Adam stepped down from the chaise and told William to wait where he was, then he walked to the front door. He expected to knock and be given entry by a housekeeper or servant. Yet, when he reached there and lifted his hand towards the knocker, he noticed the door was partly open. Perhaps one of the servants had stepped outside for a moment and was out of sight. He looked around him but could see nobody. He hesitated for some moments, then stepped inside, calling out his name in a loud voice to attract the attention of one of the servants.

Adam found himself, as he expected, in the staircase hall; a well-proportioned space with the main stairs curving upwards to the floor above. He looked around, trying to imagine why the place seemed so deserted, then tried calling out his name again and asking if anyone was there. No reply came. The house seemed dark and ill-kempt, as if its current owner had no interest in most of the rooms. It also felt extremely cold. No fire could have been lit anywhere in the house since the previous day, maybe even longer. Still no sound other than Adam's own breathing. Was the place really empty of all life? If the rector was out, would he not have left someone in charge in his absence? Something must be very wrong.

It was time for Adam to make a decision. He could walk away and leave the house unattended. That would surely not be right. Alternatively, he could try to discover the reason for the state in which the property had been left; search through all the rooms and risk someone's wrath if he was discovered doing so.

Adam made up his mind to search. Where to start? After a moment's pause, he turned to the right and opened a door which proved to lead into a dining room, as dimly lit and cold as the hall, mostly because of the shrubs growing up against the window. He then tried the room to the left side of the hall, noting as he opened the door that the space was fractionally warmer and that one wall was entirely covered by bookshelves. When he turned to enter the room properly, Adam saw the rector's body hanging from a noose of thick rope attached to a hook in the ceiling; a fitting which must once have served to suspend a candelabrum which was no longer present. In a horrid simulation of life, the draught produced by the opening of the door now caused the corpse to swing slowly around, as if the dead man was turning to see who had dared to disturb what would now be his eternal rest.

To one side of the rector's body, a chair had fallen over and one of his shoes lay at a little distance. The merest glance revealed that the man had hanged himself by standing on the chair and stepping off. The short drop would make the noose either break his neck or choke the life out of him. From the appearance of the corpse, Adam concluded the man's neck had been snapped, causing death to follow almost immediately. The public hangman could not have done a better job.

Adam was about to go back outside to tell William to go for help when he noticed a letter propped up against a glass on the table to the left of where the body hung. It was thick, obviously composed of several sheets, and addressed to "Sir Adam Bascom, Bart". It was also marked "Most Private". Adam thrust it into his pocket. Time enough to read the contents once he had summoned help to cut the rector down. William and he could probably manage it on their own, but to have at least one other person helping would make it simpler and more dignified. He hadn't liked the rector in life, but he surely deserved the concern due to his status now, however unpleasant he may have been when living.

With William sent on his way, Adam turned back into the hall. There he broke the seal on the folded paper the rector had left and read the contents. Geddy was clearly beyond mortal help, so there was no need to return to where his body was hanging. Adam had no taste at all for the ghoulish and macabre.

It was a long letter and took Adam some time to finish. Fortunately, the rector's writing was clearly formed and all was laid out neatly on the page. For a man about to take his own life, he had been unusually calm when he wrote it.

· · ·

DEAR SIR ADAM,

I am sorry for subjecting you, or whoever else should find my body, to such an unpleasant sight, but I was left with no alternative. When I returned to my home at around noon yesterday, my housekeeper told me she had noticed you arriving at Kessingfield Hall, then departing about an hour and a half later. I have often reprimanded her for nosiness. On this occasion, I was grateful for her curiosity. Naturally, I hurried over right away to learn the purpose of your visit and what you had been able to discover from talking with my old friend and pupil, William Dalston.

You will imagine my dismay when I realised he had told you all that had passed between himself and his worthless elder son. Consternation quickly turned to horror when he said you had noted my absence and he had explained that I was supervising the regular archery practice. I have made enquiries about you and learned of the previous occasions on which you have tracked down people responsible for criminal acts. Several of those I spoke with praised your insight and quick intelligence. I felt in no doubt that you would soon take what you had learned and resolve any last doubts in your mind. I suspected you already understood who must have killed Frederick Dalston. Now you would grasp how it was done. In a way, I am relieved. I thought I could go on as before, but that has not proved possible.

Let me say, here and now, that I feel no regret for my actions, any more than I would feel remorse at killing a rabid dog to prevent it from biting innocent passers-by. For that's what Frederick Dalston was. A young madman, whose thoughtless lust for money and women had already brought misery to many. I tried, when he was younger, to instil in him some sense of decorum and morality. After he returned from Oxford, it was obvious I had failed.

William Dalston had told me of Frederick's plan to continue his depredations overseas and his demand to be given what he considered to be the value of the estate. I have been William's helper and confidant since he first inherited Kessingfield. I know the parlous state of his finances, brought about by the need to settle Frederick's many debts. To mortgage the estate heavily enough to give that evil young man what he desired would have brought total ruin on the family. I could not allow that. I owe my education and my position as rector to the present squire's father. I consoled that dear man in his last days. I also made him a solemn promise, as he lay on his deathbed, that I would watch over his *son and do all I could to keep him from harm. By this final act, I shall have fulfilled that promise to the letter.*

William Dalston has always been too soft-hearted to deal with a person as thoroughly infected with evil as Frederick. This time, too, I felt sure he would give in and do as Frederick demanded, whatever the consequences. William is a good man, a loving man. He should not have been forced to face such an endless series of miseries. Watching poor William slowly sinking under their weight has finally brought me to question why a loving God should have inflicted such a curse on a decent man. To test his faith? I do not know. Very soon, unless my whole faith has been a delusion too, I may be able to find out for myself.

In the end, it became clear to me that only Frederick's death could free his family from the wretchedness he was bringing upon them. It was, therefore, my bounden duty, as a man who has devoted his life to upholding integrity in all things, to bring that death about and to do it in such a way that no suspicion could fall on Frederick's father or any other members of his family. When the coroner's jury gave their verdict — that the wretch had been murdered by a person or persons unknown — and the magistrate afterwards described it as a robbery gone wrong, I thought I had succeeded.

Perhaps I would have stayed my hand even then had I not received further proof of Frederick's continued deterioration into evil and madness.

Recently, I received an unexpected inheritance from an uncle I had not seen in many years. I thought he must have forgotten me long ago, but it was not so. He thought me his last surviving blood relative and due some recognition via a bequest from his estate. He was an extremely wealthy man by the end of his life. The "small amount" he left me in his Will amounted to four thousand pounds.

You may think me a fool, but I hoped that this would provide a way to send Frederick on his way overseas, leaving the rest of his family to live in peace. For that reason, and that reason only, I went to see him in Norwich and offered him the whole sum, on the condition that he signed a paper renouncing all future claims to Kessingfield and agreeing never to return to Norfolk or England. I knew such a document would have little legal standing, but it was better than nothing. He did as I asked and I gave him a banker's draft for the money.

You will imagine how I felt when William told me, only two days later, that Frederick had already ignored what he had agreed with me and demanded more money from his father, backing it with the most impudent menaces.

My earnest arguments and entreaties succeeded in convincing William to refuse to pay, but I knew Frederick would make good on his threat. It was obvious the time had come to act. Thanks to William, I knew when the wretch would be coming to collect his payment. I would ensure it was the last time he caused trouble. After his death, I reasoned, what he had done would soon be forgotten. No one would suspect me of involvement. I could continue as before, as the family's most loving adviser and friend.

Your investigations have brought those hopes to nothing. I do not blame you. I know William asked you to do as you have done, but I cannot claim that I do not regret your part in the decision now forced upon me. I must ensure that Frederick's death does not ruin the family's standing in society and that neither William nor George lie under any further suspicion of murder.

You have left me with no alternative but to take my own life. By doing so, I will prevent a trial for murder and all its accompanying publicity, during which the full extent of Frederick's evil deeds would have to have been revealed.

Before I do so, however, let me beg you, with what will soon be my dying breath, to conceal what I have written here. Allow the world to continue to see Frederick's death as caused by some unknown footpad. I do not ask this for myself but as my last gift to the Dalston family to save it from ruin. No good will result from these details becoming public knowledge. I implore you, do not let this become Frederick Dalston's final and most devastating blow against his family and their reputation.

Now I am within minutes of my end, I find myself plagued with more misery than I can bear. Not for the killing, as I have already explained. What torments me is the fear that my whole life may be built on a lie. I have believed and taught that a man's sinful disposition can be redeemed by knowledge of the love of God, followed by repentance and a fresh start. I tried in every way I knew to draw Frederick away from the inner wickedness I knew possessed him. I preached, I taught, I forgave him many, many times. I tried to set him an example. I tried to show him the road he was set on would bring him to ruin. And I prayed. How I prayed! None of it prevailed over his essential nature. Is it I who have failed or has the whole basis on which my religion is built proved false? If it cannot redeem one individual, how much less can it redeem the whole world? I do not know. All I understand is that I cannot live with the torment of not knowing any longer.

For many years I have suffered from periodic bouts of melancholia. As long as you burn this letter and say nothing to anyone of its contents, my death will be

*attributed to that affliction. I have given my housekeeper leave to visit her
ailing sister for a few days. My only other servant I have dismissed with a
favourable character. Thus, I have ensured neither of them will find my body. I
have also left the front door open as an invitation for you to enter, should you
come, as I hope and expect you will, to tax me with what you probably believe
was murder. I have already explained to you why it was not. If others find me
first, I can only hope that this letter will still reach you unopened. It will be up to
you then to invent some plausible explanation of what it contained.*

*Farewell, Sir Adam. I will soon stand before the Judgement Seat, where I
hope that a merciful deity will understand the situation into which I have been
placed. If not, and I am consigned to everlasting torment, I will accept my
punishment still feeling that my actions have been fully justified. Of course, if
these final doubts of mine prove correct, there will be no Judgement Seat and I
can find eternal peace and rest at the last.*

I AM, SIR, YOUR OBEDIENT SERVANT AND WELL-WISHER,
   Simon Getty, D.D., Rector of Kessingfield.

ADAM READ THE LETTER THROUGH TWICE. AFTER THAT, HE PUT IT
in his pocket. He had much to think about, and the rector's confession
could wait until he was back home. For the moment, there was a body
to deal with, the coroner to be notified and, if possible, words to be
said to lessen at least something of the grief and bewilderment William
Dalston and his family were about to suffer.

It was William Dalston himself who hurried to the rectory at the
groom's summons, along with his butler, his footman and one of his
gardeners. The three servants cut the body down under Adam's supervision, carried it upstairs and laid it reverently on the bed. Dalston
himself could do no more than sit in one of the chairs with tears
streaming down his face.

'The Reverend Simon Geddy has been rector at Kessingfield for
more than thirty years,' Dalston told Adam, after all was completed.
'For the whole of that time, he was a close and trusted friend of the
Dalston family, beginning as a young man whose education for the

church my father sponsored. To see him end his life this way breaks my heart.'

'Is there anyone who needs to be informed?' Adam asked. 'Any close family members? You will need to see the coroner learns of his death, of course. That's the law. And there will have to be an inquest, though I imagine the verdict will be a foregone conclusion.'

'The man seemed to have no family, Sir Adam. He had never married and was not the kind of person who made friends easily. He always treated the Dalston family as his own, so we will look after him and see he is buried decently. If possible, in consecrated ground too, though that is a matter for the church authorities.'

'Had he seemed especially unhappy or melancholic of late?'

'In recent months the sporadic bouts of melancholia which had affected poor Simon Geddy for many years or more had become more frequent and more intense. The behaviour of Frederick upset him greatly, especially since he had been my son's tutor in his younger years. Perhaps the murder also affected him more than anyone guessed. Whatever the reason, he had clearly felt unable to continue. I shall miss him greatly.'

Adam had now decided that, for the present, he would bow to the dead man's wishes and keep the existence and contents of the letter he had left behind a secret. William Dalston was upset enough. To tell him now that the rector had been responsible for killing his son would be an act of heinous cruelty. It would be better to murmur the conventional words of consolation and take his leave.

During the drive home, Adam thought through the whole matter again. Much as he disliked the idea of the rector' s suicide being put down merely to melancholia, he was increasingly sure no good could come from making the contents of his confession known. The Reverend Simon Geddy was immune from earthly censure. Why cause unnecessary pain to the living for the sake of an abstract idea of truth? There was only one person he refused to deceive. It was too late now but tomorrow, perhaps after dinner, he would show his wife all the rector had written. For everyone else, none of them more concerned with the truth than with finding the story had reached a satisfactory conclusion, a suitable fiction could be found.

It was past nine in the evening by the time Adam's carriage reached his house. Dealing with cutting down the rector's body, then sending Dalston's butler to inform the coroner took most of the morning. After that, Dalston had begged him to wait until the coroner arrived, since he had been the one to find the corpse and was thus best placed to give a proper explanation of the circumstances. Speaking to the coroner and magistrate also proved to be a lengthy business. Both were full of questions. Why had he gone to the rectory in the first instance? What did he think the rector could contribute to his investigation? Why go so early in the day? To all these enquiries, Adam gave the best answers he could concoct on the spot. He explained that, since the rector had known Frederick Dalston all his life, he should have been best placed to resolve the last few points concerning the young man's death. The investigation had taken far too long already and he was eager to bring it to a conclusion. That was why he had arrived so early. He wanted to avoid missing the rector, who he assumed would probably be absent on parish business later in the day. Eventually, both seemed satisfied. So much lying had proved to be a wearisome business, but they allowed him to leave.

When he reached his home again and was admitted by his butler, Grove informed him that Lady Alice had already dined and withdrawn to her room for the night. The cook would bring him some bread and cold meat if he was hungry. The events of the day had totally taken away Adam's appetite, so he said that he would require nothing, but to thank the cook for her thoughtfulness.

Still too alert to go to sleep, Adam went to his wife's bedroom, hoping to find her awake enough for him to tell her at least part of what had taken place. He found her sitting propped up against several pillows, a guttering candle on the bedside cabinet and a book in her hands.

'Is it over?' she asked him.

'Almost,' he replied. 'I was right. Simon Geddy was the murderer. He was a coward to the end. Rather than face me and go to trial for what he had done, he killed himself. He was dead when I arrived.'

'Why did he, a priest, do such a thing? It is bad enough when a layman turns to murder, but for a priest to do it ...'

'I think he felt he had no choice,' Adam replied, perching on the edge of the bed. 'You are quite lovely, you know.'

'Don't try to change the subject, husband! If you don't satisfy my curiosity, I shall be unable to sleep. Then I shall be bad-tempered all day tomorrow and make your life a misery.'

Adam laughed softly. 'A terrible threat indeed,' he said. 'Very well, your ladyship. But be aware that it is not an edifying tale.

'As soon as Reverend Simon Geddy heard I'd been talking with William and George Dalston that morning, he'd rushed to Kessingfield Hall to discover all that was said. There, learning that William Dalston had mentioned his skill at archery, he became convinced I must now know the truth of what had happened and would soon come to confront him. Since a trial would bring it all into the open, he must have felt the only way to save the Dalston family was to prevent that happening.'

'Did he love the family that much?'

'Obviously he did. "Greater love hath no man than to lay down his life for his friend" it says in the New Testament. He clearly took that literally.'

'I still don't understand why he determined to kill Frederick.'

'Geddy had convinced William Dalston not to mortgage more of his estate to meet his son's demands, since that would be bound to result in complete ruin for himself and his other children. Frederick's response was more violent than he could have expected. Rather than bowing to the inevitable he was, by this time, so firmly set on his plan to create a new life for himself overseas, he determined to ignore all restraints and demand the money he believed he needed under the threat of disclosing everything.

'Frederick's final visit to Kessingfield Hall to present his father with his ultimatum must have been the last straw. The rector realised any attempt at that stage by William Dalston to exercise his authority as head of the family was doomed. Frederick was now hellbent on destroying everything Simon Geddy held most dear: the Dalston family's good name, his father's financial and social standing, his brother's chances for the future and his sister's prospects for a suitable marriage.

All were to be sacrificed to allow Frederick to leave for a new life in America as a rich man.

'That must have been when the rector decided he had to intervene in the only way open to him; the only way which would be guaranteed to end Frederick's madness for good.'

'So, you were correct. The cause of this murder was love. The rector's love for William Dalston and his family.'

'I suppose so,' Adam said. 'Mr Dalston had told me that Geddy viewed those who lived at Kessingfield Hall as the family he had never had. Love for your family is generally seen as admirable. In this case, however, a kind of obsessive regard for the family's honour and prospects tipped over into a supposed justification for taking a life.'

'Will you have to give evidence at the inquest?'

'I will. Tomorrow morning.'

'Then it will truly be over?'

'Did I tell you how exquisite you look tonight?'

Lady Alice smiled and pushed her husband gently back to where he had been sitting. 'You need your sleep,' she said. 'Go to your room and stop looking at me like that. I can see what is on your mind. At any other time, I would welcome it but not now, not tonight. You have a busy morning before you and must look your best. No husband of mine shall appear in public with rings under his eyes. Off now! Tomorrow is another day.'

❧ 19 ❧

A dam duly gave his evidence at the inquest, trying to appear worthy of Lady Alice by looking every inch the titled gentleman. With nothing to suggest the rector had not killed himself, the legal formalities didn't take long. Medical evidence was taken first, confirming death by ligature. After that, Adam was called, but only as the person who had discovered the body. No one knew of the existence of the rector's confession but him, and he did not mention it. He stuck closely to the facts of what he had seen and done. William Dalston was called at the end and recounted the long history of melancholia suffered by the rector. The coroner summed up briefly. The jury was directed to return the only possible verdict. The law had finished with the Rector of Kessingfield. He was now the business of the undertaker and the gravedigger.

Returning from the inquest, Adam felt too restless to stay indoors. Lady Alice had gone out visiting so he took another lengthy walk. He began by heading down the hill past the parish church and across the edge of the estate surrounding Blickling Hall. The woods were now bright with the pale leaves of spring. He watched some birds carrying twigs and grasses to their nests and reflected on the way that life went on, despite all the wickedness that men concocted in their hearts. His life would be the same. No more murders and mysteries for a long time, he hoped. He had a new wife to love, a new house and estate to enjoy and a new future to forge. It was more than enough. With these cheerful thoughts in mind, he turned back towards Aylsham on the road which passed his own soon-to-be-residence of Wrigsby Hall. It was a glorious day, though the wind, as so often in this part of Norfolk, was cool and strong enough to encourage a brisk pace. Still, it served to clear his head and begin the process of setting aside the matter of murder and returning to his normal affairs.

That evening, when dinner was complete, Adam asked his wife to accompany him to the library. He then gave orders to the servants that they were not to be disturbed. He wanted to tell her all that had happened and show her the letter that Reverend Simon Geddy had left for him. He knew she could be trusted to keep it secret if he asked her to do so. He also felt he desperately needed her support for the decision he had made.

HANNAH, THE PARLOUR MAID, HAD MADE UP A SMALL FIRE IN THE grate, since the evenings were still cool, and it glowed brightly enough to assist the four candles in the wall-sconces in illuminating the room. There was also, as he had instructed, a four-branched candelabrum set on a small table close to where they were to sit. Before he settled himself in a chair on the other side of the fireplace from where his wife was sitting, Adam lit the candelabrum and went to his desk. From there he fetched Simon Geddy's letter and gave it to his wife without a word. Then he sat in his chair and waited while she read the contents.

When she had finished reading, Lady Alice handed the letter back to her husband. She took a delicate, lace edged handkerchief and wiped away the tears on her face.

'I really shouldn't have wasted my tears on that man,' she said, 'but it's so obvious he was wretchedly unhappy, even before Frederick Dalston began his career of wickedness. I suppose, by his own last words in this letter, he must stand convicted of arrogance and self-righteous pride; neither of them are qualities becoming a man of the church. Even as he prepared to take his own life, he was still refusing to accept any blame for what he had done. By killing Frederick Dalston, he had broken the Ten Commandments and acted in a way that I'm sure he would have condemned in anyone else. Instead he attempted to describe his situation as a moral dilemma, then tried to pass that dilemma on to you, my dear. What a pathetic, desolate creature he must have been at the end!'

'You said yesterday that this was a crime caused by love,' Adam replied, 'and I agreed with you. That might apply to the killing itself, but not to taking his own life as he did. The only love there was self-love. He could not face what he must have seen as the humiliation and disgrace of appearing in court and facing the hangman afterwards.'

'What about his claim that to go to court would bring Frederick Dalston's evil deeds into the open and ruin the other members of the family in the eyes of local society?'

'Nonsense, I'm afraid. Frederick's deeds — most of them at any rate — were already well known. As for the final business with Webley, the rector could not possibly have known anything about that.'

'So that, too, was simply an excuse for what amounted to self-importance and cowardice?'

'It was,' Adam said. 'Simon Geddy must have known that, without a confession, the crime could never be laid at his door. The only thing that might be provable was that Frederick Dalston was killed by an arrow fired into his back. There was no indication of who might have wielded the bow. Nothing to link it to the rector specifically. No, my dear, he had planned his crime too well to have to answer for it in any court, save that in heaven. Nor do I believe he ended his own life to avoid causing William and George Dalston the pain of knowing him to be a murderer. If that were true, why confess at all? His melancholia was of long standing and his upset at Frederick Dalston's behaviour amply confirmed by the other members of the family. No one would have guessed the real reason unless they believed me when I told them. His confession to me was part pride — see how clever I have been — and part made in hope that he could by that means prevent me telling what I knew.'

'Will you do what he asks then? Will you keep the confession he has made secret?'

'Since I let the inquest pass without revealing anything, I can hardly produce this letter now without causing a good deal of trouble.'

'If you're going to conceal what you know, why let me read the letter?'

Adam smiled at his wife. He suspected she already knew the answer but wanted to hear him say it.

'Because there is another ethical dilemma I cannot escape,' he said. 'If I claim to have finished my investigation, people will want to know whether I had succeeded in what I had been asked to do. Had I found out who murdered Frederick Dalston and why? If I speak out and reveal the letter, you know what the consequences will be for the Dalston family. To say nothing at all will be impossible — indeed, it would mean doing what the murdered man would have wished and leaving a shadow of suspicion hanging over his father and brother. Neither of those are acceptable to me. I must, therefore, tell a series of lies and half-truths, adjusting my story each time to suit its audience. The one person I cannot bear to deceive is you. That's why I let you read the letter.'

With the letter back in his hand, Adam rose from his chair and crossed to the fireplace. There he stood, silent for a moment, before throwing each page of Geddy's letter into the fire. As they burst into flame, he still waited, watching until the very last traces were consumed.

'There,' Adam said quietly. 'Now it's truly finished.'

'You're a good man, Adam Bascom,' Lady Alice said. 'I would not have married you otherwise. Sir Daniel saw your worth from the first. He told me I could trust you in all things. I believed him then because he was an astute judge of character with many years' experience in dealing with the world. Now I have seen for myself how shrewd his judgement was. I never thought I would meet another man as worthy of my devotion as my first husband. I am grateful beyond belief to see that I have.'

NEXT MORNING, ADAM BEGAN THE WEARY PROCESS OF MISLEADING his friends and helpers about his reasons for ending the investigation. The apothecary, Peter Lassimer, was closest to hand. He would probably also be the most curious about the outcome. Immediately after breakfast, therefore, Adam sent his maid, Hannah, to the apothecary's shop to ask his friend to visit him as soon as it might be convenient. She was to add that he had finished his investigation and thought Lassimer would be interested in the outcome. Just how interested he was Adam soon discovered for Lassimer accompanied Hannah when she returned.

'I cannot stay for long,' Peter said, the moment he entered Adam's study. 'I have a shop full of people and have left my apprentice on his own. Let's skip the courtesies. Just tell me the outcome so I can return to my customers as quickly as possible.'

What Adam related to his friend began with the truth and ended with complete fiction. He could only hope it would sound plausible enough to satisfy Peter's natural curiosity. He began by explaining about Webley and how he and Dalston planned to make money by tipping off the privateers. To that he added an outline description of the unconscious part Frederick Dalston had played in Webley's secret and treasonous actions, not forgetting Peter's crucial role in uncovering the means the conspirators had been using to make contact with those out at sea. After that, he turned to fiction, claiming the ship owners who had been robbed were told by Webley that Dalston was the mastermind and he was simply the messenger. If they wanted to get their money back, they should seek out Frederick Dalston and ask him for it. When the ship owners and captains asked where Dalston could be found, Webley had produced a cunning and elaborate tale. He told them that some of the ships that had been seized had paused in their voyages further to the north so that they could take the contraband aboard, hide it amongst their legitimate cargo and transport it directly to London.

As a result of the seizures brought about by Dalston's plan, the smuggling gang which operated between Great Yarmouth and Cromer had lost heavily. It was easy to imagine what they would do as a result. Dalston left Norwich immediately, probably to hide away in his original home. The gang must have guessed what he was doing and ambushed him before he could get there.

'But wouldn't Webley himself have been in danger? Why was he still in Norwich, when Dalston had already fled?'

Adam swore quietly to himself. Trust Lassimer to put his finger immediately on the weakest part of the story.

'Remember Webley had represented himself as merely the messenger boy between Dalston and the privateers,' Adam said. 'Perhaps the smuggling gang was going to come for him as well, but we got there first.'

Peter looked doubtful. 'Wouldn't the smuggling gang have tried to get money from Dalston before killing him?'

'Did I forget to mention it?' Adam said, trying to look as innocent as possible. 'We found that someone had been to Dalston's rooms in Norwich and conducted the kind of search that leaves everything broken and tumbled on the floor. I suspect they found not only enough money to cover their losses on the contraband the privateers had taken, but a good deal more besides. I did tell you that Dalston had been extorting money for some little time.'

'Did you? I must have overlooked that. My business is doing extremely well and I have been rushed off my feet. That said, I'd better get back to the shop. Yes, yes, I understand it now. Dalston was killed in revenge for one of his money-making ideas which went badly wrong. You found who did it and why, but there's no point in going further. You'll never identify the actual murderer, if it was a member of one of the smuggling gangs.'

Adam breathed a long sigh of relief after the apothecary left. That explanation had come close to disaster. Thank goodness Lassimer was so distracted by the success of his business. With any luck, he would forget about Frederick Dalston soon. The man was too curious and sharp-witted to be easily deceived a second time.

Adam now sat down to write a letter to Ross. This should be much simpler. Ross and Wicken were delighted by the arrest of Webley, the seizing of the other conspirators and the blocking of that route out of the country for secret messages and wanted people. Compared to that, the death of Frederick Dalston would be of comparatively minor interest. Ross had been extremely helpful in Adam's search, but it had always been clear his primary concern was with espionage, sedition and the escape of the French prisoners-of-war. All Adam needed to do now was to thank Ross once again for his assistance and say that he had completed his investigation and reached the conclusion that Dalston had paid the price for his various criminal activities. Exactly who had struck him down would never be known.

Satisfying Ruth Scudamore and his mother should also be easy. In his letter to them, Adam wrote it had turned out that Frederick Dalston's death had nothing to do with angry fathers or brothers. The real reason came from a series of criminal schemes he had been engaged in. One or more of those whom he had cheated had obviously decided to put an end to his activities for good. Precisely who that was would never now be discovered.

Lady Alice came into the study just as he had finished this final letter. She laughed when he told her what he had been doing and how difficult he had found it to send Peter Lassimer away contented.

'I forgot to ask you last night,' his wife said. 'How did you explain to Mr William Dalston why you were the one who found the rector? It must have seemed odd to him that you had gone to the rectory so early in the morning.'

'The man was terribly upset, so he didn't question me very closely, thank goodness. In fact, I told him that I had been surprised by Geddy's vehemence and anger in condemning Frederick's behaviour on the last occasion when I had spoken to him of it in the rector's presence. At the time, it hadn't seemed very important. Recently, however, as all other explanations for the murder were either ruled out or seemed less and less plausible, I started to wonder whether the rector knew something about the young man's behaviour that I hadn't yet discovered. Something so upsetting that it moved him to real anger. The simplest way to find out was to ask him. I had gone there early in the morning, fearing that he might otherwise be out during the day attending to the needs of his flock. I admit it sounded terribly weak, but most of it was actually true. It seemed to satisfy William Dalston anyway.'

'Another question, if I may,' his wife said. Adam nodded in agreement. 'How did you suddenly reach the conclusion that the rector had been the one who brought about Frederick Dalston's death? You never explained that to me.'

'I realised it when William Dalston at last began to tell me the truth,' Adam said. 'The simple thing that gave me the vital clue to the mystery was when William Dalston told me about the rector's skill and interest in archery. Right away, I could see exactly how the murder had been carried out. Of course, I had to check my ideas with Dr Henshaw before I was completely certain. He had examined the body and seen the wound close-up. Fortunately, he agreed with me at once. An arrow fired at close range would make exactly the kind of wound he had found in Frederick Dalston's back. After that, two other pieces of information completed the picture. The rector had lived in the area for more than thirty years and so must have known it like the back of his hand. Dalston had also admitted that he knew his son was coming to see him that night and had told the rector about it. There was the answer!'

'You'll need to spell it out a little more for me,' Lady Alice said. 'Exactly what did the rector do that night?'

'He must have gone out well before Frederick Dalston was likely to arrive and selected a suitable spot for his ambush. He'd need to hide close to the edge of the road to have a clear shot when the time came. At the same time, it was vital he would not be seen until it was too late. He might have been a skilled archer, but the moon that night was well past full. It would have given relatively little light. Even at close range, there would be ample chance to miss, alerting the rider and sending him hurrying away. Then he would be too far off to be sure a second arrow would strike its mark. I imagine that's why he shot his arrow into Frederick Dalston's back. He needed to be able to step out fully into the road and draw his bow without being seen. The man's back would have been a suitable target, even in that poor light.'

'Could he be sure of killing with a single arrow?'

'Probably not, but once the man was brought down and badly wounded, it would be easy enough to finish him off. As it turned out, one arrow was enough. All Simon Geddy had to do was pull the arrow out of the man's back, drag him off the road and give his horse a slap across the rump to send it running off into the woods. After that, he could slip away and return to the rectory. Even if his housekeeper had heard him go out and then return, it would be easy to tell her a fit of melancholia had come upon him so he had gone for a walk in the moonlight around the garden to settle his mind.'

'I wonder why he went to the trouble to lay the corpse out so neatly?' Lady Alice said.

'I wondered that too,' Adam replied. 'The best explanation I can manage is that, seeing the man dead on the ground in front of him, some vestige of decency was strong enough in his mind to cause him to do as he did. Either that, or he suddenly remembered he was a clergyman. He may even have said a prayer over the body. The man was enough of a hypocrite to have done that, even though he was the one responsible for Frederick Dalston's death.'

'So, Dr Henshaw must also know — or be able to guess — a good part of the truth of this affair. What are you going to tell him?'

'When I left him yesterday evening, I asked him to keep the whole matter secret, explaining I didn't want the murderer to guess the method he'd used had been discovered. Since that method pointed directly to the rector, or so I reasoned, it was important not to put him on his guard. As it turned out, of course, Geddy had already guessed and decided to kill himself rather than face me. I'll call around and talk to Henshaw myself later. Doctors have to be good at keeping secrets. I know I can trust him to keep this one indefinitely, if I ask him to.'

'You just said it's all over,' Lady Alice said. 'Is that really the truth?'

'It is,' Adam replied. 'I don't imagine William Dalston or his son will want to see me again, nor shall I be in a hurry to return to Kessingfield. This is not an investigation I will remember with any pleasure.'

'Try to forget it then,' his wife said. 'As I told you before, what you need most is a period to rest, preferably a long way away from the places associated with this wretched affair. If you remember, I did suggest a lengthy holiday.'

'I do remember, my dear, and I understand how much you would like to visit the places you mentioned. Whether I can be absent from Norfolk for all that time ...'

'I thought about that after we'd spoken,' Lady Alice said. 'On reflection, I think that I allowed my enthusiasm to carry me away. It would be very nice to think that we could leave everything at Wrigsby Hall in the hands of the builders and return only when the work was complete. Pleasant, but far from practical. My limited experience of builders and decorators suggests they need a close degree of supervision. I had a letter this morning from my cousins at Kentchurch Court, near Hereford. They say they will be delighted to see us and can offer us hospitality for as long as we wish. I know you have not yet become used to being a wealthy gentleman with no need to work to support himself. Nevertheless, surely you could afford to be away for, say, six weeks without causing any problems? On our return, I can make sure the architect and the builders are doing what I requested and you can devote yourself to your various duties in the area. Didn't you mention recently that the Royal College of Physicians had asked you to investigate the latest methods of treating those poor souls who have lost their reason? I have never been to the Bedlam in Norwich, but I understand it is a terrible place.'

'More terrible than you could credit,' Adam replied, 'especially since it is supposed to be a place of healing. You are right, my dear. To find a civilised and compassionate approach to dealing with the insane is a subject dear to my heart. It is high time I turned my mind to it. Still, I'm sure I could manage six weeks away. Would you intend to spend all that time in Hereford?'

'Certainly not. My relatives are rich and live in a large house, but to stay that long would surely exhaust our welcome. What I propose is that we travel first to the Wye Valley. If you recall, Mr William Gilpin wrote a book full of the praises of the beauty of that area and I would like to see it for myself. I have been thinking where we might stay and recalled a family who came to stay once at Mossterton Hall when I was living there. I think they were distant relatives of Sir Daniel's. They were pleasant, friendly people and, as I recall, have an estate somewhere near Ross-on-Wye. If I ask amongst my acquaintances, someone will surely know their precise address. I will write to them and request hospitality for a short time. If that fails, there must be good inns to be found in that part of the world. If we leave quite soon — let us say by the middle of this month — we should be able to return by the end of

June. According to the architect, our new home should be habitable by late September. I think you should tell Dr Henshaw he can move into this house at Michaelmas, October 25th. That should be enough to allow for some delays in the building work. I will tell the housekeeper to advise the servants who are coming with us to the new house that they should be ready to move by the autumn.'

Lady Alice's enthusiasm had begun to affect her husband and he found himself almost looking forward to the journey ahead. He was glad he had something specific to turn his mind to when they returned. His wife had recognised he was finding it difficult to come to terms with the life of a wealthy gentleman with a landed estate and all the time in the world on his hands. In his heart of hearts, he doubted that he ever would.

Tracked 4T
JD100349315GB

Printed in Great Britain
by Amazon

28689490R00142